DOCTOR WHO

SCRATCHMAN

DOCTOR WHO

SCRATCHMAN

TOM BAKER

with James Goss

BBC BOOKS

7 9 10 8

BBC Books, an imprint of Ebury Publishing
20 Vauxhall Bridge Road,
London SW1V 2SA

BBC Books is part of the Penguin Random House group of companies
whose addresses can be found at global.penguinrandomhouse.com

Penguin
Random House
UK

Storyline by Tom Baker and Ian Marter

Doctor Who is a BBC Wales production for BBC One.
Executive producers: Chris Chibnall and Matt Strevens

First published by BBC Books in 2019

www.penguin.co.uk

A CIP catalogue record for this book is available from the British Library

ISBN 9781785943904

Publishing Director: Albert DePetrillo
Project Editor: Steve Cole
Cover design: Two Associates
Production: Sian Pratley

Thanks to Victoria Bennett in BFI Special Collections, and the BFI National Archive for
providing access to the film script of *Doctor Who Meets Scratchman*.

Typeset in 12/15.1 pt Albertina MT Std
by Integra Software Services Pvt. Ltd, Pondicherry

Printed and bound in Great Britain by Clays Ltd, Elcograf S.p.A.

Penguin Random House is committed to a sustainable future for
our business, our readers and our planet. This book is made
from Forest Stewardship Council® certified paper.

CONTENTS

BOOK ONE: THE LONG NIGHT

Beginning of Fear   3

Chapter One   7

Chapter Two   15

Fear of the Unknown   23

Chapter Three   25

Chapter Four   33

Fear of Running   41

Chapter Five   43

Chapter Six   51

Chapter Seven   61

Chapter Eight   65

Chapter Nine   73

Fear of the Absurd   79

Chapter Ten   81

Chapter Eleven   87

Chapter Twelve   91

Fear on Earth   105

Chapter Thirteen   109

Chapter Fourteen   121

Chapter Fifteen   133

Fear of Saving the Universe   141

BOOK TWO: SCRATCHMAN

Chapter Sixteen   145

Chapter Seventeen   153

Fear of Lies   165

Chapter Eighteen   167

Chapter Nineteen   177

Fear of the Devil   187

Chapter Twenty   189

Chapter Twenty-One   195

Chapter Twenty-Two   201

Chapter Twenty-Three   209

Chapter Twenty-Four   219

Fear and Friends   227

Chapter Twenty-Five   229

Chapter Twenty-Six   239

Chapter Twenty-Seven   245

Fear of Death   247

Chapter Twenty-Eight   249

Chapter Twenty-Nine   259

Chapter Thirty   267

Chapter Thirty-One   275

End of Fear   281

Epilogue   285

PS From the Doctor   289

Acknowledgements   291

BOOK ONE
THE LONG NIGHT

BEGINNING OF FEAR

The Time Lord was late.

He was in trouble, and he'd been summoned to the Convocation of Oblivion to account for his actions. His august peers had gathered in a tall tower in a tall city to hear one of his tall stories.

'He's going to say he saved the universe again,' huffed one to another, running a finger around his stiff collar.

'It's still where we left it, isn't it?' his friend sneered. He'd been a junior archivist for three thousand years, and, in his experience, the universe continued much as it always had done.

'As if that's enough to stop him,' hissed his friend, looking around at the crowd of collared lords, buzzing like angry wasps woken from a nap.

'Always gets out of punishment by claiming to have snatched existence from the jaws of something or other, and yet –' the archivist cast his eyes up at the endless universe twinkling beyond the skies – 'you don't see the stars going out, do you?'

'No doubt he'd claim that was down to him,' huffed a revered Time Lady. They all laughed, little laughs as dry as toast.

'We're in for a load of nonsense and braggadocio,' she continued. She was put out that she'd been disturbed from her hobby of collecting dust. 'But I don't see him getting off so easily this time.'

These were the Time Lords of the planet Gallifrey and they were the most powerful creatures ever to exist.

They were waiting for the Renegade to enter, to confess his crimes. This time he'd gone too far. And they were going to put a stop to him, finally and forever. A hush fell over the room. The hush of a guillotine sensing the tumbril roll near.

A light stabbed down onto the stage, and a figure staggered into the beam, pinned there like a butterfly.

A Zero Nun left her seat in the front row, striding up to the Renegade, and bowed to him with exaggerated courtesy. 'Have you anything to say for yourself?'

'Good evening,' I said, through gritted teeth.

I was in trouble.

As my brain adjusted to the pounding intensity of the bright light, I tried to work out what to say to them. My people allowed me to go wandering the universe, tinkering here and there, but occasionally they'd call me to account for my actions. Normally when I overstepped the mark for some trifle or another.

'Your recent actions endangered the entire universe,' the Zero Nun informed me.

Yes. Something trivial like that.

The crowd seethed. There was a hunger to them. They were a bloodthirsty bunch.

'Come now, have you nothing to say for yourself?' Her tone was coaxing, as if she was speaking to a sulking, backward child.

There was the exact sound of a thousand Time Lords leaning forward on their benches. Waiting. Waiting for me to fall.

'Well, Doctor?' the Nun pressed. 'We are offering you a chance to account for your actions. Surely –' and she baited her trap with honey – 'surely, Doctor, you can't have meant to put us all in danger? We've allowed you certain freedoms, and you can't have intended to repay us with such recklessness. Can you now?'

'Well …' I began. I had something to say. Of course I did. It just wasn't what they were expecting. 'You will allow me to speak freely?'

'But of course!' The Zero Nun smiled like a haunted tree. 'No doubt you'll have an excellent explanation. After all, I'm sure I vouch for all of us when I say that we'd hate to have to wipe you from existence.'

My audience nodded sanctimoniously, all the time sharpening their knives.

'Come now, Doctor,' the Zero Nun prompted. 'Let's get to the bottom of this together.'

'All right,' I told her. 'But in order to do so, I need to teach you about fear.'

'Fear?' she blinked. That got her.

'Yes.' I addressed the entire chamber. 'You see, even the Time Lords are afraid of something. And tonight, I'm going to show you what that is. Are you sitting comfortably? Of course you are. And I'm rather afraid that's the problem ...'

CHAPTER ONE

A peculiar breeze drifted through the fading daylight on the island. The strange wind howled around the field, circling like a cat before settling down.

A sheep observed all this, curiously. Confirming her worst suspicions, a large blue box pushed its way out of thin air onto the grass. The ewe shook her head sadly and trotted away.

A door in the blue box opened, and I stuck out my head.

'Did you hear what that sheep was saying?' I said. I'm the Doctor and some people find it hard to believe I'm a Time Lord from the planet Gallifrey (although I try not to let it show unless there's company round). I was dressed with careful carelessness in my usual tumble of velvet, tweed and corduroy – a natty little outfit all held together by a long flowing scarf in the same way that an unreliable parcel can be tied up with string.

'What was the sheep saying?' A very pretty young woman walked out of the blue box. Her name was Sarah Jane Smith and she adored a good question as much as I adored her. Before wandering the universe, she'd been a journalist, and her questions had been of the common-or-garden 'and what will this mean for the working mother?' variety. These days her questions were often along the lines of, 'Why is that tentacle trying to kill us?' So she didn't mind asking about talking sheep. Not really.

'Talking sheep? I say!' A young man came out of the blue box, blinking heartily. He wore a duffel coat, wellington boots and a look of constant surprise. His name was Harry Sullivan and he was a polite boy who'd been sent to a reasonable public school before being issued with a blazer and a medical degree and sent out into the wide world to make the best of things. A child at heart, he was cursed with a hapless enthusiasm that had vicars' wives putting a protective hand on their best china.

Harry's excitable disposition didn't allow him to get over many things in life. Certainly, he'd never got over the fact that my little blue box could go anywhere in the universe. He knew that it was called a TARDIS and that through a rather charming mistake it looked quaintly like those old police boxes he used to see on street corners; he vaguely grasped that it could travel in time; but he could never hide his disappointment that the TARDIS didn't look like a proper spaceship with rockets and so on. Instead it tried to be as small as possible on the outside whilst remaining literally huge on the inside. Why did it do this? Perhaps, I suggested, because she's shy.

I had taken a few, bouncing steps across the heather and was now staring at the beach beneath us. The island looked picturesque enough, but there was something in the air. I watched the waves sweep across the empty beach and I couldn't help shivering.

'Did the sheep perhaps tell you where we were?' Harry prompted drily.

'She told me that you were going to say that.'

'Of course she did.' Sarah was wearing a long, flowing floral print dress and sturdy leather boots. (This was not her first trip with me.) 'And where are we?'

'We're just off the coast of Scotland. Probably the Scilly Isles.'

Sarah gave me a firm nudge with her elbow. 'The Scilly Isles are nowhere near Scotland.'

'Well, they're near enough if you're not from Earth,' I announced. 'From a certain distance everything seems terribly close.'

'Oh, of course.' Sarah rolled her eyes at Harry, and Harry rolled his back.

I could sense I was being mocked and broke into a broad grin.

'Why has the TARDIS brought us here?' asked Sarah.

'I'm not sure,' I admitted. I brought a hand to my eyes and surveyed the landscape. 'Perhaps because of that field,' I announced. 'It's a good spot for a picnic.'

I led my friends in solemn procession to a flat meadow, where I brought out a vast tartan blanket. On it I laid out sandwiches and little cake stands and small bowls of trifle.

'What a spread!' marvelled Harry. 'Where did you find all this?'

'I've been keeping it in the pantry for a special occasion,' I confessed. 'Originally made it for one of Henry's wives, but the honeymoon was a disaster.' I frowned. 'Do you know! I've forgotten something.'

I stomped off back to the TARDIS.

Left behind, Harry picked up a sandwich and stared at it dubiously. 'It looks fresh,' he said. He sniffed it. 'Smells OK, too.'

Sarah snatched the sandwich from him and took a bite. 'Oh, Harry,' she laughed, mouth full. 'Live a little.'

'It's precisely because I want to live a little that I'm being cautious, old girl.' Harry adopted a tone that Sarah could never be entirely sure about. 'You must remember that the Doctor is an alien. He's probably got a special appendix that deals with food poisoning.'

'A *special appendix*?' Sarah had found a pork pie. 'Harry! You're supposed to be a doctor.'

'Well,' mumbled Harry. 'You know what I mean.' He nibbled at the edges of an egg-and-cress sandwich.

The two of them settled back on the blanket, looking up at the perfect late afternoon sky. The sea rolled nearby and the two of them started to feel at peace, relaxed, even drowsy.

'You know what,' declared Sarah. 'I might just take a nap.'

'Good idea,' mumbled Harry.

'We don't normally get to do that. All my travels with the Doctor, we're so busy being shot at and transmogrified that we never get the chance for a little doze.'

'Maybe our luck's changed.' Harry's voice was little more than a whisper on the breeze. 'I feel completely at peace.'

At that point something startling happened, and Harry Sullivan sat up.

'What the devil is that noise?'

'Good news!' I bounded back into the meadow. 'I've found my ukulele.'

After a few minutes of fiendish strumming, I'd driven Harry away down to the beach where he was setting up a game of rounders. Sarah was lying across my boot, listening to me plucking my ukulele like a Christmas turkey.

'Bet you didn't know I played, did you?'

'I'm still not sure you do.' Sarah took a bite out of an apple and considered. 'Is that a tune?'

I looked affronted. 'It's "I'm Leaning On A Lamp Post At The Corner Of The Street".'

'Really, Doctor?' asked Sarah quietly.

'Oh yes, it was popular during the French Revolution, you know.'

We sat, watching Harry fall over on the beach while putting down stumps. I played on. After a while, Sarah gave me one of her Penetrating Looks, and I began to feel like one of her interview subjects. I was beginning to pen my resignation letter when she finally asked her question.

'We're not really here for a picnic, are we, Doctor?'

'No,' I agreed. 'Something's brought the TARDIS to this place. And I want to know why.'

'Something good? Something evil?' She paused, and sighed. 'It's going to be something evil, isn't it?'

'Oh, probably,' I grinned. 'Just in case, let's not make any sudden moves.'

Down on the beach, Harry paused in the art of setting up stumps. He frowned. Harry left intuition and so on up to Mother, sisters, and Sarah Jane Smith. But there was definitely something up in the air. He heard the distant call of a cuckoo. And there was something else: a distant sound carried on the air – half the creak of a haunted house door, half the crack of giant's knuckles. Harry shivered and then forced a smile. 'Ready when you are!' he called up to us.

So, we went and played rounders together on the deserted beach. Harry had gathered sticks and used them as stumps. They poked up through the sand, reminding me of the fingers of a giant skeleton. Despite my enthusiasm, and Harry's endless cries of 'Bravo!' there was something in the air. The sea crashed on the shore, birds called warnings to each other, and the wind tugged at Sarah's hair.

I could see her attention wasn't really on the game. She was probably trying to work out what was coming next. Something moved far out at sea, a slight underwater glint. She turned to look at it, and, as she did so, she quite missed my best shot.

'I've hit it!'

'Very good,' she said dutifully.

'It went over your head. Weren't you supposed to catch it?'

'That was the idea, old girl,' Harry chided. He was so awfully eager, like a games teacher who wasn't going to last a term.

'The ball's gone into that field,' I said, hoping someone would go and get it.

'Well, you did hit it a terribly long way,' Harry said, politely but firmly.

'I did, didn't I?' I accepted my fate. 'I'll just go and fetch it.'

I strolled through the field, hands deep in my pockets, trying to whistle away my forebodings. The sun was setting, and taking its time about it too. This was a nice enough island on a nice enough planet and all I had to do was find a missing ball.

I asked a passing scarecrow.

'Excuse me, sir.' I doffed my hat. 'Have you seen my ball?'

The scarecrow didn't answer, but then again, I didn't expect him to. Something about the poor fellow caught the corner of my eye.

'My word!'

The scarecrow was dressed as a vicar. His tattered black cape flowed in the wind, a homburg hat was pulled down over his turnip head. Splotches of mould blossomed in a ghastly approximation of eyes and mouth. Clutched in his tattered gloves was the missing ball.

My life was full of so many remarkable coincidences that I barely remarked on them any more. I was struck by this man of straw preaching to the sparrows. It simply seemed natural that my ball had ended up lodged in the hay-preacher's hand.

I reached up for the ball. Peculiarly, it did not come free. Somehow the scarecrow had a strong grasp on it. I gave a firm pull and still the ball did not come loose.

'This is both embarrassing and unusual,' I admitted. 'Please may I have my ball back?'

The ball fell into my hand.

I doffed my hat. 'Thank you,' I said, and headed back for the beach.

The wind stirred around the straw vicar, tugging at his vestments. When I looked back, it seemed as though the scarecrow's head had turned slightly to watch me go.

Sarah and Harry looked up as I scuffed my way across the sand towards Sarah and Harry. 'I got the ball back! Technically I'm out.' I pointed to the field behind them. 'I've been caught by a scarecrow.'

'What scarecrow?' remarked Harry.

'You can't miss him. Scarecrow dressed as a vicar.' I turned back to look at the field. 'Or maybe he was a vicar dressed as a …'

The field was empty.

We played some more rounders. Or, rather, Sarah hit the ball a lot and Harry and I scampered amongst the dunes. From the way I kept fumbling my catches, Sarah could tell I was preoccupied. Mind you, I'm always preoccupied.

'You keep glancing back at that field,' she said.

'I do, don't I?'

'Perhaps it really was a vicar?'

'I know what I saw, Sarah.'

'But scarecrows don't go wandering off. Not unless they've got another appointment.'

'Maybe the farmer came and took him away,' suggested Harry gamely. 'I can't see any crows, can you? That scarecrow was clearly doing too good a job. Yes, that was probably it.'

Sarah and I regarded Harry.

'I think the light's going,' I said eventually. 'Let's have some trifle.'

We could hear the kettle screaming as we tottered up the beach to the meadow.

'Lovely sound,' I said, picking up the pace. 'There is nothing quite so urgent as tea.'

We reached the meadow.

We stopped.

My picnic was wrecked. Smashed plates, broken teacups, crumpled cutlery. A tottering pile of sandwiches had been pushed into the ground. Slivers of glass floated in a beached trifle.

CHAPTER TWO

We surveyed the brutal ruins of the picnic.

'Oh,' said Sarah, and it was the saddest of 'oh's.

'Presumably a herd of cattle,' Harry ventured.

I ignored him, striding over to the still intact gas stove. I turned the kettle off. I cast around for the tin teapot, digging it out of a clod of mud. It had been flattened.

'Alas, poor teapot.' I put it down sadly on the grass. My misgivings about this place were growing.

'You do hear about cows doing this sort of thing,' Harry went on. 'Maybe they saw the colour of your picnic blanket and that drove them wild or something ...'

'And then they stole the picnic blanket?' Sarah pointed out. The blanket was indeed missing. She took my arm. 'I am sorry.'

I nudged a pancaked pork pie with my shoe. 'This was not cattle,' I announced. 'Those are tyre marks.' I found the matchstick remnants of my ukulele, and held them dangling in the breeze, like a banshee's wind chime. 'No leaning on a lamppost today.' I dropped it back to the ground. 'Someone is trying to warn us off.'

'This way.' Sarah followed the direction of the tracks through a gate. 'I think it's a bit bigger than a car. We're looking for a tractor wearing a picnic rug.'

We trudged through the fields. There was something oppressive about the island's emptiness. The fields were huge and barren, churned up in muddy furrows. The clouds pressed down on us, squashing flat any hedgerows or trees, reducing the landscape to an endless brown morass under a bleak heaven.

'Cinereous,' I broke the silence.

'Huh?' Even Harry had managed to lose himself in his thoughts.

'Your language is capable of marvellous little cul-de-sacs,' I declaimed. 'Cinereous. A splendid word for describing just such a sky. The colour of ash, of spoilt milk, of nothing.'

'It feels like it's waiting to fall on us at any moment,' suggested Harry.

I jammed my hands further into my pockets and tried a jaunty whistle, which curled up and died in my throat. 'I could point out it's an optical illusion, but really …' I reached a brown gate in a brown hedge and passed through into another brown field. 'I can only agree with Harry. Things must be bad.'

Sarah and Harry trooped obediently after me. Sarah paused to scrape the mud from her boots on the gate.

'Ah-ha!'

My cry attracted her attention. She turned and ran towards me and then stopped.

We were not alone in the field.

'Four scarecrows,' I said. 'I told you there were scarecrows.'

'Yes, but four of them, and no crops?' Harry was incredulous. 'That seems like overkill.'

I could tell Sarah didn't care for the scarecrows. The creatures seemed to be surrounding us. The four figures were spaced out in a loose ring. A tattered dress fluttered from the tallest one. The other three were shorter, almost the height of children.

'Some family outing,' Sarah said. 'It feels like they're watching us.'

Harry seemed cheerfully unconcerned by them. He bounded over to one of the child-sized ones and started rearranging its bonnet. 'If you don't mind me asking, young miss, where are your crops?' he asked. 'Surely it's a bit early for a harvest?'

'It depends what you're harvesting,' I said grimly.

Sarah looked curiously between me and the scarecrows. Strange the way that the wind made it seem like they were moving. It really was uncanny.

The old-fashioned tractor was the only splash of colour in the farmyard. Even in the thin grey light it was a measly place, broken barns running down into tired sheds, all leaning for support against a farmhouse that couldn't even remember the better days it had once known. Its thatched roof was balding, and driftwood shutters banged against the glassless windows.

'Welcome to Wuthering Heights!' exclaimed Sarah as her boots sank into the mud.

Harry wrinkled his nose. 'It smells terrible.'

'You're too much of a Londoner.' Sarah nudged him in the ribs and squelched towards the tractor. 'Aw, Harry, that's just a good old countryside smell.'

Harry was dubious, and so was I.

The tractor was messily parked in the middle of the yard. My picnic blanket was wrapped around one wheel and lay sinking into the mud.

I issued a piercing whistle. 'Hello! Is anyone at home? I say, have you a picnic blanket I could borrow?'

The wind continued to whip around the buildings. There was no sign of life. The shutters continued to bang.

'This whole place looms,' remarked Sarah. She was swinging her arms around her.

'It does feel to me rather like a trap,' Harry ventured.

'Of course it's a trap.' I heaved open a heavy wooden barn door. 'And you're right about something else, Harry.'

'I am?'

My voice sank into a sepulchre. 'That smell is not right. Something bad is happening here.'

'Shouldn't we go?' asked Sarah. 'Just this once.'

I shook my head and slipped into the barn. Harry made to follow, but Sarah stopped in her tracks, giving out a cry.

'What?' Harry looked at the tiny black bundle on the ground. 'Oh, it's only a dead bird.'

'It's a dead crow, Harry,' she said.

Inside the barn, the strange smell was more pronounced.

'I can almost taste it.' Sarah was chewing the air.

'It's a high concentration of nitrogen compounds,' I said, poking around the barn. I wasn't going to elaborate further.

'It's freezing in here,' said Harry. He went over to an old paraffin heater, and fiddled with it hopefully. 'I suppose that barns like this are built to be naturally cool ...'

A shadow moved in the corner, detaching itself from the wall and moving towards us.

As light fell upon the figure, Sarah flinched. It was a man, his gnarled face pale and twisted. A thatch of stubble poked out of his chin. His eyes were wild. He wore a collection of ancient, dirty clothes, and moved with a limping gait. He was pointing a pitchfork towards us.

'Get out of here!' he said in a thick burr, jabbing at us with the fork. 'This is my farm! I warned you.'

'You did indeed.' I greeted the threat with careful bonhomie. 'Terribly kind of you to run over our picnic. You were trying to warn us away from here, weren't you? Why?'

The man shoved the fork at me.

'Would you care to step outside and talk this through?' I offered. I could see he was almost mad with fear.

The farmer jabbed the fork at me again. I took half a step back and gestured for my friends to get out of the way.

'We should go outside,' I repeated coaxingly, 'catch the sunset. I'd offer you a cup of tea, but my teapot is sadly indisposed.'

The farmer took another step towards me. 'Outside?' he laughed, and there was madness in his laugh. 'But *they're* outside. They're coming.'

'Who?' I asked.

The farmer tapped his nose with the canniness of a lunatic. 'Oh, they've seen you, even if you've not seen them.'

Sarah heard a noise outside. Footsteps? She used her most professionally friendly tone. 'You can tell me, who is outside? We're here to help.'

'Help?' The farmer stopped laughing, and wiped his eyes. 'There's no helping us here. We're all dead.'

The approaching sound grew louder – the squelch of boots in mud, but also a ghastly rattling, the clattering of bones in a gravedigger's wheelbarrow.

'It's too late! I warned you,' the farmer said. 'But you wouldn't listen and now they're coming.' He took a step closer, lunging at me with his pitchfork.

'Who?' pressed Sarah.

The farmer was about to tell us when there was a thud. He gave a loud groan and sank to the floor. Harry stood behind him, holding a heavy sack.

'Bullseye,' said Harry.

Sarah sat on a fence, watching me call Harry an idiot. We'd only just got back from laying the farmer out in the parlour of the farmhouse, clearing a way through empty stout bottles and putting him to rest on a sagging sofa.

'You really shouldn't have knocked him out,' I said. I'd grumbled all the way there and all the way back.

'He was threatening you with a pitchfork!' Harry was protesting.

19

I waved this inconvenient truth away. 'He was frightened out of his wits. He needed gentle handling, not a caveman's lobotomy. Also,' I ruminated, 'I could always have parried his attack with some fencing moves I learned from the Musketeers. No, that poor farmer is our only lead. He was trying to scare us away – but from what?'

'Fair enough,' murmured Harry. 'I'll go check on the patient.'

Sarah sat, swinging her feet in the air, chewing a stalk of straw. She watched Harry duck back inside the farmhouse and turned back to me. 'You're being hard on Harry.'

I was pacing the farmyard, looking for clues in the dwindling light. 'Am I? I'm not sure I approve of him shanghaiing rustics. It gets one a bad reputation in the county.'

'He thought he was saving your life.'

'Hmmm.' I was staring at the mud.

'Footprints?' Sarah asked.

'Yes.'

'So there was someone out here.' She paused. 'You're going to say "or something", aren't you?'

'Whatever gave you that impression?' I was all innocence. 'Some of these footsteps have been made by people with two left feet, or shoes of different sizes or just one shoe – one shoe and a regular indentation like a broomstick. Very odd.'

'An amateur dramatic society dressed as pirates?' suggested Sarah.

I placed my feet in some of the footsteps, hopping from one set to the next. 'I've a theory. And it's not a nice one.'

'And you're not going to share it with me just yet, so that at some point you can say you were right?'

'Would I do that?' I plunged back towards the barn.

Sarah stuck out her tongue at me, slid off the fence, and splashed behind me.

I ascertained later how Harry, feeling full of guilt and a strange foreboding, sat in the miserable front room of the farmhouse.

He'd felt his way around the farmer's head. There wasn't too much swelling. One thing was curious – the man's limbs were stiff. Harry felt for a pulse; it was there all right – but the more he examined the man, the more worried he became. The man's hair was dry, brittle, and there was something about the hands – the skin was coarse from a lifetime of labour, but the joints beneath were rigid, fused.

'When you're conscious we need to have a talk, old chap,' said Harry gravely. 'Obviously, once I've finished apologising.'

The man stirred on the sofa, the ancient springs creaking and pinging as his hand shot up, seizing Harry's wrist. 'Barn,' he said. 'Stay out of the barn.'

In the barn, Sarah and I were examining the sack Harry had used as a cosh. It had split open and was spread out across the floor.

'Harry's useful, in his way,' I admitted.

'Don't let him hear that,' said Sarah.

'I won't.' I poked at the sack with a stick. 'He's useful in the same way that setting fire to a house unblocks a chimney. Look at this.'

Sarah looked at the grey powder leaking from the sack. 'That's the smell! Revolting.'

'Nitrates. It's fertiliser,' I said. 'A particular type.'

'Really?'

'Don't touch it,' I warned. 'I believe it's homemade. I'll tell you what the recipe is later. When we're away from here.'

'Are we leaving?'

'I hope so, Sarah,' I announced. 'But I think we have company.'

Footsteps came from outside. That strange brittle, striding sound. Making their way around the back of the barn.

Harry ran into the farmyard. It was empty.

'Doctor, Sarah,' he called, 'I don't suppose there's any chance you're not in the barn, is there?'

The barn door swung wide open.

'Looks like a giant mouth,' sighed Harry. 'Of course they're in there.'

Harry edged into the barn, not liking it one bit. It was deserted. The split sack of fertiliser lay on the ground. The wind whistled and rats scurried in the hayloft above his head.

'I really don't want to be here,' he shivered.

Which was when he heard the noise. Strange, unnatural footsteps mixed with something uncannily like the scraping of bone. Turning into the farmyard, coming towards the barn. Harry stared at what was coming in horror and disbelief.

I must tell you what happened to the farmer. Left behind by Harry, he stirred on the sofa, his body dragging him unwillingly from the dreams into which he was sinking. His name was Moray – he could remember that, just. He was getting worse. At first he'd thought the aching in his limbs was old age, rheumatism – but now he knew what it was. Moray had seen it take his family. And now it was coming for him.

Whimpering in pain and self-pity, Moray drifted into a dream. He smiled, expecting to see Peg leaning over him, her tired handsome face ready to tell him she'd baked a fruit loaf.

Moray opened his eyes. The figure bending over him wore Peg's clothes. But it was not Peg. Not any more.

He screamed.

FEAR OF THE UNKNOWN

'Stop there, Doctor,' bellowed a late September Sage from the audience. 'You're an utter fraud!'

'Am I?' I was the picture of innocence. I took a step towards him, and the beam of light around me intensified. Wincing, I retreated. 'You shouldn't interrupt. I was just at a good bit.'

'You weren't even in the room with that poor unfortunate,' the Time Lord growled. 'So how can you know what happened?'

'Quite so, Doctor!' the Zero Nun simpered. 'We can hardly judge you fairly if you go around making up your evidence.'

She was supported by some vociferous nodding.

'That's your objection?' I scoffed. 'We're a race of omniscient observers! We can travel forwards in time, backwards in time, sideways in time. Our TARDIS telepathic circuits peep inside the heads of those we encounter and translate for us; it's a simple matter to check the record from time to time and fill in the blanks, especially if they're good ones. You lot, you need reminding that people on other worlds like Earth feel life instead of merely looking at it.'

There were jeers. The beam of light intensified around me momentarily, and I felt my knees buckling. The Zero Nun called for silence. 'I must admit, I was hoping for better from you, Doctor. I'm sure we all sincerely wish that we won't have to wipe you from time.'

'Oh, good.'

I couldn't help looking up. Hanging over me was the glowing Staff of Never. At a word from the Zero Nun, my existence would be obliterated. The Time Lords always liked to remind you that you were talking for your life. The Staff of Never pulsed impatiently.

The Zero Nun followed my gaze. 'Try not to worry about it,' she chided. 'But bear in mind, we must have something more substantial from you.'

'You'll have to be patient,' I cautioned her. 'I told you, you need to understand fear. You need to understand my way of experiencing the universe, and that of my friends. You have the vantage point of all of history. Nothing is unknown to you – you can appreciate the universe in all its individual moments of splendour ... And yet you don't. Everything out there is all the same to you – you've made eternity into a pâté. Well, I'm going to show you a creature that could perceive our existence in an entirely unique, completely wrong way ... Once you understand that, you'll see what you can learn from Scratchman ...'

Chapter Three

The scarecrows strode into the barn.

Harry backed away from them, diving into the shadows. He could hear rats scrabbling frantically overhead. He heard a distant scream, carried on the winds from the farmhouse.

The scarecrows moved in twitching jerks, each one accompanied by a horrific knuckle-crack of bone. Their make-do heads swung from side to side. Straw and twig bodies were stuffed into clothes – some ancient rags, others more recent: Sunday-best chapel suits, housecoats and one wedding dress.

As they shuffled in, their heads bobbling from side to side, Harry felt a mixture of horror and pity. Previous monsters he'd met were all confidence – there was something pathetic about these ramshackle creatures as they filed in and ground to a halt. They started to make an awful sound – at first awful because he couldn't put his finger on it, and then awful because he could. They were sucking at the air, plucking at it with whatever mouths they had – be it a tear in an old football, a maggot gash in a turnip, or the slack dribbling maw of a carved pumpkin.

Harry tucked himself into a corner, and watched warily as the terrible sucking ceased and those nightmare heads slumped forward. Were they slumbering? He wondered if he could sidle past them to the door? Perhaps, if he skirted the walls of the barn, he could.

He took a step. The straw matting cushioned his sensible soles. Relieved, he risked another step. Then another.

No response.

He took another step.

Nothing.

Harry grinned. He was going to get away with this.

With his next step he knocked over the old farmer's pitchfork. He had no idea how it had got in his way, but things always got in Harry's way. He made a hasty grab for the pitchfork and missed.

He watched it tumble, taking its time to reach the ground, where it landed with a magnificent clatter.

The heads of the scarecrows all snapped up, seeking the source of the sound.

Harry dived into the shadows under an old hayloft. As he did so, a scarf dropped down in front of him.

For a brief moment, Harry stared at it, doing his best boggle. Scarves, nicely knitted stripy scarves, did not as a rule just dangle down out of thin air.

'Psssst!'

He looked up. Above him was a trapdoor leading into the hayloft. Leaning over him were Sarah and me.

Seeing the search heading in his direction, Harry grabbed hold of the scarf and scrambled, kicked and was hauled up onto a bed of ancient straw where he lay panting.

'Gosh,' said Harry.

'Gosh, indeed,' I said in a whisper of a whisper.

'We were trying to get your attention,' hissed Sarah.

'I thought you were rats,' protested Harry. 'What are those things?'

Sarah pulled a face. 'Scarecrows, obviously. Living scarecrows.'

Beneath us came the sounds of stumbling feet as the creatures explored the corner of the barn, twiggy fingers scraping against the barn walls.

Harry peered down. 'Are they blind?'

I shook my head and held a finger up to my lips.

Sarah joined in with a lovely mime of a yawn and a pillow: *They're tired.*

'Ah!' exclaimed Harry and then dropped his voice at my angry look. That made sense of the creatures' strangely lethargic movements – they were exhausted.

'What now?' Sarah mimed.

'Easy,' I murmured. 'We watch. Very quietly.'

Sarah and Harry nodded. But the scarecrows beneath had stopped moving, heads tilted, trying to locate the sound.

One looked up, but only one. It seemed to focus for a moment on me and then it shuffled away.

The scarecrows were all now lurching towards the sacks of fertiliser. They descended on the one Harry had split, reaching into it, scooping the powder out with their gloved fingers. They threw the dust up into the air, then dived into the other sacks, tossing the powder until it formed a choking cloud that the scarecrows shuffled back and forth through.

The creatures became more animated, their movements less stiff. One in a ball gown began to hop from foot to foot, swishing a rotten feather boa around. The figures capered – disreputable scarecrow gents using their bowler hats to scoop up more powder, tipping it over themselves and their fellows.

Strange deformed creatures crawled into the dust – broken scarecrows with one leg, or no head, rolling and lolloping in the powder covering the ground, absorbing it, twitching and thrashing as a new stumpy stick leg sprouted, or a bulbous straw head sprang from the tree-stump neck.

It was a ghastly servant's ball, the sight of all these grotesques cavorting, the powder rising around them like smoke.

I rarely got to see monsters having fun. These creatures weren't huddled around a screen hissing about their secret plan. They were dancing, revelling. The scene was as charming as it was horrible.

Which was when we heard the cries.

The strange dance stopped, the scarecrows stepping back.

We watched in horror as the farmer was dragged in, howling and begging. The woman scarecrow we'd met earlier was dragging him by his wrists. He was followed by the three little girl scarecrows, each doing a stumbling hopscotch in her petticoats.

'Please,' the man pleaded. 'Please, you can't.'

These were the four scarecrows from the field. They'd come home.

Harry made to leap down from the hayloft, but I grabbed his hand in an iron grip. There was nothing we could do for the poor man. Not now.

The farmer grovelled in the gritty dust, whimpering with fear at the scarecrows crowding around him. The female figure holding him pushed him down to the earth, and the three little girls gripped him by the shoulders and legs. He screamed.

'I don't want this, I don't,' he wailed. 'Please, Peg, let me go – let me go …'

'We must help him, Doctor!' Sarah hissed.

I shook my head. 'I'm afraid it's far too late for that.'

One of the gentleman scarecrows dipped down with his bowler hat and scooped up some of the fertiliser. His steps towards the prostrate farmer were nimble, graceful. The scarecrow bent over the man. One hand reached down, twig fingers creeping into the man's mouth, holding it open.

The man's screams became guttural, gagging and moaning.

The scarecrow tipped the hat forward, cascading dust into the farmer's open jaw.

The farmer began to choke, spitting and chewing at the claggy powder filling his throat.

My grip on Sarah and Harry was tighter than ever. Harry leaned forward and caught the choking man's eye – he wanted the poor fellow to know that he wasn't alone. He didn't look away, didn't blink.

More powder was tipped into the man's mouth, mixing into a foaming mulch. The farmer writhed, his limbs convulsing.

The scarecrow mother and her daughters stepped back, solemnly observing.

The poor man raised up a hand, staring at it in silent disgust as the gnarled old fingers elongated and grew, stretching into long, withered points. The flesh of his hand, desiccated, fell away, the bones beneath showing themselves first as a skeleton then as a bundle of old twigs.

The farmer issued a powdery scream, and then his head snapped back, skin stretched tight over a skull that bloomed into a mottled old cabbage.

The farmer had become a scarecrow.

The entire barn held its breath.

The female scarecrow in a dress leaned down and gently took his hand.

The farmer stood up, testing his new limbs of wood and straw. Then he reached out his other palm, and one of the girl scarecrows obligingly placed her paw in it. The family of scarecrows turned and walked out of the barn, the two youngest ones trotting behind, their footsteps at a skip. They marched out into the yard, crossed over to the farmhouse and shut the door.

The remaining figures filed out after them, dispersing into the fields.

The last scarecrow banged the door shut behind it.

The dust settled behind them.

'Horrible,' gasped Sarah.

Harry made to scrabble down from the loft, but I grabbed his arm. I had to stop him from killing himself.

'Beware of that dust,' I warned. 'Don't breathe it.'

We waited as the last particles of fertiliser drifted down to the ground, and then, with a little help from my scarf, we scrambled down.

'What happened?' demanded Harry, angrily. Without waiting for a reply, he plunged on. 'We could have helped that man.'

'I'm very much afraid we couldn't.' My smile was mirthless. 'He was already infected.'

'Infected?' Harry laughed sarcastically. 'Are you saying there's a scarecrow virus?'

'If you must call it that, then yes.' Harry always liked a simple universe. 'More likely to be an engineered DNA resequencing meme, or self-replicating nanites ...'

'But I don't understand,' Harry persisted. 'Why would you want to turn people into scarecrows?'

'To create fear? Or perhaps it's someone's idea of a joke. But – if you were going to experiment on people, then this island is a splendid spot. Isolated, plenty of material to play with.'

'Material? You mean people.' Sarah shuddered and strode over to a discarded sack of fertiliser. 'And the infection is carried in this stuff?'

'Well, no,' I considered. 'I doubt the fertiliser is the means of transmission. If it was, we'd have breathed in enough particles. It's probably conveyed by something as old fashioned as touch.'

'That poor fellow,' said Harry. 'No wonder he was crazed – he lost his whole family, and then they came back for him and ... Did you say touch?'

'Yes,' I said. 'Why?'

'Nothing,' said Harry.

Sarah poked at the fertiliser with a stick. 'Then what is this stuff? Why do they need it?'

'You saw, Sarah,' I said. 'It's fertiliser. They feed off of it. An old farmer's secret – blood, fish and bone, ground down into powder.'

'Ugh,' said Sarah, stepping away from the bag.

'It's very good for geraniums,' I told her. 'Ordinarily. I'm afraid that this is made to a local recipe.'

'What do you mean by that?' Harry asked.

Sarah worked it out, and shook her head. 'No, no ...'

I nodded solemnly. 'The people on this island have two purposes. One is to become scarecrows, the other –' I lifted up the sack of fertiliser and tipped it out onto the ground – 'is food.'

Harry turned away. 'Let's go,' he said. 'I've had enough of this place.'

We stepped into the farmyard. It was silent. The unloved afternoon was slinking away, and there was a chill to the air.

'What do we do now, Doctor?' asked Sarah.

I greeted the question like an old friend. 'There are more people on this island. We find them and we warn them.' I grinned. 'And we save them!'

CHAPTER FOUR

'Civilisation!' I brought Harry and Sarah to a halt.

'A church?' said Sarah.

The church squatted on a bleak bump in the dirt track, a divide between the barren fields leading up to it and a small clutch of buildings leading down to a harbour. The distant shrieks of gulls carried from out at sea, giving the building an unsettling air. The church had been built out of sobriety and slate, and stood hunched over with age and neglect. It was stolid, meagre, scoured by the never-ending wind. Gap-tooth gravestones were scattered through the churchyard, so haphazardly they looked as though they'd fallen off the church itself, and some yew trees huddled around the back for shelter.

A close-of-business wind coasted over the hill, sending a shiver through their bones and causing me to jam my hat more firmly down on my head. 'For centuries, this is where the humble islanders have come to meet their maker!' I announced. 'Some would argue that we make our god in our own image, and if that church is anything to go by, the signs are not promising.'

'No,' said Harry dubiously. He'd been raised in the Church of England, and so felt automatically awkward around piety.

'Funny thing about yew trees,' I said. 'You always find them in churchyards. And yet many of them are several thousand years old. Makes you wonder what was there before.'

Harry shivered. 'It puts the *fear* into god-fearing, if you ask me.'

Sarah nodded as she peeped disapprovingly at the gravestones. 'Looks like Count Dracula is buried there. We're not going in, are we?'

'*We're* not. You are.' I smiled as her face fell. 'We need somewhere safe near the village, somewhere that we can defend.'

'That church certainly is built like a fortress,' conceded Harry.

'These islands often came under attack,' I told him. 'The good people needed a refuge. And will do again. I'm going to gather up whoever I can find and send them to you.'

'Can't we put them in the TARDIS?'

'Sarah,' I said. 'Even if I could find everyone on the island, and persuade them to hide in a little blue alien box that's popped out of nowhere, I suspect they'd want to come out sometime.'

'Good point.'

'Give them a warm welcome, would you? There'll probably be a tea urn in there somewhere. That's a start.'

Harry turned to Sarah and whispered: 'I say, old girl, he's got us making tea.'

Sarah blew a raspberry at me.

'Mind out for ghosts!' I said, heading down the road, whistling as I went.

I strode down into the village. 'Fog, fog everywhere!'

The twilight gloom was a world away from our picnic by the beach. There was a shiver to the air that promised a winter without the comforts of a fireside or nuts. The mist clung around my boots.

I looked at the tiny cluster of old stone houses sloping down towards the harbour. They were built to weather several centuries of storms. They looked more like retired tanks than homes.

There were no passers-by to nod to, no children playing in the street, no twitching net curtains, and, one more thing missing – no little puffs of smoke from the squat little chimneys.

'I only hope I'm not too late.'

A distant clanking caught my attention. I recognised it at once – the pedalling of an ancient bicycle. I hurried after the sound, ducking into a side street and then down a back passage into another street.

'Hello! Hello there!' I called gingerly. No sense in attracting unwanted attention.

I reached the end of a lane which faded away into the gloom. Somewhere beyond, on the bumpy track, I could still hear the creak of unoiled pedals.

'Hello!' I whispered again.

I took a few more steps into the mist. It wrapped around me, and the land around me vanished into dark grey shadows.

The distant pedalling stopped.

'Hello?' I whispered once more.

Silence apart from the wind.

I stood there for a bit, biding my time. Nothing. Ah well. When no one appeared, I headed back to the village.

The shop was small, but stuffed with everything.

I loved this sort of shop, and said so as soon as the little bell above the door had stopped tinkling.

'Good evening!' I boomed, speaking to thin air and frightening it just a little. 'I love a place that is the same size on the inside as the outside but doesn't let that stop it. Why look at all this – flypaper and mousetraps and picture postcards and eggs and, ahhhhh …' I plucked a dusty jar from the shelf, unscrewed its black lid and inhaled its contents. 'Liquorice wheels!'

'And you can put them back.'

The woman's accent was sharp as mustard and just as strong. You could pickle herrings with it.

I turned, proffering the jar to the woman who'd come in. 'Wouldn't you care for one first? Tell me – how do you eat yours, do you bite at the edges or do you unravel and nibble? I'm the Doctor, by the way.'

The woman continued to glare at me from the gloom from which she'd emerged. 'Mrs Tulloch.' She had a know-nothing, do-nothing face. Her little black eyes had spent a lifetime squinting in disapproval, and her hair was battened tightly down against her skull, afraid a sudden wind would carry it off. She wore several layers of clothes, as though when one wore away she simply placed another one on top. A tattered dress had been supplanted by a faded jumper, wrapped in an old cardigan, gathered into a dirty green housecoat, tied together by a greasy smock.

Behind her stood her inner sanctum – a living room with oilcloth table, a gas fire (only one bar lit), and a suicidally miserable carpet.

The scrutiny of her stare eroded my soul in a way that mind-drills and hypno-rays never had. With a shrug, I screwed the lid back on the jar, while Mrs Tulloch regarded me with her arms folded.

'Madam.' I plugged another bulb into my smile. 'This whole village is in terrible danger, and I suspect it has been for some time. Have you noticed people missing?'

'Can't say as I have.' She folded her arms.

'The vicar?'

'Not much of a churchgoer myself.'

'And quite a lovely farming family just over the way. You'd have missed them, no?'

'Can't say as I have.' Mrs Tulloch's arms folded themselves even more tightly. 'Got my own hens. Out the back.'

'Well, I'm terribly worried about them too. I'm worried about everyone. Tell me, is there a Mr Tulloch?'

'Gone fishing'

'Ah, when will he be back?'

'Went out ten years ago.'

'I am sorry. Lost at sea?'

Mrs Tulloch pursed her lips. 'Very likely. Where are you from – Inverness?' A lethal pause. 'Or London?'

'The fourth dimension,' I told her. 'Mrs Tulloch, you're in terrible danger.'

'Is that so?' She narrowed her currant-bun eyes.

I smacked a fist on the wooden counter. 'Mrs Tulloch, your island is being invaded by scarecrows. It's up to us – you and me – to put the word out. Gather everyone together. Tell them—'

'Get out,' said Mrs Tulloch, and she turned and vanished into her parlour.

I stepped out into the street, at a loss for words. There had to be a way to warn everyone, to get them together. To save people.

I darted off, first one way, then another, rapping at doors.

No one answered. Not a single curtain twitched.

'What if I'm too late?' I mused. 'No. I'm the Doctor. I'm never too late.'

I crossed another empty village street, and something pulled me up short.

It was a red telephone box.

Sarah and Harry, meanwhile, so I gather, crept through the church like storybook mice on their way to a telling-off. The building was fiercely cold with a damp you could taste. A series of stiff pews sat in rigid rows, facing a raised altar. Beyond it were a couple of doors.

'I hope one of those leads up to the spire. I like a turret,' said Harry hopefully. 'With a bit of luck, the vicar will have left the key lying around.'

'We're not sightseeing,' said Sarah, rattling one of the doors. 'We need to get this place ready.'

'And that's just what I am doing.' Harry was sullen. 'A spire is a good vantage point. I'll be able to see the lay of the land.'

'In the fog? At night?' Sarah wasn't biting. 'You just want to go exploring.'

'Towers are nice,' said Harry to himself, sadly.

I threw open the door of the red telephone box and peeked inside. 'How marvellously dimensionally untrascendental,' I said, squeezing myself inside. I checked the phonebook dangling from the phone by a string. '1964,' I mused. 'I need a tanner. Or a shilling. Or a penny. Or something.' Finding a coin that'd roughly do, I dropped it in the slot, dialled a number and hoped.

There was a long, slow, ringing noise. Then a voice said 'Um? Hello?'

'Sullivan!' I boomed.

Harry stood in the vestry of the church, holding an old-fashioned candlestick phone to his ear and marvelling as I addressed him in clipped, plummy tones, doing a startling impression of our old friend the Brigadier.

'I repeat, is that Dr Harry Sullivan of UNIT?'

'Um … yes, Doctor. Are you … being held hostage? Are you all right?'

'Mustn't grumble. Bad show down in the village, Sullivan, that's all. Tried to make arrangements to get the hoi-polloi to head to the farmhouse for shelter. Nothing doing, I'm afraid.'

'The farmhouse?' squeaked Harry. 'But I thought—'

'Village postmistress – Mrs Tulloch – saw through me. Sharp cookie, that one. Not a chance of putting people where they're not safe while she's postmistress.'

'Well, Doctor,' Harry said gently, 'I don't think the farmhouse is a particularly safe place. It's crawling with horrors.'

'Absolutely. Mrs Tulloch agrees with you, Sullivan. Bad show, bad show.' I could hear him trying to salute. 'How are things at the church, old boy? Looking secure?'

'Ah, yes, pretty much.'

'Capital, Sullivan, capital. It'll make splendid accommodation for the VIPs. After all – ha ha – we don't want you getting overrun with common villagers.'

'No ...' muttered Harry. 'I guess we don't.'

'Splendid work, Sullivan. Tally ho!' I dropped the receiver down, squeezed my way out of the telephone box, and wandered away chuckling.

Harry stared at the receiver and then put it down as if it was a dead gerbil.

'Oh,' he said.

Sarah stopped hunting around and looked at him. 'Are you all right, Harry?'

'I'm fine. I'm not sure about the Doctor.' Harry blinked at the telephone. 'He just rang me up and spoke gibberish. Said he'd had no luck with the postmistress, and so he wanted me to know we were only to offer accommodation here for VIPs.'

'Right.' Sarah smiled and pointed to the phone. 'Bet it's still a party line. Everyone listening into each other's phone calls to get the gossip. And the village postmistress considering it her solemn duty to eavesdrop on every single call so as not to miss a thing.'

'Ah,' said Harry, and his face brightened. 'So, now the Doctor's called me ...'

'Everyone left alive on the island will be making a beeline here, demanding VIP accommodation.'

Sarah and Harry looked around the spartan church dubiously.

'Not very VIP, though, is it, old girl?' said Harry glumly.

'There are some bags out the back for the jumble sale. I'll see if we can find some blankets.'

I stopped at the harbour front, transfixed on the tail-end of a beautifully melancholy sunset sinking into the sea.

Then something pulled me away from my reverie.

That terrible noise I'd heard earlier – the squeak and clank of an unoiled bicycle chain. Somewhere out there to my right? Over among the heather? It was dreadfully loud.

I turned, just at the last minute, and saw a bicycle barrelling down the harbour towards me. I smiled – a policeman. Perfect. I held up a hand in greeting, and then snatched it back.

The policeman was a perfectly dressed scarecrow. An old oil lamp smoked away where his head should have been.

I threw myself out of the way, and the bicycle sliced past me.

I staggered up from the cobbles and turned to see the scarecrow pedalling furiously back towards me.

I ran.

FEAR OF RUNNING

'Doctor, I have to ask – why all this activity?' enquired the Zero Nun. There was some huffing agreement from the audience of Time Lords. 'You spend all your time running from things, running towards things, running here there and everywhere. Aren't you ... exhausted?'

There was mocking laughter at that. Of course there was.

'Running? I'm running now!' I did a few steps on the spot, just to show her. 'Running for my life! But so are you. Even sitting still – you're running. We're all running. All the time. Just being alive is running. Even when we're standing still, every molecule in our bodies, in creation, is racing. So, the physical act of running really is just joining in the fun of the universe.'

They did not like that.

I staggered under the weight of their disapproval as the light burnt into me. I could hear them baying. If there was one cardinal rule the Time Lords lived by, it was never joining in with the rest of creation.

'Hear me out,' I begged. 'You might think this is a distraction, all a bit of fun, but it's important.'

'I believe you, of course I do.' The Zero Nun advanced, smiling with both of her teeth and neither of her eyes. 'But I worry that not all of the audience is entirely persuaded.'

'Oh really?' I said through clenched teeth. The grinding beam of light eased off, just a little.

I squinted out at my audience.

The whole bag of humbugs tried to give their best impression of giving me the benefit of the doubt. Really, they were checking their watches and wondering when they could don their black caps.

'I'll tell you what you need to know about running,' I told them. 'I've met quite a few emperors. They're all the same: murder their way to the top of the heap, declare that they own the world ... But then, the next time one of them looks at themselves in the mirror, their reflection stares back at them, and it says, "Really? You thnk you're safe now?" And that's when they're finally afraid.' A terse hush had fallen over the room, and I made the most of it. 'I'll let you into a secret – they're really the ones who spend all their time running. From that moment on, they are running for their lives. And the one thing you can never get away from is yourself.'

I let that sink in.

'So, where were we? Ah yes. Running ...'

CHAPTER FIVE

At the church, Sarah and Harry stood in the porch, watching the sunset.

'No one's come,' said Harry.

Sarah nibbled at her lip. 'Do you – do you think it's just us left?'

'You mean has everyone else been turned into scarecrows or ground down into food?'

'You didn't have to spell it out.' She jabbed him in the ribs.

Harry rather wished he still had his coat. The night was going to be a cold one, and all he had to rely on was a blazer. Still, Sarah did look very handsome in a duffel coat.

'Did you find any jumpers in those bags of old clothes?'

'Why?' asked Sarah. 'Are you cold? Do you want your coat back?'

'No, no,' Harry politely lied twice. 'I just fancied seeing if there was a fisherman's jumper back there. Thought I might look dashing in one.'

'There are some,' said Sarah. 'They smell of mackerel.' She took hold of his arm and steered him away. 'Tell you what. There's something we can do. And I think you'll like it.'

*

Meanwhile, as mentioned, I was still running. I ran through a field. Mist had risen in thick walls around me. Night on the island was a terrible, starless murk. Even the distant gulls had fallen silent.

The scarecrow on the bicycle pedalled indomitably behind me, its smoking oil lamp the only relief against the gloom. Occasionally, it would reach out a claw, to pluck at the nape of my neck. There was something about the creature that was primally terrifying. It had something of the grave about it, like a half-decayed nightmare dug up and set on my heels.

My feet betrayed me, and I tumbled down a bank and onto a sand dune, torn at by gorse. I staggered to my feet and stumbled through the sand. All was quiet. Had I shaken the thing off?

And then came that dreadful clanking of chain, and a sulphurous light glowed in the mist.

I ran on, swallowed up by banks of fog. I was totally disoriented. Which way was the church? Left or right? Which way was the sea? Would I only know when I got my feet wet?

My eyes, adjusting, decided that that was definitely the sea in front of me. Was there something – glinting – beneath the surface?

A rattling alerted me – the policeman was coming at me fast across the stone-hard sand.

I picked a direction and ran, the froth of the sea churning around my boots. If I could just keep going along the shoreline, maybe I could reach a landmark or something.

And then I heard it. Drifting loud and clear on the evening air.

The tolling of a church bell.

'Good old Sarah,' I said, and struck off towards the sound.

Up in the belfry, Sarah and Harry were tugging at the bell ropes, sending peal after peal echoing out across the countryside.

'It's very loud!' proclaimed Sarah.

'What?' cried Harry.

Sarah smiled at him fondly, and he nodded.

'It's very loud!' he told her. He stepped back from the ropes, rubbing his arm. 'I don't know about you,' he groaned, 'but I'm deaf and tired.'

Sarah nodded, massaging her ears. 'If that doesn't send out the alarm, I don't know what will.'

She peered out of the tower. Lights were dancing in the mist below.

'It's working!' she said. 'They're coming.'

As Sarah and Harry reached the porch, people bustled towards them, led by a furious woman in a horrid coat. The Mrs Tullochs of this world are always at the front of every queue.

'Let us through!' she shouted, all puffed up for a fight. 'We demand admittance.'

'Splendid,' beamed Harry. 'You must be our VIPs.'

'Well, that's all right, then.' Mrs Tulloch deflated a little, and pushed him out of the way.

She stood in the church and looked around it dismissively. 'Not put the tea urn on, have you?' she sniffed. 'Come on, Sophonisba, seems we have to do everything. You may as well make yourself useful.' She pushed a dowdy woman out of the crowd before she could protest. 'A fine to-do this is,' she snarled. 'Call yourselves the authorities?' and then she said, 'Well!' as only a woman who has spent decades scrubbing a doorstep can say 'Well.'

Sarah turned to Harry. 'And you're welcome,' she whispered.

Harry nudged her in the ribs.

I was running across a marsh, the wet bog gobbling at my feet. I still wasn't sure if this was a brilliant tactical move or a terrible mistake. I'd evaded my pursuer, but, as so often happens in the English countryside, things which appear very near prove, in fact, remarkably hard to get to. The marsh ended in an unpromising ditch and a hedge woven from thorns.

I wriggled through a small gap and plunged into a large field. Unlike the others, this had been planted, ranks of corn rising above my head, whispering and gossiping in the wind. Glancing up at the feeble moon, I picked a direction and stuck to it, racing on through the stalks.

The rustling of the staves was eerie, and I couldn't shake off the feeling that I was being followed, followed by something breathing down my neck. I couldn't resist the impulse to turn and see what it was. It was this glance over my shoulder that saved my life.

A blade jabbed through the air, snicking a chunk out of my coat.

I turned to face the creature. It was dressed in a moth-eaten soldier's uniform, topped by a gas mask. It was holding an ancient rifle, fitted with a wickedly sharp bayonet.

I held up my hands, calling for a moment's peace. 'Wait!' I told the scarecrow. 'You know, I can't stand the idea of being stabbed by a rusty blade.'

Another stab. I ducked back, and held up my scarf, warding the scarecrow off. 'Stay back, or I shall have to use this.'

Dropping the rifle, the scarecrow leapt forward. Two bony claws seized my face, cold ivory scraping across my cheeks and rusty old nails digging into my flesh.

Agonised, I stared up at the empty face of the creature, and then yanked one end of my scarf. The other had looped around the scarecrow's feet. The creature flailed, staggered, and fell backwards.

I was already away and running.

'The natives are getting restless,' Harry muttered.

As well as a lot of questions about the threat they were facing, there had been a lot of fuss about the setting up of the tea urn, more fuss than Harry could have dreamed possible. A trestle table had had to be found and set up, then a tablecloth, then cups. An old labourer had enquired hopefully about sugar, and one very tired woman was asking if there was perhaps any milk.

'I bet Mrs Noah had exactly the same problem catering the ark,' agreed Sarah. She was watching Mrs Tulloch sweep some dried flowers into a bin as she laid out some drab plates and saucers. 'Amazing how people's thoughts turn from imminent danger to crockery.'

They went over to the porch and peered out into the gloom. Sarah shivered.

'Feel like we're being watched?' asked Harry.

Sarah nodded. 'Something's out there, waiting.'

A young farmhand approached, cap literally in his hand. 'Excuse me miss, you haven't seen the teaspoons, have you?'

'Of course. I think Mrs Tulloch has them,' Sarah said maliciously.

She turned back to the porch. Harry was standing there, looking out at the mist rolling through the churchyard.

'We'd better close up,' he said. 'I don't like how it feels out there.'

'Me neither,' Sarah shivered. 'Hurry up, Doctor, hurry up.'

Harry heaved the door shut.

They were locking me out!

At that moment, I'd reached the churchyard. There was, I thought, something so cheering about seeing a church lit up like that. Midnight Mass on Christmas Eve. Welcome, weary traveller.

As I crunched up the path, four figures slipped from out of the shadows to block my way. The scarecrows of the farmer's family.

'Oh, hello,' I said sadly. 'Ordinarily, I'm fond of children and children are partial to me. I'd just like to say how sorry I am that I got here too late to save you—'

Two of the scarecrow children flung themselves at me, the sharp thorns on their fingers headed for my eyes.

I dodged their attack and continued my run towards the church. But another of the unearthly creatures gripped my leg.

I could feel the thorns scrape and stab into my shin, and I gasped in pain. I kicked my leg out at a gravestone, scraping the nightmare child off on it, and broke into a limping run.

I grasped hold of the heavy iron handle on the church door, and discovered to my horror that it wouldn't turn. I was trapped outside.

'Help!'

Sarah and Harry heard my cries, but found their way back to the door blocked by Mrs Tulloch. Her arms were folded.

'But that's the Doctor!' protested Harry. 'We've got to let him in.'

Mrs Tulloch shook her head. 'You said it had to be locked.'

'And now it has to be unlocked!' said Sarah.

I turned to find the scarecrows fencing me into the porch. I wrenched a parish noticeboard off the wall to use as a makeshift shield. 'Really now, why can't we all get along?'

A scarecrow lunged at me, and I swiped out with the board. The thin edge cleaved the creature's head from its body. I watched it roll and topple and bounce along the gravel.

'I'm so terribly sorry about that.'

The scarecrow knelt down, picked up its head, and put it back in place.

'And now I'm less sorry about that.' I reached behind me, grabbing hold of a threadbare umbrella from a rack. Shaking the umbrella as a sword and wielding the noticeboard, I backed up against the door and kicked it firmly.

'I say!' I called behind me. 'Sarah, Harry! Could you see your way clear to letting me in?'

The scarecrows got closer. The farmer's wife reached out for me, the sharp sticks of her fingers bristling to caress my cheek. I fell back against the door, and was amazed to feel it give way. Involuntarily, I reached out for something to steady myself and grabbed hold of the scarecrow's apron. I heard a tearing of old cloth as I fell back inside the church.

Sarah and Harry were dragging me across the flagstones by the arms, yelling at each other to shut the door. As the door slammed shut, I saw something remarkable.

I sprang to my feet, shaking Sarah and Harry by the hands. 'Thank you both!'

Then I turned to the congregation who were staring at me in alarm.

'Dearly beloved, good evening. I'm the Doctor and I realise tonight has been a bit of a shock. Yes, we really are under attack from animated scarecrows, but I have excellent news.' I held up the torn apron and beamed. 'I know how to defeat them!'

Three scarecrow children stood outside the church door.

More figures stumbled and shuffled into the churchyard and came and stood beside them. A row of blank turnip heads and sack faces staring balefully at the door.

The smallest of the children stepped forward and tapped on the door with its skeletal hand.

Tap. Tap. Tap.

When there was no answer, the next child joined it and they both knocked together.

Tap. Tap. Tap.

And then another scarecrow came forward and knocked.

And then another.

And another.

CHAPTER SIX

The islanders stood listening to the loud, steady knocking on the church door.

I was leaning against a stone pillar. Sarah and Harry edged over to me. They were sipping weak tea from weak green utility cups.

'Mrs Tulloch makes a less than agreeable cup of tea,' said Harry.

'Well, she's a less than agreeable woman,' I replied.

'This plan of yours for defeating the scarecrows ...?' asked Sarah coaxingly.

'Currently, I only know a way to undo them. That's not the same as having a plan.' I was examining the apron. 'One can know the breaststroke. Doesn't mean one can swim the Channel.' I held up the tattered apron. 'This is the key to it!'

'An apron?' Sarah had adopted her Humouring Tone.

'Did you see what happened to the farmer's wife after I tore it off her?' I prompted.

'We were busy shutting the door,' Harry muttered, rubbing his elbow. 'I bruised my arm.'

'Well – she fell apart.'

'She ... I beg your pardon?'

'She went quite to pieces,' I confessed. 'Their new bodies are terribly unstable. Take away the clothes and they just disintegrate.'

'Really?' Sarah frowned. 'Isn't that a bit …'

'Silly?' I said. 'Not at all. Whatever it is, it's still adapting. It can lose an arm or a head and that's fine, but it relies on a solid core. Elementary mutagenics.'

'Oh, of course,' said Sarah solemnly.

'They just need to find a proper casing.'

'Let's pray they don't get their hands on a suit of armour,' said Harry.

'You're right there, Harry.' I slapped him on the back and he winced.

'So what do we do, Doctor?' he asked. 'Go around debagging them?'

'Moths,' suggested Sarah.

'Don't be silly,' said Harry.

'You were suggesting taking their trousers off,' Sarah snapped back at him.

'Well, yes, but all the same, old girl, moths?'

'Moths! Yes, of course, that's it. Clothes moths!' I dashed up and away, collaring three terrified islanders. 'Hello! I'm the Doctor, and I'm in urgent need of any old woollens …'

Harry looked at Sarah. Once more they were left in my wake.

'So,' he began.

'Yes?'

'Moths?'

'Moths.' Sarah smiled. 'Doctor,' she called to me, 'if you're actually serious, out the back there are some bags for the Bring and Buy.'

'Are there?' I beamed. 'I do adore a jumble.'

A few minutes later, the aisle of the church had been cleared, more trestle tables had been set up, and a vast mound of old clothes had been spread out. The ladies of the island were sorting through under Harry's uncertain eye. 'What we're looking for is larvae.'

The tapping continued on and off against the church door. I was sitting cross-legged by the altar, dismantling the tea urn. Sarah was standing over me.

'You know I trust you, don't you, Doctor?' she asked.

'Mmf,' I replied. It was the best I could manage. There were three important screws balanced on my lip.

'And I'm sure your plan is going to work splendidly ...'

I issued a more considered *hmmmf*.

'But wouldn't it be easier to, I don't know, burn the scarecrows or something? Wouldn't a flame thrower be easier than ... um ... what are you calling this?'

I popped the last important screw back in and grinned. 'An Artron Incubator!'

Sarah shook her head sadly.

'No? I'll think of a better name,' I promised. I always valued Sarah's support. She put up with my strange ideas. 'For now it's important that you know that this will work. I can't be certain until I can examine one of those scarecrows up close – and we can't do that because they're so deadly – but what we're dealing with behaves like a mutagenic virus. It adapts whatever it comes into contact with.'

Sarah thought about that for a moment. 'Oh,' she said.

'Oh indeed,' I agreed, and tapped her nose. 'We're going to stick with my way. We're going to incubate, weaponise and deploy a plague of moths.'

Mrs Tulloch was sorting through some old jumpers. She'd already slipped a couple to one side, just to look at later at home. Despite getting first dibs on the annual jumble, she didn't let her secret pleasure interrupt the thick scowl on her face.

'You there, Kirsty Campbell, I saw you fingering those socks. For now, these clothes are God's property. Shame on you.' She wagged a stern prophet's finger. 'Give them here. I'll look after them.' She took the socks – they really were quite nice – and slipped them into the bag alongside the jumpers. 'If you ask me, this is all nonsense. Scarecrows indeed!'

'I understand your scepticism,' said Harry, who'd wandered up behind her. 'But these creatures are all too real. They're nightmares.'

Mrs Tulloch made a noise that suggested that she herself wouldn't have been at all frightened.

Which was when, with a mighty crash, one of the stained-glass windows shattered and a scarecrow started to force its way in.

Mrs Tulloch gave a mighty shriek, overturning the trestle table.

The rest of the villagers gathered behind her, joining in her panic as the creature struggled and squirmed its way through the gap, turnip head and tree-stump claws grasping at the air.

Mrs Tulloch gasped in horror. 'What is that unholy thing?'

'I'm afraid that's your vicar,' said Harry.

In the vestry, Sarah ran up to me. 'Doctor! Something's up!'

I was busy pulling an ancient vacuum cleaner apart. 'Oh, probably just the scarecrows breaking in.'

'Yes,' Sarah glanced through the door. 'It's the vicar.'

'Homing instinct, poor thing. Be it ever so humble … This bit's fiddly, give me a hand? I'm sure Harry can deal with things.'

'I'm not sure about anything,' said Sarah.

Harry had grabbed a candelabra and was shaking it at the vicar.

'Back, Reverend!' he was shouting. 'That's an order.'

The scarecrow continued to squirm and push itself through the window.

Harry jabbed the candles at the vicar. 'I'm warning you!'

The scarecrow made a swipe at Harry. It caught his bruised arm, and he dropped the candelabra.

Sarah came running. 'Harry, wait!'

'It's all right, I've got this!' Harry assured her, and bravely, nobly, heroically, picked up the candelabra and shoved the fire into the vicar's face.

'No, Harry!' cried Sarah.

'I'm fine,' Harry reassured her, watching calmly as the vicar burst into flame. 'Problem solved.'

He stood back to admire his handiwork. Some of the villagers applauded and slapped him on the back. But the applause died down as the scarecrow continued to writhe and flail. 'I say, old girl, I have killed it, haven't I?'

'Harry, the Doctor says that the scarecrow virus adapts to whatever it comes into contact with.'

'Right. What does that mean, exactly?'

The burning bundle of twigs pulled itself through the window and flopped to the floor. It landed neatly and stood there. A pillar of flame which advanced on Harry.

'It means it's now living fire!'

The burning vicar lurched towards Harry, its hands stretched out in supplication. With each staggering step, cinders drifted up around the creature, the damp celestial air filling with thick, oily smoke.

Harry was riveted by the thing, even as he ducked out of the way of its arms. The turnip head was hissing like an old apple on a bonfire and something was foaming and dribbling out of the welts in it.

Harry felt the urge to apologise to it, to what it had become. Even though it had no eyes, it still seemed to be staring at him. An arm flailed towards him, he ducked, and it left black marks in the pillar where his head had been.

Dazed and winded, Harry sneaked a glance at the villagers, wondering if someone was coming to his aid. Instead they stood there, their faces blank with horror and incomprehension. Harry was backed into a corner, hands spread out on the cold stone tiles, looking up at the creature bearing down on him.

Someone grabbed him by the shoulder. It was Sarah, tugging him out of the way. The two fell into each other, moving back at a crouch as the burning vicar scattered pews, hunting them.

'It's quite all right to scream, you know,' said Harry.

'I'll bear that in mind,' Sarah said, pulling him back.

She was still casting around for something, anything to defend them with, when I appeared from nowhere and threw a fire bucket full of sand over the vicar. It had taken me a while to find it, but it was really most effective. The creature thrashed and smoked and toppled to the floor in a pile of smouldering twigs.

I turned back to a stunned Mrs Tulloch. 'How thoughtful!' I said, snatching up a green curtain she was holding, and threw it over the body. I then proceeded to jump up and down on the smoking bundle. 'There. I believe I've extinguished him. Don't thank me.'

'Sorry about setting light to him. Honest mistake,' said Harry. 'But, Doctor, won't the wretched thing just become sand?'

'Sand is inert. Fire is not.' I smiled sadly, my machine tugging again at my attention. 'And moths are another matter.'

A few minutes later, and I had unveiled the first attempt at my Artron Incubator. The islanders looked sceptical, and I supposed I couldn't blame them. My invention was, after all, made out of an old fish tank, a vacuum cleaner, and the parish's beloved tea urn, connected to a few bits from the vicar's old bicycle. It was set up on the altar.

'Is that it?' Mrs Tulloch announced.

'Of course not!' I braved her withering gaze. 'Why, in order for an Artron Incubator to incubate, we need some Artrons.' I pronounced this firmly and hoped the matter closed. 'Sarah, I need you to go to the TARDIS and fetch me an Artron Power Pack. Harry – I need you to go to the village shop.'

'My shop?' Mrs Tulloch was indignant. 'You want to go to my shop?'

'Excellent point!' I agreed. 'And thank you for volunteering. Mrs Tulloch, I need *you* to go to your shop and bring me back some sugar.'

'You want me to go outside?' She was aghast. 'With those things out there?'

'Then Harry will go for you. Just give him your key.'

'Haven't you got enough sugar here?'

'All told, we've about a dozen lumps, barely enough for a good cup of tea,' I said. 'And we need all the sugar we can get.'

Harry and I stood behind a pillar.

'You know what to do?' I asked. 'How's your arm?'

Harry looked away. 'Bit stiff,' he admitted. 'How's your leg, where the scarecrow caught you?'

I examined my boots, but said nothing.

'We're both infected, aren't we?' said Harry.

'Oh, possibly, possibly.' I put on a brave show. 'But it should take a while before it shows. And by then we'll have dealt with this business.'

'Yes, of course,' said Harry, casting a dubious eye at my invention. 'Good.'

I handed over the shop keys and looked at him seriously. 'Don't be long, Harry,' I said.

'I won't be,' he vowed.

I found Sarah perched on the font, peering through the broken window. The scarecrows were silent now, standing vigil amongst the tombstones, the mist rolling around them. 'How do we get past them exactly, Doctor?'

'Well ...' I helped her down off the font. 'I'll be at the front door creating a diversion. You're nipping out the back.'

I stepped out of the church and looked up at the dark sky.

'Lovely night for it!' I said, waving my hat at the scarecrows. 'I've been sent out here by the Village Cultural Committee.

If anyone's interested, you're welcome to an organ recital. We're doing requests.'

The church organ blasted up, the bells tolled and the watching scarecrows began to converge on me.

Meanwhile, a tiny door at the back of the church creaked open and Sarah and Harry dashed out into the shade of a yew tree. The door creaked shut behind them. Sarah turned left, Harry turned right.

'Good luck, old girl!' called Harry.

'Good luck, old boy!' Sarah called back.

Both vanished into the night.

At the front of the church, I stood in the porch, toying with a yo-yo and listening to the strains of 'The Bonnie, Bonnie Shores O' Loch Lomond'. 'There's nothing like the classics, is there?' I remarked to the scarecrows advancing on me.

The lead scarecrow – a nightmarish figure in waders and oilskins – shuffled into the light cast from the porch. It stood there, bony fingers grasping at the air.

I regarded it curiously. 'Getting hungry, aren't we?'

The scarecrow just stood there, old leather football head swaying from side to side, the plucked stitches stirring in the wind.

'I don't know what you are precisely.' I frowned at the empty head. 'Besides hungry. What is it that you really want?'

There was silence from the scarecrow. I watched my yo-yo descend to its full length, then snapped it back.

The scarecrow lunged suddenly forward and made a grab for me.

I hurled myself back through the door, and it slammed shut with a thundering echo. Villagers piled pews up against it, the heavy timber squealing as it was dragged across the stone tiles.

I admired their handiwork. 'I love a good barricade. It reminds me of the Siege of Leningrad. We've only one problem – our visitors are coming for dinner. And we're on the menu.'

Mrs Tulloch took this latest news with a sniff. 'And what are you going to do about that?'

I gave her a mirthless smile. 'Hope we can hold out until my friends get back.'

CHAPTER SEVEN

As Sarah told me later, she didn't dawdle on her way to the TARDIS. The night was cold and ominous. She looked out at the moonlit sky and admired the way that the stars were reflected by the sea, almost like they were trapped beneath it. As she crept along the shore towards the TARDIS she felt herself relax. Yes, the island may be full of eldritch horrors, but it also held a certain beauty.

Sarah grinned, remembering her colleagues at *Metropolitan* magazine. Travel was always something you did with the aid of a brochure. It took a fortnight, your luggage would go missing and the hotel cooking wouldn't agree with you.

Instead, Sarah travelled from one planet to the next, never the same sky, never the same suns, never the same sand to squeeze between her toes. In all that time there'd been no guided tours, no trips, and no planning, but an awful lot of adventure. No souvenirs, and definitely no time to send postcards. (Although, having said that, a few years ago she'd received a mysterious postcard at her desk. It had been a grim, rainy day when the postcard had arrived. It was dog-eared, with a faded view of Mauritius and a 1924 postmark. The really odd thing was the message on the back. 'You'll do all right,' it had said. In her handwriting.)

Sarah reached the meadow, kicking her way through the sad remains of our picnic. The familiar, reassuring shape of my time machine perched just around the corner. Home! The blue box had parked itself dramatically overlooking the beach. She patted it.

She shivered. There was something not quite right about the machine's hum. Warning. She risked a glance over her shoulder. No. Nothing behind her but that empty field and the beach beyond.

She looked back at the TARDIS. What if something lurked behind the ship? Listening to her every move? Waiting to pounce? She forced herself to smile. She was being silly. Silly! And yet … she remembered me saying something to her about the TARDIS being telepathic. What was it trying to say?

Plucking up every scrap of courage she sneaked a peek around the left hand side of the box. Nothing. She checked the right. Also nothing.

Not yet daring to relax, Sarah unlocked the door of the box. Warm, bright, friendly light spilled out. She slipped inside, and closed the door behind her.

Only she didn't quite close it. A figure slipped from the shadowy hedgerow and inserted a finger of bone into the door.

Sarah stepped through that tiny wooden door into a large hotel lobby of a space. She always found it impressive. She'd seen spaceship flight decks at the cinema – they were gun-metal grey and bristling with buttons. Not so the TARDIS, I'm pleased to say.

As anyone knows, the controls of the TARDIS were concentrated in a tiny pedestal, not much bigger than a desk, which left plenty of space in the control room for a homely collection of chairs, a hat stand and a cuckoo clock, which was just how I liked it. My TARDIS had been built to go places, but she did so in a whimsical sprawl.

Sarah crossed over to the control console and tapped one of the few buttons I allowed her to touch. A screen glowed on the wall and, with a few more presses, a map lit up showing her where to go and look for an Artron Power Pack.

'Fine,' said Sarah. 'Second workshop.'

Sarah was going down a rickety spiral staircase. Despite its size, the TARDIS didn't do lifts. Instead her tastes ran to an endless winding set of stone steps, halfway between a magician's turret and a stairway on the London Underground. Sarah stopped counting at eighty-odd steps and just let her feet take her. Much the best way with the ship's inner dimensions, I find.

My TARDIS's rooms are constantly rearranging themselves like ornaments on haunted bookshelves. I'm not sure that's how they're supposed to work, but we've grown used to each other's caprices. The art is to enjoy the journey and accept what you're given. But that's part of the fun.

At the bottom of the staircase, Sarah saw a poster for a Buster Keaton movie and a little illuminated sign indicating the workshop. She turned left and found herself in front of a tiny door. It had the number 23 on it in brass letters. There was a letter box. A door knocker. A little fake stained glass. And a cat flap. Clearly, an Acacia Avenue somewhere had woken up one day missing its front door.

Sarah opened the door and stepped into an echoing hangar. She got a feeling for the size of it from the old biplane tucked away in a far corner.

'I guess this is Workshop Two,' she remarked to herself, stepping over an abandoned train set. In the middle of the room was a small secretary's desk. She opened the bureau, rifled through some unpaid bills and a startling offer from the *Reader's Digest*, and located a hidden drawer, covered with old pencil shavings. At a push, the drawer sprung open, and the cleanest, whitest light she'd ever seen spilled out of it. A neat little plinth rose up from inside the desk. On it nestled three glowing green cubes.

'Artron Packs,' said Sarah happily to herself and took one.

She turned back and made her way glumly to the spiral stairs, only to find they'd been replaced by an escalator.

'Thank you,' said Sarah.

Sarah stepped back into the main room of the TARDIS. She was whistling again.

The tune died in her throat. The familiar hum of the TARDIS had gone. The ship was silent, her footsteps echoed. There was a cold breeze stirring the air. The door to the outside was open, mist drifting in.

Sarah stopped dead in her tracks. 'But I thought I closed the door...'

Even at the time, back in the church, I felt a shiver down my spine.

I didn't know it, of course. But something had crept inside my TARDIS.

CHAPTER EIGHT

'Excuse me, what are you doing?

A tiny, fluffy woman was leaning over me. She looked tired, as though everything about her – from her grey hair to her pale grey skin to her spinster-green crinolines – had been through the wash once too often. Yet, despite the drabness, something about her sparkled.

I grinned and continued assembling a makeshift Reticulator in a nice quiet corner of the church away from the suspicious glances of Mrs Tulloch.

'It's just,' the woman continued in her soft Morningside tones, 'I've been told you're breeding supermoths. Apparently to devour the scarecrows' garments?'

I nodded.

'Forgive me, but that's not how moths work,' she said.

'Not currently.'

'Indeed. And what's to stop them from attacking us?' She allowed herself a tiny smile. 'From attacking our clothes?'

I stopped work on my Reticulator and gave her my full, delighted attention.

'The first enquiring mind and the first intelligent question I've been asked, and –' I sniffed the air – 'I notice the organ has stopped playing.'

'Yes.' The little woman flushed modestly. 'I'm pleased you were enjoying my modest playing.'

'You played excellently.' My compliment was genuine.

'Thank you. Mavis – Mrs Tulloch – she doesn't like me to play,' the woman admitted. 'She commandeers the organ at most services. And does so really well, most admirably. She refuses to learn the new settings of hymns. Good to keep them going. Commendably traditional.'

'I'm sure she is.' The lady had extended a gloved hand and I took it. 'I'm the Doctor, delighted to meet you.'

'Miss Sophonisba Mowat. And,' she prompted with gentle firmness, 'you were going to tell me some more about this machine of yours. It looks highly … original.'

'Well.' I resumed work on the Reticulator. 'Let's call it the Mighty Moth Machine. Mark One.'

'Mark One?' Sophonisba leant over the machine and nodded approvingly. 'I'm not sure there'll ever be another.'

'You have an enquiring mind, Sophonisba!' I exclaimed, looking up from a capacitor.

'Not enquiring enough,' she lamented, 'if I've missed my home being turned into a living nightmare.'

'Whatever alien intelligence is animating those scarecrows, it is cunning, conniving and terribly clever.'

She started. 'Alien?'

'It works slyly. Turns your isolation on this island to its advantage. It's built its forces slowly so you wouldn't see.'

'Alien.' Sophonisba cogitated gravely on this. 'Doctor, you sound as though – and this is probably rude of me – but you do sound somewhat alien yourself.'

'Somewhat,' I agreed genially.

'Oh, well …' She smiled a dainty smile. 'If I can accept that the island is overrun by living scarecrows, then it's not so hard to accept that Martians look like members of the Bloomsbury Set.'

'It would explain Virginia Woolf's cooking,' I agreed.

Outside in the churchyard, a crowd of scarecrows stood, ghastly heads tilted back, sucking away at the night air. Three of them staggered away, picked up something heavy, and then tottered towards the porch.

There came a loud and heavy pounding on the church door. The barricade of pews jumped.

'What are the scarecrows using, do you think?' Sophonisba asked. 'I was picturing tombstones. Are they perhaps using one as a battering ram? Is that too ghoulish of me?'

I looked at her. 'It's as well to be prepared.'

The thumping continued.

'The beats are getting fewer and further between. Do you think it'll be safe for us to sneak out there?'

I shook my head. 'That would be like a ham sandwich running towards a Labrador.'

'Oh dear.' Miss Mowat frowned.

'What can you tell me about the island?' I asked her.

'Well, it's never seemed a happy place,' she confessed. 'When I came here, I thought it was the most beautiful place on Earth, but there's something to it – a feeling in the air. It has a terrible history.'

'Does it indeed?' I put down my screwdriver and gave her my full attention. Terribly histories are my favourite kind.

'Oh yes, going right back to before Saxon times. An archaeologist found a remarkably preserved Viking boat buried out in the harbour. The whole crew was still on board. They died rowing away from something. So the story goes.'

'It so often does.'

'There's a whole history of plagues, of curses, of raids. James VI thought a spell had been placed on it, and took great joy in exiling people here. None of them lasted long. Others came here looking for a lost treasure.'

'Didn't find it, did they?'

'Oh no, but their deaths gave rise to a fair few sea-shanties. This place has a terrible reputation among sailors. There's a Spanish galleon out beyond the sandbanks, and it was joined by a fair few wrecks during the last war.'

'Fascinating,' I told her. 'I think there's been something wrong with this island for a considerable time.'

'What sort of thing?' she asked.

We both looked over to the door resounding to the ominous beat of tombstone against oak.

'Ah well.' Miss Mowat indicated my sprawling machine. 'So tell me more about how this contraption is going to save us all.'

I'm afraid I seized the chance to show off, even if just to an audience of one. 'Well, these moths are going to live at a terribly fast metabolic rate. This machine will accelerate their life cycle by several hundred per cent, poor dears.'

'You do know that moths breed quite quickly, don't you?' Miss Mowat put in. 'So, if you speed that up ...'

'Well, yes, there is a tiny chance that these creatures could descend like a biblical plague all across Europe.'

'I see.'

'A very tiny chance.' I held up a finger and thumb. 'Hardly any risk at all. Certainly compared to the last machine I built. Anyway, I'm trying to train the moths.'

'You are?'

'At a genetic level. What I really need is a microscope. All I have is a discarded pair of reading glasses.'

'So having a microscope is important?' Sophonisba Mowat nodded, straightened and shuffled off to the vestry.

Out of the corner of my mind, I could see Mavis Tulloch. She was standing on the font, peering through a window into the gloom of the churchyard. She did not like what she saw. She was scared and, for the first time in her life, she did not feel in control. She'd ruled this island for most of her adult life. In all that time she'd never been scared or confused. Things she didn't understand had always had the decency to get out of her way (poor Mr Tulloch included). She'd spent the last few weeks refusing to believe that the order of things was changing. Now she found herself adrift and oddly unable to reassert herself. From time to time a villager would approach her to ask what was going on, and she heard herself snapping unfamiliar words: 'I don't know.' She could see the effect this was having on the villagers and she didn't relish it. Nor did she admire the way that I'd decided to take Miss Mowat into my confidence. Something, she decided, would have to be done about this.

She slid off the font and sidled over to Harriet McEwan, one of the sourer fishwives. She began in age-old fashion: 'I'm not one to gossip ...'

'Of course not,' replied Harriet, leaning in.

'But, if you ask me, our Miss Mowat is already overfamiliar with our new arrivals. What does she know?'

Miss Mowat brought in a bag and handed it to me. 'You said you needed scientific instruments,' she said. 'This was in the jumble sale.'

I plucked a box from the bag. '*Every Boy and Girl's First Science Kit?*'

'It includes a microscope. I think it's broken,' said Miss Mowat. 'And some slides, but they're none too clean. It comes from Harry Perkins, and that child is quite the devoted nose-picker.'

'I see.' I eased the cover off the box, looked inside, then slid it all to one side. My attention was riveted instead by what the uninitiated might conclude was an eggcup for an acorn at the bottom of the bag. 'Oh wonderful – a flea glass!'

'Probably the vicar's,' Sophonisba remarked. 'He is – he was – a bit of a botanist.'

I screwed the flea glass into my eye like a jeweller about to appraise the Koh-i-noor diamond.

'Sophonisba,' I said gravely, 'I'm going to try and re-sequence the DNA of an entire species with little more than a magnifying glass.'

'Do you think you can do it?'

I regarded her solemnly. 'I shall have to squint.'

Mavis Tulloch slipped from group to group, topping up tea here, handing out a slice of bread and butter there. All served up with a garnish of mistrust and suspicion. Wherever she went, another nervous glance would wander over to me, my machine, and the terribly attentive Miss Mowat.

'Mavis is getting restless.' Sophonisba's tone was warning. 'I can tell. When she thinks you've been on the phone for long enough, you can hear her tutting down the line. It's most distracting.'

I looked up from my glass. 'I'm sure she doesn't miss a thing. If only she could isolate nanogenes we'd be in business.'

Miss Mowat smiled and cleared her throat. 'I rather think it's us she's trying to isolate. You may have to stop a mutiny.'

I followed her pointing hand to where Mavis was muttering at three old fishermen and casting acid glances in my direction. Occasionally she'd exclaim 'Moths!' and the men would murmur in agreement. I had started enough rebellions to recognise dissent brewing. Something clearly needed to be done.

I put down my microscope and strode over. 'Ladies and gentlemen, If I could have your attention.' I gestured to the hole in the window. 'That's our weak spot. We need it to be airtight. Find something to block it. A tea tray should do. But failing that, use your imaginations.'

The fishermen nodded and started casting around for something to use. They made some suggestions, all of which I agreed with heartily. This, as I'd intended, provoked Mavis Tulloch's ire and she started to come up with four different things that, as anyone could see, would be vastly better for fixing a broken window.

'But of course!' I exclaimed. 'Mrs Tulloch, I don't know how you do it! Superb – how idiotic of me to suggest plugging a gap with a tea tray. I defer to you, I really do. Splendid! Keep up the good work!' And then I wandered back to my machine, favouring Sophonisba with a big wink.

'Masterfully done,' whispered Miss Mowat. 'That's bought you some time.'

'It has, hasn't it?' I said, squinting again at the glass. 'But there's no tea tray big enough to keep out the winds of change.'

'By the way, where are your friends?'

'Good question.' I looked up from my work, worried. 'They've been gone a long time, haven't they?'

CHAPTER NINE

At that moment, Harry was creeping through the abandoned streets of the village, trying to follow the directions I had given him while repeating my instruction: 'Watch out for scarecrows.'

A creaking noise attracted his attention. In the shimmering moonlight a figure appeared through the fog. It was a policeman on his bicycle.

Harry had the instant urge to hail the figure, but something in the jerky gait of the figure and the strange glow that poured from its head pulled him up sharpish. He ducked behind a water butt and watched the policeman approach and sail jerkily past.

'I say!' exclaimed Harry. 'A scarecrow riding a bicycle, that's quite something.' He felt a moment's terrible pity for the policeman who'd found himself so outlandishly transformed, but also an amount of childish wonder. That was the thing about Harry Sullivan – there was no malice in him, just an urge to grin at everything until it grinned back.

Harry watched the ghastly policeman pedal away then broke from cover and headed towards the village store. He looked up at the sky, at the hunter's moon peeking through the clouds, and said grateful thanks for its light.

It helped him to find the shop without too much trouble. The street was quiet as a grave. He rattled the door. It was locked, of course. Mrs Tulloch was too careful. He felt in his pockets. Where was that keyring?

He didn't notice, but a figure stepped out of the shadows behind him. It was a scarecrow, dressed in a fisherman's oilskins.

Harry sniffed. There was a strange tang to the air. If he'd been a bit sharper, he'd have realised it was the smell of blood, fish and bone. He failed to find the key in his pockets and went round again. Left jacket pocket, right jacket pocket …

The figure behind Harry stepped closer. Under the hood a skull peered out, the jaws opening.

Harry found the keys at last. Two of them. And, of course, one lock. Harry picked a key. Tried it in the lock.

The figure took another step towards Harry, stretching out arms of bleached ash.

Having no joy, Harry gave a tiny tut at the unfairness of the world, and tried the other key. That didn't fit either.

The scarecrow paused, savouring the moment. That terrible skull seemed to grin.

Harry went back to the first key. For some reason it worked now. Well, wasn't that just his luck?

The scarecrow lunged.

Harry opened the door and stepped through, smiling at the jolly tinkle of the bell above the door.

The scarecrow followed behind him, bony fingers brushing Harry's shoulder.

Shivering slightly, Harry pulled the torch from his pocket and turned it on, sweeping it around the village store. He noted a rack of magazines and newspapers; why, there was the *Boy's Own Paper* and there was *The Ensign*. Dear old Jack Harkaway, prepping for adventures with the chaps of the First Remove. Seized with nostalgia for a forgotten childhood hero, Harry stepped forward to pick up the paper.

The scarecrow followed.

As it did so, the edge of its oilskins caught against the old latch of the door. As the scarecrow lunged, its coat pulled away, falling apart at the well-worn seams. For a few moments, the scarecrow continued to lunge, but its exposed body of wood and bone crumbled away to dust.

Harry, lost in childhood, put aside the enticements of *The Ensign*. Something – a noise? a groan? a clatter? – had recalled him to the present. 'Stay awake, Sullivan,' he chided himself.

With renewed purpose, he headed for the grocery counter, stepping over the oilskins that, so he presumed, someone had left lying on the floor. He advanced on the counter, waving the beam of his torch across the supplies. He saw half a shelf stacked with bags of sugar. 'Splendid!'

What Harry had failed to notice (and he'd already failed to notice quite a lot) was another scarecrow creeping in through the door. This one was wrapped in a tattered dress and a widow's bonnet. The scarecrow was desperately hungry. It grasped for poor Harry like a beggar after alms.

Harry, oblivious as ever, swung up the counter flap, ducking through. The flap knocked the scarecrow back. Harry marvelled at all of the groceries on display, and rushed forward to help himself. The scarecrow rallied and lunged again. Harry let the counter flap drop behind him. The flap caught the edge of the dress, and yanked it from the frame of the skeleton.

For an instant the scarecrow stood there, a bundle of sticks and a bonnet. Perplexed, it reached out for Harry ... Then it turned to dust.

A few minutes later, Harry had armfuls of sugar. He had piled the little paper packages up on the counter and topped the pyramid off with a jar or two of sweets. At first he went for mint humbugs but then plumped for jelly babies. He knew I would approve.

He regarded his haul proudly. 'Well done, Sullivan,' he told himself. He tried gathering it all up and realised he had rather more than the rucksack he'd brought with him would allow for. Seemed a shame to leave it all behind.

He threw his torch beam around the village stores and his eyes alighted on a promising side door which led to an outhouse. He stepped past a gurgling water closet and into a small garage open to the elements. It was piled high with firewood. In a corner was a scythe, a coiled length of hose, and, joy of joys, a wheelbarrow.

'You're just the ticket,' Harry Sullivan told the wheelbarrow and seized it, bouncing it into the shop.

Behind him, a figure moved out of the darkness of the shed. It was wrapped in a cloak, with an old sheep's skull for a head. It paused to pluck up the scythe and then fluttered after Harry, silent and deadly as Death.

Harry was loading up the wheelbarrow, his torch perched on the counter, motes of dust dancing in its beam. He was stifling the urge to whistle jauntily. Things were going jolly well and not a peep of a scarecrow. 'Sometimes,' he thought, 'the Doctor really does over-egg the pudding.' Dear old Harry.

Loading done, Harry grabbed the barrow and began to negotiate a path out of the shop. The wheelbarrow bumped up against something. He pulled it back and yanked it around.

Behind him the scarecrow with the sheep's head raised its scythe and whisked it through the air.

Harry bent down to hoist the wheelbarrow up.

The scythe whispered over Harry's head, snicking at the tips of his curls.

A moment later, Harry lifted up the wheelbarrow, marvelling at the balance. The squeak of its wheel masked something creaking behind him. He wheeled about and made for the door.

Behind him, the scarecrow made ready to swing its scythe once more – as the wheelbarrow jerked to a stop. Something was wrapped around the wheel. Harry bent down to see what it was.

The scythe whipped through the air where Harry's head had been, but Harry didn't notice; his attention was firmly fixed on the old rag or whatever it was, caught in the axle. Harry gave it a yank, pulling it firmly free. There was a satisfying tearing noise and he found the rag was in fact part of a long, dusty cloak. How odd that Mrs Tulloch should leave all these old clothes lying around. Dusting his hands, Harry threw the raggedy cloak to one side.

He straightened up and wheeled his way buoyantly towards the door. Time to get back to the church.

Behind him the denuded scarecrow still clung to its scythe. It tottered around impotently and then dissolved into a mound of dust. The scythe swayed in mid air and then clattered to the floor.

Truly, Harry Sullivan lives a charmed life.

Or, at least, he had up until this point.

FEAR OF THE ABSURD

My audience on Gallifrey was growing restless. Clearly they didn't yet find Harry Sullivan's antics as charming as I did.

Booing has never been invented on Gallifrey. Because we don't have opera or rail replacement buses, we've never really had the need. The worst you'll get from us is a cough, or a silence so cold it could keep milk fresh.

Lady Pralamandavarvar, an expert in Xeno-Lepidoptery, began to heckle. 'You were proposing to use a Gallifreyan power source to re-engineer a species of insects?' she yelled. Clearly, if she'd had the power, she'd have had me executed on the spot. 'It's monstrous! It's nonsense! It's monstrous nonsense!' Her ceremonial collar shook. 'Did you even consult a single authority on how to carry out this absurd plan? Did you make research plans, or conduct tests? Can we see your notes?'

'I'm afraid I didn't make any,' I confessed. 'I simply ... Well – I made it up as I went along.'

My audience was aghast.

'I think he's making it all up now!' simpered the Zero Nun, playing to the crowd.

I waited for the scattering of laughter to die down.

'If I am making it up,' I said, 'perhaps you should ask yourselves why. Look at those villagers—'

'Why should we?' thundered Lady Pralamandavarvar. 'They're just a bunch of stubborn idiots who refuse to recognise the danger they're in.'

This time I was the one to laugh. She didn't understand why. Of course she didn't.

'I fail to see what's funny.' There was no pacifying her. 'We've let you improvise your way through the universe. It's just not good enough, not any more.'

There was a considerable amount of muttering at this.

'Perhaps you should continue with your fable,' suggested the Zero Nun, clearly paying out a bit more rope for me to hang myself with.

I bowed to her.

Chapter Ten

The scarecrow stepped into the control room of my TARDIS from behind the door. Standing there, in Sarah's home from home, it looked absurd as well as frightening. The comforting, warm lights of the ship showed up the creature's ridiculously rag-taggle garments – a tattered smock complete with bird-pecked shirt. The head was an old flour sack without eyes or mouth, with the word 'NETHERCOTT' printed upside down. One hand was a gardening fork, the other an old chimney brush. The creature stood there, swaying slightly, its hands reaching out towards Sarah, almost begging.

Sarah felt sorry for it. 'Hello?' she said. 'Are you all right?'

The creature took another step towards her.

Sarah spoke again, using a tone she used for the squirrels in Hyde Park. 'Is everything all right? Can I help you?'

The scarecrow made another shuffling step. Its head was bowed, its hands were stretched out. It was a supplicant.

'What can it want from me?' Sarah thought. 'Are the last traces of its humanity looking to me for comfort?'

The creature stretched out its fork hand. It was trembling.

Sarah reached out to take the hand. 'What can I do?' she asked it. Then the corner of her eye noticed something.

The wall behind the creature was in darkness.

Which was odd. No, not odd, wrong. The TARDIS didn't tend to shadows. A gentle light always glowed from the walls of the ship. Sarah had found it disconcerting at first. In her bedroom there were no windows – there was just a light that turned itself down gently as you settled down to sleep, washing the room in a quiet rose glow. But here – here in the control room everything was always a sterile white. Except that there was a pool of shadow behind the scarecrow.

The creature took another step towards her, and Sarah snatched back her hand.

As the creature moved forwards, the shadows behind it rippled and spread.

Sarah turned on her heels and ran.

The creature followed, darkness flowing out behind it like spilt ink.

The TARDIS, my poor ship, had been invaded.

You know, Sarah actually spent some moments worrying about how upset I'd be. Monsters just didn't invade the TARDIS. This was a home, a sanctuary. The monsters were kept firmly outside and here was where you came to plot, to plan, to laugh once it was all over. And she'd left the door open and a monster had strolled in ...

Sarah was running down a long TARDIS corridor, the creature shuffling behind her. Its gait was awkward but steady. Sarah was tiring, the scarecrow wasn't. She could hear the pattering of her feet, the puff-puff of her breath, the gentle hum of the ship, but beyond that came the relentless clump-drag-stump of the scarecrow ... and something else.

The corridor was long and straight, and the ship had forgotten to put any doors in. Occasionally the TARDIS does this – corridors pottering away to infinity. I've no idea why she does it, but they were perfect for a good walk and a think without distraction. 'A door always appears when it's needed,' I'd once told Sarah airily, words which she now repeated bitterly as she ran.

She'd clearly made a terrible mistake – there was nowhere to hide, nowhere to shelter, no side turns to take – just endless corridor. Ahead was brightly lit infinity; behind her were the scarecrow and its shadow, implacable, constant.

Sarah kept running, telling herself that she'd been in worse messes. Something pulled her up, made her waste a few seconds on catching her breath. The light up ahead wasn't quite so bright, was it? Maybe there was a door looming?

Then she realised, and a dread chill entered her spine. The shadows were spreading up over the ceiling, the walls, the floor, racing ahead – long fingers just waiting to close around her. And there was a sound that came with it, the whispering, crackling of treading on fallen leaves.

Sarah found another spurt of steam. She needed to outrun the shadows. The scarecrow continued behind her, *shuffle-clump-stump, shuffle-clump-stump*.

At last she came to a door. She rattled it. It was locked. Why would I lock a door in the TARDIS?

She turned back to see where the scarecrow was. At first she couldn't see her pursuer, so lost was it in the murk surrounding her, and then it sprang out of the darkness at her.

Sarah stifled a cry as that faceless face with the upside down NETHERCOTT hovered over her. It emitted a dreadful sucking, pulling at the air. One of its arms brushed against her shoulder.

'Door,' Sarah said, with quite wonderful calm. 'Please, come on.'

She rattled the handle once more, and the door flew open. Sarah tumbled through and slammed it shut behind her. Plunged into brightness, she screwed her eyes tight as she threw her whole weight against the door.

'Right then,' she said and hunted around for a lock. Logically there must be one, because it had been locked in the first place. But now it was just an ordinary TARDIS door. She hunted around for something to wedge it shut with, something to hold the creature back – but no, there was nothing.

The door bulged. The scarecrow was throwing itself at the door. She felt the impacts. She knew how tireless the creature was. Still, it was on the other side of the door. That was a good thing.

Sarah decided to make the most of the situation. She leant back against the door, closed her eyes for a moment, gathered her breath. Then she opened her eyes and took in her surroundings.

'Oh my,' she said.

Sarah was in a very large room that felt like an empty water tank. Steel walls glowed gently around her. In the distance, steps led up to a little gantry running around the room. She wondered where the exit was.

There was something about the floor – it appeared to be a series of strange tessellations, interlocking tiles that glowed, bathing the metal ceiling in a dancing swimming pool of reflections.

'What is all this?' she wondered. 'Do I take three steps and then fall into a pit of piranhas? Why is this even *here*?'

I wasn't there to explain, so she knew she'd just have to work it out for herself.

The door behind her shoved and buckled. Sarah heard the creaking and splintering of futuristic space alloy. She looked down and saw a black puddle seeping around her feet.

For a horrific moment she wondered if she was bleeding from a wound she'd not even felt. Had she been stabbed through the door and not noticed it? Was that it? Was she impaled? Was she dying?

Then she realised – the puddle was a spreading darkness. It had seeped and crept under the door and was now making its way into the room. As it moved, a whispering noise trickled with it. Sarah twisted her head to one side and then the other and realised the darkness was soaking into the walls like they were blotting paper. She snatched her hands away from the shadows, feeling, to her horror, a slight stickiness to them – as if the darkness was a tar baby.

The door splintered. The scarecrow was scrabbling at it, tearing at the edges of the hole with its strange gardening fork. Its head burst through.

She watched the pathetic bundle of sackcloth with its upside down NETHERCOTT swing left and right, tasting the air. It snapped at her.

Sarah staggered away, and realised she was standing on the tessellating floor tiles. They lit up and shifted in colours and shapes as she moved from one tile to the next. She froze in sudden panic. What if she'd already taken two deadly steps?

'Think! Think! There's obviously a pattern.' Sarah jumped across to another tile. 'Let's be old fashioned. Avoid the lines and tread on the squares – let's go for that.'

Sarah started to run – albeit a tad gingerly – across the floor. The tiles lit up and glowed as she went, a strange dancing pattern which would have been quite beautiful if only she hadn't been in imminent peril.

Behind her, the scarecrow broke into the room, shuffling and staggering onto the board.

Disappointingly, lightning didn't strike the creature. It strode over the tiles in pursuit of Sarah, and lights swirled around it, quite ignoring the whispering darkness that followed it – more, in fact. As the shadows whispered towards the floor, the patterns glowed more brightly and the shadows retreated, hissing and spitting like hot fat.

As Sarah ran, more lights sprang up from the floor, the patterns washing over the steel sky far above her. The patterns and the purpose of the room baffled her. It wasn't trying to kill her, so what was it for? She reached one of the walls and started clambering up the iron stairway. She turned to try for just a glimpse of the pattern behind her, and her pursuer grabbed her ankle. It started to pull.

Sarah wedged herself into the metal stairs and gripped on tight. The scarecrow pulled, exerting its terrible strength on her.

Sarah wiggled and yelled at the creature and then struck back with her other foot, sinking it right through that upside-down NETHERCOTT. The scarecrow didn't cry out or flinch, but it gave her something to push against. She drove her foot further into the crunching mass of the creature's face and propelled herself back up onto the stairs, scrabbling free and scampering up, up onto the little walkway that went around the tank.

Unfazed, the scarecrow reached the bottom rung of the staircase and began to climb implacably behind her.

Sarah got ready to run around the gantry, but then the distant floor caught her attention and she stopped.

And she saw, now, what she'd been running across.

CHAPTER ELEVEN

Besides the sheep, there was no one around to notice that something was wrong with the sea.

The mists cleared and the ancient, chilly waters of the ocean began to bubble and then went flat and still. A perfect circle glowed beneath the waves. A hand shot up out of it. Then an arm. Something rose from underneath the sea and strode towards the shore.

Another, identical figure emerged and waded after it. The two figures, silver and impassive, stood on the shoreline, taking stock of the night. They stood there, their heavy feet sinking down into the wet sand. Waiting.

Meanwhile, at the back of the church, the pounding on the door had reached a crescendo and the barricade was shivering under the pressure.

'We're surrounded! They're breaking in!' wailed Mavis Tulloch.

Another staccato rap came from the back of the building.

'Interestingly,' I said, 'that wasn't a scarecrow.' I hurried over to the back door and unlocked it.

Harry was standing there, panting, holding a wheelbarrow.

'Hello,' I said. 'I was wondering if I could borrow a cup of sugar. Won't you come in.'

Harry rushed in, and I slammed the door behind him.

Mrs Tulloch immediately descended on Harry's haul. 'Here, I hope you paid for all that.'

'I left some cash on the counter,' Harry vowed, faintly outraged that he'd even been asked.

'I shall count it when I get back,' said Mrs Tulloch gloating at unimaginable riches, and holding out her hand for her keys. I had already grabbed hold of Harry, who was forced to throw them to her hurriedly, as I swept him away.

'This is Miss Sophonisba Mowat, she's been helping me,' I said, introducing him. 'This is Harry Sullivan, he's terribly good at errands, you know.' Then I started delving into Harry's wheelbarrow, pouring bag after bag of sugar into a gramophone horn I had adapted into a funnel. Sophonisba and Harry came over to help, reaching into the wheelbarrow. I swatted Harry's hand. 'Wait!' I cried. 'You can't put that in there.'

'Why not?' said Harry.

'That,' I said very gravely, 'is a bag of jelly babies.' I took the sweets from Harry's hand and offered them round. No takers.

A small group of curious villagers gathered about my admittedly peculiar device.

'What happens now?' asked Sophonisba.

'We turn it on,' I said. 'With a bit of luck, the moths will be drawn to the infected villagers, and they'll be very hungry.'

'How do we know the moths will stop at the scarecrows?' Harry couldn't hide his doubts.

'We'll soon know if the curtains vanish.'

I flicked a switch, and my machine leapt and gurgled into life. One old man from the village was operating a pump rigged up from the organ's bellows. Another was pedalling the vicar's bicycle, which was propped up on bricks. A long conveyor belt had been assembled from my scarf. The machine began to glow and emit a crackling, whining sound.

I sank back into in a pew, throwing my legs up on the bench in front. I let out what was either a Tibetan meditative prayer or a long sigh, I'm not sure which. Something had been worrying me. 'Funny thing,' I said.

'What?'

'Well, Harry, have you noticed how many of our adventures recently – they've been about things fiddling with humanity, producing abominations. Professors and giant wasps and militant potatoes and mad scientists and shapeshifters and androids and so on …'

'And now scarecrows?'

'Precisely. Trying to work out what makes a person a person and if there's another way of doing things. There isn't, of course, but something's driving them to try.'

'Well,' Harry opined, 'isn't that always happening to you?'

'Not really,' I ruminated. 'It's like someone's found a loose thread in the universe and is tugging at it. I wonder why?'

'To get your attention?'

'Oh, if you want to do that –' I pushed my hat down over my eyes – 'you've only to send me a nice card.'

Realising I was heading off for a nap, Harry smiled weakly at the old fishermen pedalling and pumping the bellows and looked warily at my machine. 'I do hope Sarah hurries up.'

My voice drifted up from under my hat. 'So do I, Harry. So do I. But at least she'll be safe in the TARDIS.'

CHAPTER TWELVE

In the TARDIS, Sarah Jane Smith was gazing down at the floor of the great chamber and trying to get her poor mind to take it all in. She had never seen anything like it – and she'd seen a lot.

It was one of the strangest rooms in my ship, and a room I kept locked for a good reason. The tiled floor was made up of little irregular squares, glowing with different lights. It was only at this distance that she could see that the lights made a pattern – more than a pattern.

Each tile was a picture. And the pictures interlocked. Sarah was looking down at a vast jigsaw. Only, and this was what grabbed her breath, the jigsaw was of her.

Each piece she'd stepped on was a different chunk of her life. There she was, a schoolgirl – with her best friend, laughing on the pier. There were her poor, dear parents. There was that horrid picture from her first press pass. Her dungaree phase – well, her first of many dungaree phases. There was that charming idiot from the sports desk who kept failing to ask her to a match because girls did not like football. Her cluttered desk at *Metropolitan* magazine with everything in the right place and her name on a little placard. Her name in a newspaper. She and

Aunt Lavinia eating ice cream. An MP shrivelling like a salted slug under her questioning. So far so normal – then things got weird. There she was in a medieval tapestry, then in a mug shot, glimpsed through security cameras on several worlds, standing next to a naughty-looking octopus at a peace conference, at the UNIT Christmas Party (as the alien-fighting organisation was Top Secret, everyone else in the picture had been blacked out), there she was running through a space station, across an exploding minefield, carried in the arms of an Egyptian Mummy, and posing while happily hitting her android duplicate with a lump hammer.

What stunned Sarah even more than what she'd seen was that the jigsaw didn't stop there. There she was on a street corner clutching a stuffed owl; there she was in a garden centre (looking a little older, but then she'd have to be if she was in a garden centre); older still, running from an exploding school; running from an exploding quarry; and, there she was, holding a young boy's hand, looking even older and still running. She didn't seem to stop running. Some of the pieces weren't in colour, and shifted a little, like novelty school rulers.

'I guess that's my future,' thought Sarah, and tried not to peek at the end. She wondered what the purpose of it all was.

As she watched, some of the tiles flickered and shifted. There she was on a beach at dawn. There she was, yelling at Harry. Then she was, running through darkness, her head turned to look at something swooping towards her. The tiles around that piece flickered and went dark.

'That's not good,' said Sarah. She refocused her attention on the scarecrow advancing on her, beadiness in its lack of eye. 'I reckon this is your fault,' she accused it.

The scarecrow didn't say anything, but lunged towards her. Sarah backed away, throwing herself around the corner of the walkway. The creature swiped, but she ducked and bolted away like a hare. The scarecrow dragged itself around the corner.

Sarah Jane Smith ran on.

The scarecrow did not feel tired. It still had plenty of nutrient. It had long ago stopped feeling pain, exhaustion or frustration. The poor thing knew only that it had to hunt – to find others and to either consume them or infect them. Its life was simple, its life was good.

It had once had to worry about so much more, but this was no longer the case. The scarecrow lived only in the present. Its instructions had been to get inside the craft, to infect it, and hunt down anyone inside. It was doing this implacably, unstoppably.

The woman, its prey, was running out of places to go. The metal walkway they were on had only one way out and they had passed it. All the creature had to do was to continue moving forward. Its quarry would eventually run out of places to go. She would fight back, she would cry out, she would plead. These things did not matter because she would die.

The scarecrow moved on.

It realised that the woman had stopped moving and was instead shouting at it and pointing. The reaction seemed strange behaviour for prey, hard to process. Was it a trap? An attempt to distract? The scarecrow summoned up a forgotten feeling – it allowed itself to be curious. What was the woman doing? She was pointing, pointing at the floor beneath them.

The scarecrow turned and looked down.

At first the scarecrow wasn't sure what it was seeing. The floor showed pictures. It knew this, it just did not care very much about pictures. You cannot hunt pictures, you cannot kill pictures, you cannot infect pictures.

The prey kept pointing at the floor. She was shouting and she seemed *angry* and *sad*. That was it – those were the words the scarecrow needed.

It looked again at the pictures, trying to work out what was in them. Some of the pictures showed a little girl in a skirt and heavy coat, walking along a beach, splashing in the sea, running through a field. In other pictures was the same girl, a little older, a little serious, surrounded by books. Then she was pictured with a handsome young man in a soldier's uniform (no, a sailor's uniform, that was it). Then the two of them together underneath an arch of flowers – their wedding day, all their friends around them. The little cottage they called home, the young man heading off on his ship, the young woman – so serious without him – working away, reading her books, feeding her animal (a *kitten*, that was it). The young woman walking through the village, or just sitting in a field, hands around her knees, attention drifting between her book and the sea.

The scarecrow considered how serious the woman looked. The scarecrow looked at the next pictures, of the woman reading a book about planting a vegetable patch and then digging one. A whole tile was devoted to her marrows. Then a sudden jump or two in time. The woman older, sadder, quieter. The kitten now a rangy old tom, curled up on her lap. The other chair by the fireside empty, gathering dust. The seasons moved on across the tiles and in all of them, the woman was alone. Then a change – the woman walking home, looking worried. The woman seeing something, something bad over her shoulder. The woman running. The woman hammering on the door of the village store. The face of Mavis Tulloch looking through the frosted glass window but refusing to open the door. The young woman pressed up against the shop front, seeing something coming towards her … And then the last picture was of a scarecrow, a scarecrow standing on a metal walkway looking down at a jigsaw.

The scarecrow realised what its life had been. That it was all here beneath *her*.

'That's me,' she tried to say, but all that came out was a guttural sucking noise. The scarecrow realised she had no voice, no face, just a jumble mockery of a body and a sack for a face that said NETHERCOTT.

The scarecrow looked up at her victim, who'd pointed all this out to her. At Sarah Jane Smith. For a second, the scarecrow felt rage and fury. And, for a moment, she didn't know what to do. Was she still going to kill her prey? Or was she going to ask for help?

The prey took a step towards her, her hands out, her face – it was a real face, not a sack – sad. 'That is you, isn't it?' Sarah said gently.

The scarecrow tried to speak again, but still the words would not come. The scarecrow shook herself, her stupid, cruel hands reaching up to poke and push at her burlap face. She felt nothing. She was nothing. She realised then that she didn't have eyes, so how could she see? She had a sudden memory of her father telling her to try not to think about her tongue, and for a few minutes her tongue had been all she could think about and she'd laughed then, and now the memory brought her nothing but pain – no, not pain, just an emptiness where sadness should have been.

There was a lot of emptiness in her now, the scarecrow realised. The information in that straw head was patchy. It felt like so much had been sifted and thrown away, and just a few husks remained. She remembered Mum was a woman with an apron dusted with flour. Dad was a gruff man who worked on the farm and pretended to begrudge buying his daughter books. Then there was her husband, the man who owned that little cottage with all the roses. His name was Alexander. Where was he? Why couldn't she recall what happened to him?

She realised with a shiver that she could not remember her own name.

Her attention returned to her prey. She realised that, while she'd drifted away, Sarah Jane Smith had been edging past her, trying to escape. Her instincts kicked in, and she lunged forward. Sarah ducked to one side, saying that she felt sorry, that she wanted to help. The scarecrow almost believed her. But then Sarah shoved her, shoved her hard against the railing.

The scarecrow reached out to Sarah with her imploring, stupid hands. She was trying to ask for help, to say that she was trying her best, that she would make amends, if only Sarah could help her stop wanting to kill her.

But instead Sarah Jane Smith, still mouthing 'sorry', kept pushing her, until the scarecrow felt herself toppling over and backwards. The weight of her top-heavy head took over, dragging the rest of her body with it, and she smashed down onto the flickering floor.

For a moment, the scarecrow lay there. She did not feel pain. She did not feel despair. She felt angry.

The scarecrow hauled herself up onto her feet, and got her bearings. She looked up and saw Sarah running across the walkway and out. Dragging her feet behind her, the scarecrow followed.

Sarah was running through the darkened corridors. She felt bad about what had happened to the scarecrow. Once she'd realised what the pictures in the jigsaw meant, she'd realised what the scarecrow was, who it had been. She had felt desperately sad for it.

The scarecrow had looked at the patterns on the floor, but it hadn't responded to them. It just made a couple of noises.

'Hello,' she had said, stepping towards it. 'I'm sorry. My name is Sarah. I can't imagine what you've been through.'

'Take my hand,' she had said.

The scarecrow had reared up, striking at her. Sarah had darted back, trying to push it off her, but the creature had just kept coming at her.

So, acting out of panic and fear, she had pushed it away, over the railing.

'I didn't mean ... it was an accident ...' she kept saying to herself as she ran.

The darkness was spreading through the entire ship. The light was struggling to be seen through the walls. Sarah paused for breath and wondered what it was; was it just shadow, or was it – glistening? She reached out to touch it, to try to work out if it was as sticky as pitch, then snatched her hand back.

The darkness was swamping the ship, and with it came a musty smell that hung in the air like spores. The normally sterile, off-pink glow of the walls became a murky sunrise – a Shepherd's Warning, if ever she'd seen one. She had to get out of here, somehow, but she was now thoroughly, miserably lost.

She reached a T-junction and gathered her wits along with her breath. She had to get out, get that power pack back to the Doctor. She just had to.

The clatter of bones drew her attention. Something was crawling towards her out of the darkness – the broken body of the scarecrow came creeping, broken and horribly wrong.

She ran on, turning left, and the tolling of a bell soon caught her attention. It was a splendidly mournful sound that echoed down the corridors, as though the TARDIS were throwing a funeral for itself.

She turned into a vast, forgotten ballroom, her footsteps echoing on the sprung dancefloor. Dustsheets covered the rows of chairs and the grand piano. An uneaten wedding cake had long ago collapsed into itself. For a few moments the room glowed with pristine whiteness. And then the darkness spilled out of the regimented circular patterns in the walls. The whole ship was going dark.

She ran through the ballroom, feeling the floor sag beneath her, uncomfortably aware that the shadows were puddling around her feet.

The tolling of the bell was getting louder and somehow more urgent. 'How can a bell sound urgent?' thought Sarah, heading towards the sound. It was giving her something to focus on.

She almost didn't notice the door. It seemed to be an ordinary grandfather clock, tucked into the corner of the ballroom, but it had a little knob in the case.

'Ah well,' thought Sarah. She turned the knob – the whole case of the clock swung open and she stepped forward into a world she hadn't been expecting.

Sarah was inside a bell tower. She seemed to be halfway up it. Beneath her were cascading rows of interlocking cogs – a vast mechanism that ticked and counted eternity. A huge pendulum swished through the air, arcing a graceful path between cogs. A narrow mahogany staircase ran up the inside of the bell tower. Sarah scampered up, heading towards the chiming of the bell.

The higher she climbed the more deafening the ticking, wrenching sounds of the clockwork became, almost drowning out the incessant tolling of that bell.

'What I wouldn't give to shut all this up for a moment,' she thought.

She climbed higher and higher, trying to work out what she'd do when she got to the top. Was she trapping herself?

'Oh no.'

A door into the clock opened above her and the scarecrow crept in. It stood almost upright once more. One of its arms dangled long and limp, but the other was firm. It started down the stairs towards her.

Sarah froze. Something rooted her to the spot, something primal, something of the little girl that lay at night too terrified to check for monsters behind the wardrobe door.

'This is ridiculous,' she told her stubborn feet. 'There's a monster right there. Do something about it!' But her body wasn't listening to her.

The scarecrow lurched implacably towards her. Two steps away it stopped, regarding her with its flour-sack face.

'Please,' said Sarah. 'There must be something inside you that's still human ...?'

The scarecrow seized hold of her, picked her up, and threw her into the abyss.

Sarah fell so quickly she didn't have a chance to scream. Something swiped past her in the darkness and she grabbed at it. She felt an enormous wrench, as though her arms were being pulled from their sockets, and then a crushing pressure across her ribs.

This is it, she thought, I'm falling into a giant cog and that's it for me. Perhaps the Doctor will one day wonder why his clock's a few seconds slow and that'll be it.

(Oh Sarah Jane – I'd never forget you!)

The crushing pressure against her lessened, and yet the sensation of movement did not. Sarah still felt she was falling. She was even more puzzled when there was a sharp jerk and she seemed to be falling in another direction entirely.

Sarah realised that she was clutching on to the giant pendulum. It was weaving its way in a stately madrigal through the vastly complicated arrangement of cogs and regulators. Spinning around inside its bearings, Sarah tried to get hers. This wasn't helped by the way that her fingers were slipping down the pendulum.

Squinting, she forced her eyes to adjust to the stygian gloom. At the far end of the pendulum's slice, it was just a short jump between two cogs to another staircase. She let the pendulum go a couple more times and then, trying not to cry out loud, she launched herself into thin air. She could see the walkway coming up towards her—

Something snatched at her collar. At first she thought it was the scarecrow, but she realised she'd become snagged on a tooth of one of the giant cogs and she was being pulled up into it. Sarah dangled like a mouse hanging from a cat's paw. The walkway was just out of reach. The cogs were grinding with the effort of hauling her up. If she could just grab hold of the pendulum again, she stood a chance of it dragging her free. She grasped for it. No luck.

However, the movement tugged at the hood of her coat. Harry's was a very sensible duffel coat from a lovely old-fashioned department store. It had put up with a lot in its life, but it had never expected to be its wearer's sole means of support.

The hood gave way with a loud tear, and Sarah found herself falling through the air once more. As she twisted, she could see the pendulum coming up towards her, the large hard disc on a collision course with her skull.

At school Sarah had only ever hated one teacher. His name was Mr Doyle and he'd insisted that 'his girls' (as he referred to them in greasy fashion) jump over wooden horses and shin up ropes and dangle from parallel bars. Most of the girls had suspected that Mr Doyle was a terribly unhappy man with murder in his soul. It hadn't surprised her in the least when poor Mrs Doyle was later found tucked behind the hot water tank in his attic. Anyway, Sarah's rugged hatred for Mr Doyle had meant that she'd always made it to the top of the rope, always dangled the smartest on those bars. And right now it was pure muscle memory hatred for the miserable man that threw her arms out right now, grabbing on to something. It turned out to be the railing at the side of the staircase.

She clambered onto the staircase and shakily took to her feet once more. The chiming of the bell was extraordinarily loud above her, and she went on climbing until she reached the bell tower.

'No bell,' she realised. 'Curious.'

Then she saw it. A small portable record player sat, the shellac disc spinning away. She lifted the needle. The tolling of the bell stopped.

'Oh, Doctor,' she sighed.

Then her breath caught. That terrible wisp at the back of the neck that told her she was not alone in the bell tower.

'I know you're there,' said Sarah.

The scarecrow stepped from behind an arch. It had been waiting for her.

The scarecrow stepped from behind the arch. She found her prey curious. If it had been her, she'd have turned and run, run away from all this. But not Sarah Jane Smith. She kept going. The scarecrow remembered younger days, when her father had a dog that was always sticking its head into burrows hunting for rabbits. Never giving up.

The scarecrow paused. She remembered loving that dog. She remembered crying for days when the poor thing had died. She remembered these things. But she did not feel any of these memories. They were all dull, faded like the pattern on a too-washed plate.

She spread out her arms, feeling something moving inside her sawdust innards. The darkness was there – it flowed out through her arms, through the gaps in the flour sack, the darkness spreading out and worming its way into the machine that was around it. She had a mission and she was finishing it.

She watched as the air grew dark and she felt a numb satisfaction. It was nearly done.

'No!' the voice startled her. 'Stop it!'

It was Sarah Jane Smith, yelling at her. 'Whatever you're doing to the Doctor's TARDIS, stop it at once.' She stamped her foot and the scarecrow remembered uppity children like that in her class.

Yes. She'd been a schoolteacher. A whole clutch of memories came rushing back. Her brain felt something like enjoyment. She just had to let the last of the darkness flood out of her and then her work would be done and she could remember—

'I said, stop!' It was Sarah Jane Smith again, angry, shoving her aside. How did she know Sarah Jane Smith's name and not her own?

The scarecrow no longer cared. She jabbed her muddy fork of a hand at Sarah, impatient for the work to be done.

Sarah recoiled from the scarecrow's attack, its pitchfork stabbing into the stonework behind her with a bone-jarring scrape. She darted round to the left, risking a peek out of the arched windows. Outside the clock was an impossible vista of fluffy clouds, like she was in the Giant's Castle in *Jack and the Beanstalk* – not in the eaves of a colossal grandfather clock at all.

The darkness continued to drift out of the scarecrow like a haze of flies. She could hear the whispering of it over the ticking of the clock. That was why the creature had come here; hunting her was just a secondary purpose – it had come to infect the TARDIS.

Now it lashed out at her again. Sarah dashed over to the record player, snatched up the record, and snapped it brutally across her knee. Then, putting all her weight onto her left foot, she lunged forward with the shellac dirk, slashing across the clothes of the scarecrow, snicking open the tied bundle of twigs which formed the creature's chest.

The scarecrow stopped moving and looked down at itself, an almost comical tilt to the sack head, a frown forming in the ETHER of NETHERCOTT.

The scarecrow who'd once been a teacher looked down, bluntly aware that she no longer had a stomach or internal organs. Just a gathering of sticks. The old cord around her chest was cut, but if she no longer had a heart, what did it matter?

And yet there was a terrible feeling building inside her. She remembered when the storms had come that terrible winter and the whole village went to watch North Cliff taking that terrible pounding from the waves. At first it had looked much the same as ever, and then, after one mighty wave, the cliff had started to slide away, one big slice after another crumbling, sliding, smashing into the waves and vanishing under the water.

The same thing was happening to her now. She was falling apart, slipping away into nothingness.

Sarah looked at the writhing creature, watching its arms paw at the air. Sarah recoiled in horror as the wooden limbs peeled back, revealing little shanks of bone that then turned to powder.

The creature fell backwards, toppling down the stairs and into the bowels of the clock.

The last thing the scarecrow saw was Sarah Jane Smith's look of sheer horror. Then she flipped over and over, falling into the cogs of the great clock.

The last thing the scarecrow heard was the snapping of twigs as her body was crushed into matchsticks.

The last thing the scarecrow thought as what remained of her brain turned to dust was, 'My name was Joanna.'

FEAR ON EARTH

'Why do you have to keep saving Earth?' one of the listening Time Lords called out. There was some scattered applause on his behalf. 'What's so special about it?'

'I'm often asked that question,' I said, fixing that individual with a glare. 'People do so love to invade the planet Earth, which seems unfair on the place, as it has problems enough of its own. The people for a start – they frequently stump me. And yet ... there's something about them. Have you ever met a human? Talked to one? They're so very curious.

'They're so wonderfully eccentric – give me a vicar with a deadly secret hidden in his library; give me a little old lady who plays the bingo every day and goes home to tend a monster in the cellar at night; give me a monk who greets every dawn with a pious invocation to the dark and ancient ones; give me a young girl selling sticks of rock who delights in short-changing her customers. Earth has a plethora of peculiar people – all of them so fascinating, so interesting, and – when they turn to evil – so wonderfully muddled. For every mad maniac with an unthinking army, there's a quaint old widow who poisons a single bloater-paste sandwich at every tea party.'

I let them try to get their heads round that lot. It took some doing. Gallifrey doesn't really do eccentrics. It's why some of us leave.

'Another thing about the Earth – the sights! So many seas crash against so many shores. There are the terrible temples of hidden knowledge in the Hindu Kush; there are the great and hidden icy tundra beneath which something dark and mysterious slinks slowly towards Doomsday; there are queues at bus stops and there are little glass screens behind which little men scowl and tell you that it's not their problem. All of these places huddle under the same sun and in each and every one of them, along with the danger and the terror, there is something that thrills the soul. Maybe it's the distant waft of chip shop vinegar, or the pop of a cork, the wink of a guard as he locks you in at night, or just the quiet smile of the tired woman behind you in the queue who tells you it's all going to be all right eventually. What's not to love about each and every one of them?'

The mood in the room was grim, but I was in full flow. I could sense the beam of light around me intensifying, but I refused to be stifled.

'I'm trying to teach you the value of a planet – one single planet in a universe of billions,' I told them. 'Take Earth's history – so full of miserable devils concocting terrible plans in hazy rooms. Ignore them – they get in the way – and instead appreciate the magnificence there. To take tea in the Hanging Gardens of Babylon; to chat with the Sphinx before she took her vow of silence; to go to the theatre in Athens and laugh so hard you forget how uncomfortable the seats are; to sit with an artist, ask her what's new, and maybe leave her some money for the electric bill before taking her daughter out for ices on the pier.

'That's the thing about the Earth. I'm trying to make you love it, to see the value of it. Every time I land there, even in its darkest corners, there's something new and delightful. Something worth defending. Something that brings me back.'

'That's all very well, I'm sure,' sniffed the Zero Nun. 'But what about the rumours we've heard about your special relationship to the planet. Aren't you its self-appointed guardian or something?'

'It was you Time Lords who sent me there!' I reminded her.

'Did we?' purred the Zero Nun, pretending to search her memory. 'Ah yes, wasn't that after your last trial? Weren't you exiled there to learn the error of your ways?'

Oh they lapped that up, and banged the bowl for more.

'It's true!' I admitted over the hubbub. 'But all planets deserve defending. And it's not for you why I defend the Earth … It's not even for myself. I defend it because it's a juicy currant bun and it's my duty to keep the flies off.'

'Are you telling us –' the Zero Nun gestured up at the Sword of Never hanging over my head – 'that you'd risk obliteration, you'd risk the universe, just to save a planet?'

'Yes,' I told her, and felt the room go cold.

'That,' she said with grim finality, 'Is a decision no Time Lord would ever make.'

'No,' I snapped back at her. 'Because you're too afraid to. And I'm going to tell you why you're wrong …'

CHAPTER THIRTEEN

Sarah was running through the night, arms aching as she clutched the Artron Pack to her chest.

As she approached the church, she froze.

There was something wrong with the churchyard. The stiff silhouettes looming out of the night weren't gravestones. Standing perfectly still, arms outstretched, were a dozen scarecrows. Waiting.

Crouching low, she skirted around the drystone wall to the back of the churchyard, and climbed over it. Her foot caught a loose pebble, and she winced as it skittered down the wall. She jumped the last three feet. To her ears the impact was like a bomb going off, but maybe, just maybe, no one had heard it.

She slunk towards the vestry door, one eye on the figures waiting at the front of the church. None of them had moved.

Her heart in her throat, she crept up to the door, and tapped on it. Gently.

'Doctor, Harry!' she whispered.

Nothing.

She tapped again. Louder.

Still nothing.

Panic edged closer. What if the scarecrows were creeping up on her? What if there was one behind her? What if they'd already got inside the church? What if the Doctor and Harry were already dead?

She took a deep breath and she knocked again. Firmly.

Harry's voice drifted through the door. 'Sarah, is that you?'

'Of course it's me, Harry.' Her voice flooded with anger and relief.

With a clunk, Harry unlocked the door.

As it swung open, a figure detached itself from the yew tree and lunged at her.

Harry opened the door to see a scarecrow fighting with Sarah. It had an arm around her waist and was crushing the life out of her. Sarah flailed as it shoved her forward, forcing its way through the door. Harry grabbed an ornamental crucifix from the wall, and smashed it brutally down against the creature, lopping off its straw arm. Harry struck again, pushed the creature outside and kicked the severed arm after it. Then he slammed the door shut, turned back to Sarah and held her closer to him.

'Am I glad to see you,' she said into his collar which smelt comfortingly of aftershave.

'Hello, old girl,' he said. 'I say, what have you done to my duffel coat?'

I was terribly pleased to see her. She began to tell me about the state of my poor TARDIS. But I was a little preoccupied with my moth machine, and I'm afraid to say I cut her off.

'You're all right, though, aren't you, Sarah?'

'Yes, but listen—'

'Then that's all that matters.' I took the Artron Pack from her, and wired it into the device as casually as an battery into a torch. 'You got here just in time – once I've flooded the distillation chamber with Artron Energy, we can unleash the moths.'

'That's wonderful news,' said Sarah. 'But—'

I sent her off to help Sophonisba and Harry then returned to my machine. We really were pressed for time.

Left to her own devices in the middle of the church, Sarah kicked a pew. 'Great Doctor, that's fine, Doctor, don't worry about what I've been through, or your TARDIS,' she muttered lethally. 'Just fiddle with your Heath Robinson madness. What does it even do?'

'Nothing sensible, if you ask me.' Mavis Tulloch had sidled up to her. 'It's nothing but a waste of time and good sugar.'

Sarah's natural inclination to disagree with anything Mrs Tulloch thought allowed her to immediately overcome her own objections.

'Mrs Tulloch! Hello!' Sarah's forced smile brought a little brightness into the room. 'How is everyone holding up? You're doing your best to keep morale high?'

Sarah's tactic worked. 'Ah!' Mrs Tulloch exhaled. 'I've done my best. I always do.'

'Of course you do,' Sarah agreed solemnly.

'But – and I'm not alone in this worry – can that contraption really save us?'

'If the Doctor says it can,' Sarah assured her, 'then it will.'

'I'm sure, I'm sure,' Mrs Tulloch purred like a malicious tabby. 'You're a loyal friend.'

The two women smiled at each other insincerely, and Mavis Tulloch pottered away to tell a few select islanders, in absolute confidence, that the Doctor's friend thought he was a fraud too.

'Oh, wonderful,' Sarah said to herself angrily.

Harry came over to her. 'Put your foot in it with Mrs Tulloch, did you?'

'Both feet,' said Sarah. 'She overheard me doubting the Doctor's machine.'

'Shame on you, old thing,' said Harry. 'After all, there is absolutely nothing ludicrous about it.'

At that moment, the Artron Incubator emitted a belch and a puff of purple smoke.

Sarah and Harry both started laughing, the first proper laugh they'd had in hours.

'At any moment,' Sarah said seriously, 'specially bred moths are going to surge out and destroy the scarecrows, and we're all going to look really silly.'

'I once owned a flea circus,' Harry announced mournfully. 'The fleas ran away.'

'You didn't name them, did you?'

There was a tiny pause from Harry.

'You did, didn't you?'

The machine started to glow. There was a small bang, and I emerged through a cloud of sparks, sucking my fingers.

'It's actually working!' I cried delightedly. 'The moth's life cycle has been sped up by several thousand per cent. All we need is a moment's calm, and we'll know for sure …'

The machine glowed brighter. Inside the fish tank, you could just see a cloud of tiny black dots, buzzing back and forth getting ready to spill out …

With a crash, the front door of the church gave way.

A figure pushed its way inside, forcing the piled-up pews to one side.

It was the scarecrow of the farmer. But he'd changed since last I saw him. He was no longer a collection of spindly twigs and rags, but a magnificent mahogany creation, a living statue. His clothes hung off a solid frame, his well-toiled muscles captured in wood, a solid world-weary face staring out at the world. There was something twisted through the grain of the wood, a metallic glint.

Of course, everyone was screaming and backing away and asking me what to do, but I was trying to think. What did the farmer remind me of? Had the scarecrows been only a trial run?

Was whatever was loose on this island now finding its true form? And if so, what was it?

Sarah was tugging at my sleeve and demanding an explanation.

'They're evolving,' I told her. 'Fascinating. Only, if they're building themselves stronger bodies, they may be out-evolving their weakness.' I looked miserably at my machine, still shaking and glowing away. 'And I need just a little longer for my clever moths.'

'Is it too late to raid these old pews for woodworm?' Sarah asked.

The villagers cowered back from the farmer. All except for Mavis Tulloch, who shoved her way through the crowd to regard it. She was, I could tell, about to do something terribly unhelpful. In a crisis, always be afraid of someone who isn't afraid. Unless it's me, of course.

'Well,' she snapped at the farmer. 'And what do you want?'

It was how she'd greeted customers to her shop for decades, putting them in their place as they stepped over the threshold. Unlike them, the farmer did not cower. He gestured outside, where a dozen scarecrows stood among the tombstones. Then he pointed at me. Then he pointed outside.

The gesture was unmistakeable.

'They want you, Doctor!' said Harry.

'Word about me gets around so fast,' I sighed.

Mavis gave me a look. A woman used to pricing things by the pound, she'd worked out my exact value, and considered it very low.

'All right,' she said to the farmer.

A silence fell over the church.

I noticed that none of the villagers were looking at me.

Well, apart from one. Sophonisba was protesting vociferously. 'You can't give the Doctor to them! He's helping us!'

There were a few nods of agreement, but still no one looked at me. I could read the room. I was tomorrow's chip wrappings.

Mrs Tulloch pressed home her point. 'Of course they want him,' she sneered, jabbing a finger at me. 'He's behind it all, you'll see. They've come to rescue him. He's been laughing at us the whole night – he's been lurking around, causing all this madness, and now he promises to save us. And with what? Moths! I ask you. Moths! Give him to them!' she cried. 'Then they'll leave us alone.'

I've been in a lot of rooms where a terrible decision is made. It hovers and swoops through the air, at first unthinkable, unspeakable, and then it lands.

I looked at noble Miss Mowat, at Sarah, and at Harry, who was clearly working out if someone needed a piece of his mind. I smiled at them all. Perhaps it wasn't my strongest smile, but it urged them all to stay still. After all, my little machine was still puttering away.

For a few moments an uneasy silence hovered between the villagers. A small, old fisherman detached himself from the crowd and crossed over to stand with my friends. He regarded Mavis Tulloch with rheumy, defiant eyes.

'This is wrong,' he said, his voice as quiet and firm as the sea. 'You know it is.'

Then, nodding to Sophonisba, he walked up to the farmer.

'Away with you,' he said. 'We've had enough.'

The farmer regarded him for a long, wooden moment.

Then he lashed out with a smooth, brutal chop. Felled silently, the old man's broken body toppled to the ground and lay still. Horror-struck, the cowed villagers gathered sullenly behind the grim figure of Mrs Tulloch. The farmer's arm was already back by his side, as though it had never moved.

If only I could have done something to prevent it.

Things had gone far enough. I stepped forward, past Sarah and Harry and Sophonisba, tipped my hat to Mavis, and came to a halt in front of the farmer. Sarah darted after me, but Harry held her back.

'I cannot bear a scene.' I rapped the farmer on the wooden shoulder. 'Shall we go?'

Outside the church, I sniffed the night air and considered my options.

The line of scarecrows hemmed me in.

They could kill me, of course they could. That was entirely possible.

On the other hand, my Artron Incubator was due to hatch at any moment. Perhaps, there'd be enough time – if I could stall proceedings a little, or maybe if they executed me very slowly. Ordinarily, I'm not partial to a long and lingering death, but I'm always prepared to make exceptions.

Waiting nervously for something to happen. I spend a surprisingly large amount of time waiting for things – sometimes the end of the world, sometimes a bus. The feeling is always pretty much the same. Anticipation, a nervous glance at the horizon, a hope that something will turn up.

The farmer pointed back to the church.

His meaning was clear.

Wait and see.

Inside the church, a furious Sarah shrugged Harry off and turned on him. 'What were you doing? Letting him go like that!'

'Steady on, old girl,' Harry cajoled. 'Don't you think the Doctor's up to something?'

Sophonisba fluttered nervously between the two. 'I suppose, he was trying to prevent further bloodshed. And if he's right, then his marvellous machine will save us at any moment.'

'We need to save him.' Sarah had had enough of capitulation. 'I'm going out there,' she announced, pointing to the door that still stood ajar. 'Who's with me?'

'Strangers turning up, bringing trouble and telling us what to do.' Mavis Tulloch used the tone she employed when someone asked if they could have their groceries on credit. A glance at the islanders told her they were wondering if they'd made an entirely correct decision, so she made up their minds for them. 'I'm fed up of it. Aren't you?'

There were murmurs. No one likes being caught out on the wrong side.

Having quelled any rebellion, Mavis decided she needed to do something showy. She crossed over to where my machine was puttering away to itself.

'This thing,' she sneered, 'has been a waste of everyone's time – and *my* sugar.'

Sarah and Harry started forward but before anyone could stop her, Mavis gave my machine a good, hard shove, and it slid off the table and crashed to the floor. The lights went out. The fish tank cracked. The lid of the tea urn fell off, rolled along the tiles and then with a slow, circling clatter, fell still.

Mavis Tulloch turned to the parishioners triumphantly. 'Good riddance to bad rubbish,' said her old slug of a smile.

Harry, Sarah, Sophonisba stood frozen. Everyone stared at the wreck of the machine. Some had the decency to lower their heads in shame.

The farmer pointed to one of the scarecrows. The creature stepped forward. It was garbed in a woeful pair of trousers, drawn tight with string, and a flowery blouse. In its hand was a small jar. I saw what it was up to and cried out, but without pausing, the scarecrow threw the jar into the church.

The jar sailed through the open church door and smashed onto the floor, sending a powdery ash spilling out.

'Get back!' shouted Harry, recognising it before the niff of nitrogen caught at his nostrils.

But the dust shot up in clouds. Sarah had adored pantomimes as a child – this was the big puff of smoke out of which a genie would appear. It hung in the air, and the villagers cried out.

Sophonisba ran into the throng, pushing people out of the path of the dust. The islanders were stumbling around, blinking and bemused. 'Gas!' she bellowed. 'Poison gas!'

The men of the island had gone off to war, and the few who came back admitted to seeing terrible things. They reacted instinctively to the warning, racing up the steps to the quire where Harry and Sarah stood.

'Look at you all!' sneered Mavis Tulloch. She'd been the first out of the path of the cloud, of course, but that didn't stop her denouncing the men with all the joy she'd once had handing out white feathers.

As Sarah tried to work out what she could do now, a fisherman stumbled forward out of the cloud, bent double and coughing, rubbing at his watering eyes.

He held up his hands, staring blankly as the flesh bubbled and coarsened and twigs pushed their way through the sagging pores of his skin. Before he could call out, ivy burst from his mouth, leaves and all, vines wrapping around his face, hardening and coarsening. He took one staggering, agonised step, his legs twisting into old tree stumps, his arms sagging limply.

'The villagers are already infected,' Sarah gasped.

Harry dashed over to the ruins of the Doctor's machine, shaking it. It glowed feebly, sputtered, and then did nothing.

Harry turned to Mavis Tulloch, fury in his eyes. 'What have you done?' he cried.

I stared in horror at the sounds of chaos inside the church. At the cries of humanity dying.

Two scarecrows stood either side of me, holding me firmly in place. I pushed my feet into the gravel, poised to spring away from them, but the creatures' strength was too great.

'Let me in there,' I pleaded.

The farmer regarded me, his posture curious, and slowly shook his head.

There are times when I can do nothing. Nothing more than stare at the gravel, silent and furious.

In the heart of the cloud, Sophonisba was grabbing arms and sleeves and shoving the islanders out of the door, into the fresh air, scarecrows be damned.

I turned to the farmer. My smile gave my eyes a very wide berth. 'What are you up to?'

The farmer did not reply.

I pretended he had, though. 'Your infection is frightening but terribly impractical. Mutating human beings into abominations? That can't be the end game, can it? What are you working towards?'

The islanders staggered out of the church, heaving and choking, Sophonisba at the rear, shouting at everyone to take deep lungfuls of the stinging night air. The group pulled to a halt in front of the scarecrows. Sophonisba greeted them with equanimity and me with relief. She stepped forward, a shepherd protecting her flock.

'Doctor! Good evening.'

'Miss Mowat!'

'These are not friends of yours?'

'Absolutely not,' I vowed. 'I'd cross my hearts, but as you can see my arms are indisposed. I often get tied up in my line of work.'

'What a life you must lead.' Sophonisba turned to the islanders. 'Go home. I'm between them and you. You heard me. Go.'

The villagers backed away, sidling around the sides of the church.

Sophonisba, wary, gentle, maintained eye contact with me. 'We both know I can't protect them,' she whispered, with a certain steel. 'But if you must say nonsense, say it with authority.'

'I quite agree.'

She glanced over to where the islanders were pooling at the edge of the churchyard, and shooed them. 'It appears they are to be allowed to leave unmolested. Have we you to thank, Doctor?'

I shook my head, wary, as I looked between the farmer and the other scarecrows. They stood among the tombstones, stiff and still and waiting. Waiting for what?

I had a nasty suspicion.

One of the islanders coughed. Then another. As the cough spread like a ribald joke, they looked around with panic and alarm, eyes wide with fear and horror.

I turned to the farmer. 'Enough of this.'

Still the farmer did not move.

'Enough!' I shouted.

'I don't understand—' Sophonisba gave a little bee-sting cry. She stretched out a hand, pained. I stared at her hand aghast, watching as her flesh hardened, twisted and splintered. The change raced from her fingertips down to the wrist and then consumed her arm. She clutched at her throat, the fine flesh there already thickening. Her mouth made small puckering attempts to breathe, then froze into a skeleton's grimace. Her eyes went black, the skin on her face setting, mould blooming over the oaken surface.

The other islanders were in similar distress, bent over, pawing at the air, as they changed horribly. The creatures that emerged from the transformation were more like rood-screen carvings than scarecrows. All their fine old individuality sanded down, their souls frozen in wood, wood that glinted with hints of metal.

It took a while, but eventually, mercifully, the desperate cries of pain stopped, and the horrible twitching of limbs stilled. The scarecrows were joined by a group of villagers, standing in a silent row, their faces open in what could have been just an 'oh' of surprise, but looked like a horrible wooden choir screaming in silent and perpetual agony.

I had made myself watch.

All of it.

CHAPTER FOURTEEN

Harry and Sarah stood inside the church, horrified.

'We have to do something to help them,' Sarah whispered.

'It's too late for them.' Harry's hand found hers and gave it a squeeze. 'They were already soaked in the petrol, and something lit the match. All the villagers are gone.'

'Not good enough,' Sarah informed him. 'At the very least we have to free the Doctor. There must be something.'

They were disturbed by a sudden movement. A tiny creak.

Harry turned towards the pews, stiff as a setter. 'Sarah, old girl,' he was positioning himself between the pews and her. 'I don't want to alarm you, but we're not alone in here.'

'I can hear that,' muttered Sarah. 'Who is it?'

A figure emerged from the shadows.

My attention was riveted by what had happened to the villagers. I watched the creatures finding their feet, testing their new limbs, sucking at the night air.

'I was right,' I said, and for once I didn't enjoy it. 'The infection has adapted, it's becoming more practical. But there's an intelligence at work behind all this, isn't there? Someone

attempting to teach me a lesson. And I don't care for the subject.'
I turned to the farmer. 'Somewhere close by there's a malevolent
scapegrace grinning like an idiot, isn't there? Probably in a cloak,
with grand schemes, vast plots, but no idea at all what life means.
Someone who has never returned a library book late, walked a
dog, or even felt that tiny bliss that comes from having the right
change. Someone who has done this terrible thing simply for fun.'

A creature of an entirely different sort made its way out of the
church, tiptoeing like fate. It came not with a stride, or a gloat, but
with a skulk.

It was Mavis Tulloch. Shaken, horrified, sly she tried to edge
past the creatures who had once been her neighbours. She
employed the creep of one desperate not to be noticed.

'Mrs Tulloch,' I whispered. She didn't even turn her head, just
kept sidling past.

'Oh, you're all right,' I growled. 'They've not noticed you.
They're too busy trying to grasp what's happened to them. The
people you've lived alongside all your life. But you don't care
about them, do you, Mavis? So, run. Run away and don't give us
another thought.'

And Mavis Tulloch did run. She made it out of the churchyard
silently, slipped through the lych-gate, and, at the last moment, it
shut behind her with a bang like a pistol.

The newly born creatures in the churchyard turned towards
the sound, a dozen wooden blank-eyed faces sucking hungrily at
the air.

'Run and don't stop,' I called.

Mavis Tulloch took to her heels.

I watched the villagers lumber after her, their footsteps as
stiff as clockwork soldiers. I turned to the farmer and nodded
ominously. 'Let's hope she's got a stout pair of shoes on under
those petticoats.'

Sarah and Harry crouched inside the church, watching.

'So, that's it.' My voice carried to them over the threshold. 'There goes Mavis, taking Sarah and Harry with her. The others are all dead now, changed into monsters. There's no one left alive inside that church. So shall we go wherever it is we're going?'

Peeping over a pew, Sarah saw the farmer nod, and watched as the two scarecrows holding me wheeled about and marched me away.

'They're taking the Doctor!' hissed Harry.

'I've got eyes,' whispered Sarah.

The other scarecrows started to file out of the churchyard.

There was a football rattle of a noise behind Sarah.

Sarah started, at first assuming it was a scarecrow. But the noise was coming from the ruins of the Artron Incubator. Sarah hurried over to it, rifled through the pile of smashed junk and plucked out an old petrol can that was rattling. Harry darted towards the altar and whipped the cloth from it, a magician's marvel that, sadly, no one else was there to applaud. He threw the cloth around the can, muffling the noise.

'Let's hope no one's heard that racket,' Sarah said.

Out in the graveyard, the procession of scarecrows made their way towards the coppice gate. I hoped Sarah and Harry were all right. I'd heard the popping sound from inside the church and it made me think all was not lost. I had to pass them a message. I thought for a moment and then smiled, pleased with myself.

I wouldn't have been quite so pleased if I'd noticed that one of the scarecrows had turned away from the file, and was making its lurching way back towards the church.

Sarah and Harry crept onto the porch, watching me vanishing into the mists of dawn.

'We have to do something,' said Sarah.

'Good grief,' said Harry.

'What?' Sarah threw him a look.

'The Doctor's arms! He's signalling!' Harry exclaimed. 'It's Boy Scout semaphore!'

Sarah stared. Even though my arms were pinioned by scarecrows my hands were – well, they were busy, making little flapping gestures. I'm never one to miss an opportunity.

'Surely that's pins and needles? That can't be a code.'

'DO … NOT … WORRY … ABOUT … ME …'

'Really?'

'STAY … SAFE …'

Sarah smiled sadly, and wondered if Harry was making it up just to try to cheer her up.

Harry squinted. The light was low, and the scarecrow procession was being swallowed by mist. 'I could do with some field glasses … Ah yes … PLEASE … LOOK … AFTER … MY … MOTHS.'

'As last words go, that's a bit desperate.'

'Wait, there's more.' I had almost vanished from view. 'I … REALISE … THINGS … ARE … SOME … WHAT … DIFFICULT … RIGHT … NOW … NEVER … THE …' Harry stopped.

'And?'

'He's gone.'

For a terrible moment, the two friends perched glumly on the porch. Sarah had been abandoned by me in distant times and on alien shores before. These things happened. Smith family lore was that a great-uncle really had nipped out for a tin of tobacco and not been seen for five years. She wondered sometimes if he'd met me. I'd refused to be drawn.

'The Doctor really doesn't want us to rescue him?' she asked Harry, who was leaning sadly against some notices for an evening of light music.

'Well, I don't think so. There's not much we can do, is there? Cheer up, old girl. It's always darkest before the dawn.'

'Isn't it dawn now?'

Harry squinted at the meagre light and conceded the point. 'You're going to make me do something heroic, aren't you?'

'Wouldn't dream of it.'

'Oh, good,' Harry said without enthusiasm.

The two were silent. That comfortable silence that occasionally falls between two good friends who are often locked up in dungeons.

'Please look after my ...' Sarah beamed. 'Moths!'

And she was off.

'Oh no,' said Harry.

Sarah was back among the ruins of my machine, searching for the oil-can Harry had wrapped in cloth. 'The Doctor's Moth Machine.'

'What about it?'

'That can was making a noise.'

'The Doctor's inventions tend to. It normally means "Take Cover".'

'Found it!' Sarah held up the bundle and started unwrapping it. She pulled out the oil-can and peered at it. 'It could be about to blow us all to Timbuctoo.'

Harry nodded. 'Do you think anything much ever happens in Timbuctoo?'

'Once this is all over, we'll go there,' Sarah promised. 'Ah-ha!' She shook the oil-can, making Harry wince. It was rattling.

'Sounds like it's full of popcorn.' Harry was baffled.

Sarah gave it another shake. The noise was now like bullets. A gunfight between gerbils.

'That's not popcorn,' Sarah laughed. 'This can is full of scarecrow-attacking moths.'

'Very angry moths.'

'Yes! Harry, the Doctor's experiment worked!'

I was dragging my feet along the path, leaving what I hoped was a magnificent trail through the gorse and morning dew. Admittedly, I'd be spending the next week picking briars out of my socks, but then, if I was doing that, I'd still be alive and so it was just something to look forward to, wasn't it?

The procession of scarecrows – wait, I really must find a decent plural for them: a discovery of witches, a parliament of owls … a scratch of scarecrows? Now, why did I think that? – marched towards the shore.

My mind was racing off in five different directions. I normally did some of my very best thinking like this – under guard or in chains or facing imminent death; a mixture of all three was ideal. Whatever I was dealing with here – an infection? a nanovirus? – hadn't just been engineered to be cunning, it had also been designed to be cruel. My job was to stop it, to overcome it, to remove it.

But how?

I dragged my feet a little more and started to whistle 'Colonel Bogey'.

Sarah and Harry dashed out of the church, holding the angry oil-can between them.

'Have we got a plan?' asked Harry.

'Absolutely.'

'Are you lying?'

'No, no, no.' Sarah's mind was spinning almost as furiously as mine. Appraising the trail, she could tell that I was being led towards the beach. The beach where the TARDIS was. She didn't like the idea of that. Especially since she hadn't had a chance to tell me what had happened to the TARDIS. One problem at a time.

As they reached the edge of the churchyard, a scarecrow stepped out of the shadows and lunged towards them.

Harry gave a yell. Sarah dropped the can. The scarecrow stabbed at them with its hands, each one studded with dirty old nails.

Harry dived to the gravel path, rolling behind a gravestone. He scrabbled around in the dirt and threw a handful of marble chips into the face of the scarecrow. While it was momentarily distracted, Sarah launched herself through the air onto its back.

'Harry!' she called. 'The can!'

Harry grabbed for the oil-can. The scarecrow kicked it away. Harry lunged after it, landing painfully on his bad arm. The scarecrow kicked him in the ribs and Harry pulled a face.

The scarecrow turned on Sarah, grabbing her in its razor-sharp arms and throwing her against the churchyard wall. Pinned to the wall like a butterfly, Sarah kicked and flailed with a toddler's vim, but her vision clouded as she struggled for air.

Then Harry popped blearily into view. 'Good morning,' he said politely, and uncorked the oil-can.

An angry buzzing cloud of insects soared from the spout to engulf the scarecrow.

Choking and dazed, Sarah had the presence of mind to croak: 'The lid! The lid!'

'The what?' said Harry. 'Oh!' He jammed the lid back on the oil-can and leapt clear of the crowd of angry moths surrounding the scarecrow and Sarah.

Sarah, still held in the creature's arms, felt it rear up like a dying tragedian, and then topple forward. She saw the tombstone looming towards her. Twisting aside, she avoided having her brains dashed out all over Kenneth Mackenzie, Esq., and instead saw the moths settling on the crumbling, thrashing limbs of the scarecrow.

The body was deflating and shrivelling, a wretched balloon the day after a birthday party. Their work done, and now fully grown, the escaped moths soared up, up into the morning skies, leaving nothing but a pile of dust behind them.

'Crikey!' exclaimed Harry. 'That's done for the poor fellow.'

'I'd love to know what the Doctor's done to those moths,' marvelled Sarah.

Harry helped her up, and she didn't fail to notice that he was searching her body for any scrapes, scratches or punctures.

'I'm fine, Harry,' she said, dusting herself off. 'It didn't get me.'

'I'm relieved,' said Harry. 'And the Doctor's genetic jiggery-pokery worked. We've still got our clothes on.'

'I'm relieved too.' Sarah smiled. 'I'm really very fond of your duffel coat.'

I stood on the beach, admiring the sunrise. It was nice to be imprisoned for once somewhere with a pleasant view; so much more rewarding than meditating on a gloomy cellar wall.

'Turned out nice again,' I remarked to one of the scarecrows.

It did not reply.

I repeated my remark to the scarecrow on my right with a similar lack of success.

We'd been here for nearly twenty minutes. A little that-a-way the stumps of Harry's rounders match were just emerging from the tide. Which meant the TARDIS was somewhere behind me. Taking me there had not been their purpose. I deduced that whatever we were doing now was waiting. Waiting for something.

The farmer stood at the edge of the surf, sturdy tree-trunk limbs sinking into the damp sand. It was looking out to sea.

Something was coming.

Harry and Sarah crept through the grass near the dunes.

'This is rather like being in the Marines,' enthused Harry.

Sarah somehow doubted that. She raised her head cautiously above the dune and surveyed the beach. She could see me, surrounded by scarecrows, the sinister figure of the farmer towering over them all like a pagan god.

'They're all just standing there,' Harry observed. He'd reclaimed his duffel coat and it made things somehow easier to bear. 'Do you think they're waiting for something?'

'Luckily we have a plan.'

He winked at her. 'You mean, creep up and throw moths at some scarecrows?'

'Honestly,' Sarah smiled back. 'You didn't have to say it out loud.'

There was no sign of a ship sailing into view on the horizon. There was no sign of a starship descending through the pink clouds. But I just knew something was coming.

Something more than the distant furtive footsteps I could discern across the hiss of the tide. Two sets: one in leather boots and the other in wellingtons creeping closer. Ah ha. Well, I'd told them to stay safe. But they never would, of course, the dear old things.

'Do you know what Charles Dickens said about the sea?' Sometimes I can be very loudly facetious. 'When Mrs Lirriper the Landlady saw the sea she cried, "To think it's been rolling ever since and that it was always a-rolling and so few of us minding." Fancy that!' I looked round for approval. 'And all at no extra charge. That was Dickens' genius. To put the wisest words into the mouths of landladies.'

For a few moments, silence, apart from the sea breaking on the shore and then retreating. I squinted at the waves – there was something glinting under the surface, I was sure of it.

With extreme difficulty, I checked my watch. 'Goodness me,' I said loudly. 'A trifle early for it, but somewhere in the world, it's always rescue o'clock.'

At which point, Harry Sullivan came running over a dune, yelling like a banshee and whirling his arms like a dervish, if dervishes popped to the seaside in duffel coats.

'Harry!' I bellowed with delight.

Two scarecrows marched towards Harry, both of them slicing the air – one with a mallet, the other with an axe.

Harry tripped over his wellingtons and fell on his face, just as the two blades met each other where his neck had been.

The scarecrows stepped closer to the prostrate Harry and raised their weapons again...

Sarah Jane Smith came pelting from the other side of the beach, shaking an unstoppered oil-can.

A thick black treacle of insects poured out of it, so dense they blocked out the sunrise. For a moment, the moths drifted wistfully out to sea on a breeze and then, with a furious rustling of wings, rallied and descended on the scarecrows.

One after another, the scarecrows vanished in an explosion of sawdust.

The farmer turned on me, and raised a fist. Before he could flatten me, he too vanished under a cloud of insects.

'Oh dear,' I said as the creatures went to work. 'I think I may have made my moths a little over-eager.'

The farmer flailed beneath the swarm of insects, then fell to the sand, sinking into it. The moths tore into his old overalls. His frame was sturdier, but the only advantage it gave him was that it took the poor creature longer to die.

Their work done, my pitiless moths fluttered away across the island.

Harry picked himself up and headed over to me. 'I say, Doctor, are you all right? That went rather well.'

'It did, didn't it?' I was clapping my arms around my shoulders trying to get some feeling back. 'Do you know, I swear I now have one arm longer than the other. Hello, Sarah Jane, well done with your moths.'

'Your moths, Doctor.' Sarah bounded over to wrap me in a hug.

'They're not going to wipe out all of civilisation, are they?' Harry asked.

'No.' I watched the swarm drift along the beach. 'I engineered them with a short and busy lifespan. The worst that'll happen is a few holes in some favourite jumpers.' I held up my scarf, examining it for nibbles. 'And maybe the odd dining table.'

'What about the villagers?' Sarah had picked up one of Harry's stumps and was scribbling in the sand. 'Can you save them?'

'Nobody can. Reversing genetic manipulation of that sort – pretty unknown in this universe.' I found a sandbank and sank down on it. 'There were some lovely people. And I promised that I'd save them.'

'You did all you could!' protested Sarah. 'Your moth machine would have been ready earlier if it hadn't been for Mavis Tulloch…'

Just at that moment, further inland, Mrs Tulloch stopped running, exhausted. The creatures that had once been her neighbours had stalked her tirelessly across the island and finally she'd reached a hill.

She stood there, panting, as angry as ever, jabbing fingers at the creatures that pressed in around her.

'You're all weak,' she snarled. 'That was your problem. Why, look at me, I'm fine. Not like you.'

The scarecrows had by now formed a loose circle around her.

'What do you think you're doing?' she cried. 'Keep back.'

But they stepped closer, fingers of twig and bone brushing at her face.

'Keep your hands off me!'

The empty makeshift faces of the creatures looked impassively down at her as they pressed ever closer.

Mrs Tulloch felt a rare moment of panic as the creatures closed in, but something gave her hope. The creatures were all groaning and shifting. Weak. That was it. She could see it now – their arms were falling back, their heads were lolling, feet freezing into position. They were spent.

Mrs Tulloch smiled triumphantly. She'd always despised weakness. A little gap had appeared in the circle around her. She prepared to step through it. She'd come back later with some firewood and finish them off.

As she reached through the gap, the heads of the scarecrows snapped up, looking at her one last time. The creatures took one final step towards her, wrapping her in their thorny embrace.

Mavis Tulloch screamed for a long time. But there was no one there to hear her.

The next time anyone walked past – and it was a long time off – all they thought was what a strange sad tree there was, perched on the top of that hill.

Back on the beach, two silver giants burst from the tide and stood there, surveying the three people on the shore. Water streamed from their metal joints as they waded ashore, their blank metal eyes sweeping from side to side, their polished faces glowing in the sunrise.

Sarah and Harry gasped and fell back.

I held out a hand in greeting.

'Good morning!' I said. 'I'm guessing your craft's parked under the bay for reasons of stealth. Very sensible. Although possibly a danger to shipping.'

The Cybermen had arrived.

CHAPTER FIFTEEN

The Cybermen made their way through the foam to stand towering over me. Their giant bodies were entirely encased in dull metal that absorbed the morning light. Their heads were the worst thing about them: smooth, silver helmets with no nose – just two blank discs for eyes and a slit for a mouth. It made them look pitiless.

The silver giants regarded me with their blank, patient stares.

A third creature swilled up from the sea. It was subtly different. The sides of its helmet were black, and the metal was eerily transparent, exposing the terrible secret of the Cybermen. These were not robots – they had once been men. And you could still see the desiccated skull lolling inside the helmet, covered with wires and bolted into place.

The Cybermen had wanted to live for ever and had ended up as the ever-living dead. Once, long ago, on the planet of Mondas, the people had begun to die out, and had sought to prolong their existence by replacing their rotting flesh. This relentless surgical mania had gone on until one day they somehow eradicated their souls. The exact location – or even the existence – of a soul is hard to pin down, but somewhere, during all that drilling and gouging and cutting, the Cybermen had removed their souls. Perhaps they had been numbed by one of the many circuits sewn into their brains to allow them to control their splendidly strong new hands, or maybe it was one of the drugs coursing through their agonised nervous systems. But suddenly the Cybermen lost their emotions, and wandered anaesthetised through existence. They were, for a while, living husks – devoid of purpose. And then, gradually, the software stitched into their brains took over and gave them a new reason for living – a set of goals aligned to logic. The Cybermen had wanted to survive, and so survive they would. More than that, they would prove that they were superior to organic creatures, simply by converting them too.

There were problems with this approach. As they discovered among their own population, not everyone surrendered willingly to conversion. More seriously, it took up a lot of resources. Cybermen had to be built from the finest of materials. They had to be adaptable. They had to be superior. They had to have the strength of ten men, they had to walk in the airless vacuum of space.

They began to invade worlds, not just to convert the population with zeal, but also to seize their mineral wealth in order to make more bodies. The fault in this plan (whisper it) was that the more worlds they invaded, the more minerals they needed, and the greater their need for yet more raw materials. And so, they wandered the stars, trapped in a ghastly pyramid scheme of their own devising. They'd wanted to live forever, instead they'd ended up tinned like pilchards. Such is progress.

Staring at the Cybermen, three silver giants standing utterly unmoved by the breathtaking sunrise on a beach, a penny dropped in my head and it dropped very loudly indeed.

'The scarecrow plague!' I exclaimed. 'Of course. You've been offered something you cannot refuse, something you'd find irresistible. Unlimited armies! What's being tested on this island is crude, but already it's adapting – imagine being able to turn an entire world into Cybermen overnight. That's what you're longing to do, isn't it?'

The lead Cyberman nodded, its skull lolling forward just a little in its helmet. 'It is efficient,' it said in a dead, metallic rasp. Somewhere inside its skull a light glowed as it spoke. 'Where are the test subjects?'

'Ah, bad news,' I smiled, pointing to the stick-like ruins on the beach. 'I've dealt with them. Even the later versions.' I kicked the remains of the farmer. 'I'd write this plan off if I were you. If you thought being allergic to gold was embarrassing, just wait till people find out you're irresistible to moths.'

The Cyberleader considered. Having no emotions, it was not easily put out. 'No matter,' it continued equably. 'They were simply prototypes.'

'Let me guess.' I started pacing. 'You've been offered this virus in return for obedience to a higher power, haven't you?'

'The Cybermen do not obey,' the leader said.

'You also don't think outside the tin, old chap.' I patted one on the shoulder with a clang. 'This island has been home to a brilliant, absurd leap that you clockwork soldiers could never dream of.'

'Cybermen do not dream.'

'Exactly! You do not do so many things. Do not smile. Do not think. Do not walk on the grass. Life must be terribly limiting for you.'

I realised that Harry was signalling to me frantically in Boy Scout Semaphore (DO NOT UPSET THEM. LET'S RUN). I held up my hand for a moment's peace from Harry's terribly loud sign language. 'So, tell me, Cyberleader, who offered this to you? And, why have I been brought here?'

The Cyberleader straightened up and tilted its head until the skull rolled to one side. 'You have been brought here to suffer.'

'Splendid. What happens next?'

'We are waiting,' said the Cyberleader. There was a small pause, the ghost of regret. 'For orders.'

'That's just not good enough,' I snapped. 'Tell me – who offered you this plague? I would like a word with them.'

The Cyberleader did not reply. Instead he tilted his head up, just a little. He appeared to be watching the clouds. The reverie lasted just a moment.

Then the Cybermen turned and walked back into the sea. As they submerged, the seas around them surged and frothed, and lit up with a great and terrible light.

'Is that it?' Sarah, confounded, stepping breathlessly forward. 'Have the Cybermen gone?'

'So it would seem,' I sighed. 'But it's not a victory, Sarah Jane.'

The sunrise stopped, and the sky went dark. The churning sea froze.

A figure stood on the beach. It hadn't appeared. It had always been there, and yet it definitely hadn't been there a moment before.

You could see through the figure, but what you saw through it was like peeping into Dante's kaleidoscope. Glimpsed through the figure, the placid sea was a lake of fire, the beach was paved with skulls and the dunes became burning rocks.

With every step the figure took, the sand blackened.

There was nothing substantial about the figure. It had the rough shape of a man. Of all things, it appeared to be waving at me, a jaunty wave that was somehow the most sinister thing I'd ever seen.

'What is that?' Sarah asked.

'It doesn't belong here.' I raised my voice to the creature. 'Do you?'

The figure spoke, the voice a distant rasp down a phone line. 'I do not. But I shall.'

'You're from some other dimension, some other universe, some other way of life – looking to sneak into ours. It won't work.'

'It will,' the voice continued. 'It will because you will help me.'

'I shan't, you know. Haunting this island is one thing. You may have made a small peephole into this reality, but I shall make it my business to seal it up. This plane of existence is getting on quite well without whatever magic you have to offer.'

'I disagree.' The fluttering shape drew itself up. For a moment it was the height of the sky and the width of the horizon, and a great, screaming darkness poured out of it. Then it was once more a shimmer the size of a man.

'No ...' I fished around in my pocket for my yo-yo. 'Doing deals with the Cybermen? You may as well try and explain the meaning of life to a cash machine.'

'I would rather do a deal with you, Doctor.'

'I thought you wanted me to suffer?'

'And having suffered, to see how I can make all things better. Come and visit me. You will be my ambassador.'

'I certainly will not. You've nothing I want.'

'Haven't I?'

The creature stretched out an arm. The air behind it hissed with endless night.

Harry Sullivan looked down at his chest. 'Oh dear,' he said. 'I was afraid of that.'

A tree trunk burst through his stomach, branches spreading out and wrapping themselves around him. His flailing arms twisted and sagged, and the skin of his face blossomed and bloomed into moss as the skull underneath became that of a dead and ancient ram.

Sarah screamed.

The shadow watched the transformation calmly. 'He has been infected. You knew this, Doctor.'

I nodded.

'You knew?' cried Sarah, staring angrily at the piteous figure of Harry.

'He did,' the shadow announced. 'He kept it from you. He wanted to spare you. He had hoped to find a cure. But Harry Sullivan is of my realm now.'

The figure snapped its fingers, a rude customer in a restaurant.

The ghastly remains of Harry Sullivan jerked towards Sarah, imploringly. 'Sarah,' he said, reaching out a hand. She flinched. And the scarecrow vanished.

'Oh, Harry,' gasped Sarah. 'I'm sorry.'

The figure addressed itself to her. 'You have the Doctor to blame. But your friend can be rescued.'

'Doctor, we've got to get him back!' demanded Sarah.

I didn't like what was on sale, and shook my head. 'Be brave, Sarah.'

'Be brave!' snorted Sarah. 'Harry was infected. He ...' And then she remembered her hand when she'd touched the shadows on the TARDIS wall, coming away sticky with something she couldn't see. 'Oh, no.'

'I see you've remembered.' Without a face, the creature smiled. 'You are of my realm too.'

I reached for Sarah, but the creature got there first. Its arm expanded, filling the beach with a vista of bone-bleached trees and a coal-black sky raining fire. Sarah backed away, but the rippling shadows swept over her, plucked her up, and she vanished screaming into the nightmare.

And that was it. Sarah and Harry. Both of them gone.

Now there was just the creature and me, standing on the beach.

'I could take you along with your friends, of course.' The creature folded its arms. 'But I want to see what you do. You could seal the hole in my reality. It would be the sensible thing.' It leaned forward. 'But then, what of your friends?'

'You're absolutely right,' I agreed. 'Up until a few moments ago, I would have let you be. Your incursion into this dimension? A cursed island! And a few Cybermen with ideas above their station. That's hardly a bridgehead. The deaths on this luckless place? A tragedy, but a blink compared to the damage you could do. And, if you'd left well alone, then, perhaps, I'd have boarded up the breach and let it pass. But no.' I took a step towards him and lowered my voice. 'You've stolen my friends.'

'Yes,' The figure seemed to smile. 'Only a fool would try and rescue them.'

'Well, I'm that fool.' I grinned. 'And I'm coming to get them.'

I turned away and headed for the TARDIS.

I didn't bother looking back. I knew the creature would be fading with the dawn.

I stepped into my time machine and we went on our way. We had work to do.

The new day broke over the island, but there was no one there to see it.

The island was empty, abandoned.

FEAR OF SAVING THE UNIVERSE

There was uproar on Gallifrey. The Cybermen in league with a creature from another reality that was attempting to invade this dimension?

'Surely Doctor, you could see the danger the universe was in?' The Zero Nun prowled the stage beside me, being very reasonable, very loudly. 'Your only option should've been to seal the rift between universes by destroying the Earth.'

There was a lot of nodding agreement.

'No,' I told them. 'I had to save my friends.'

At that, there was a sort of palsied eruption. The beam of light tightened its grip around me, and I fought to breathe.

'Instead of which you went haring off on another of your adventures?' An old Chancellor heaved himself to his feet. 'Inexcusable. Your duty was simple: forget your friends, forget your pet planet – save the universe.' A smug little bank manager's chuckle. 'After all, isn't that what you do?'

They waited for me to answer, but I was in too much pain even to blink. The light around me dimmed a little.

'Well, Doctor,' prompted the Nun as I took a breath. 'What have you to say for yourself?' Her malicious pleasantry reminded me of someone – the unctuous hatefulness of Mrs Tulloch. The idea amused me; Mrs Tulloch would have made a good Time Lord – a creature of no imagination, no ambition, no love.

I rallied. I needed to convince them of what was at stake.

'I am trying to show you how I've changed,' I began. 'When I left this place, I was still very much a Time Lord like you. I never set out to save the universe. On my travels I may have saved the odd little world, stopped a few wars. But it was you – you, yourselves! – who were responsible for the first time I saved the universe. You packed me off to that dreadful chalk pit of a world to save everyone from the Master and his Doomsday Weapon. You needed me to stop him, because you knew the Time Lords would have been first up against the wall when he took control of it.'

My Time Lord audience went silent. The Sword of Never buzzed menacingly over me.

'Yes,' I said. 'You're not above a bit of meddling yourselves, when it suits you.'

'But surely,' purred the Zero Nun, 'that was different.'

'Was it?' I asked, innocent as milk. 'How?'

'Well,' piped up Lady Pralamandavarvar. 'With the universe in peril, you should have called on us for help.'

'And with your collective refusal to dirty your hands, you'd either have quietly wiped the Earth out, or just packed me off into that dimension hoping I'd sort things out, which is precisely what I did anyway.'

'Even so,' the old goat of a Chancellor gave a complicit smile to Lady Pralamandavarvar. 'We have to be careful, don't we?'

'Oh, indeed, Chancellor,' I said. 'You have to be very, very careful. Especially when you're voyaging into the unknown ...'

BOOK TWO
SCRATCHMAN

CHAPTER SIXTEEN

I stepped from the TARDIS and suddenly realised I didn't know who I was.

No. Not a clue.

Well, that was odd.

I frowned.

The journey had been a difficult one.

It didn't take me long to realise that something had gone wrong with my lovely ship. As soon as I stepped inside I could tell.

'Hello, you dear thing. Have you been redecorating?'

When I'd left, the TARDIS control room had been a shining white library, humming like an aunt in a butcher's queue. Now she was dark and foreboding, her empty spaces ticking ominously away. Dense vines covered the walls, poking and jabbing their way into the floors and the ceilings.

It was cold and grim and no longer felt like home.

'Something's up.' I swept some creeper from the controls and prepared to play them, a concert pianist confronting a saloon bar pianola.

Only the machine did not like me. Normally the two of us, we have a rapport (she knows where I want to go, even if she refuses to send me there), but this time the levers were sluggish and the dials were weary. The ship's engines groaned as I engaged them, filling the chambers with agonised wails.

'I know, I know, you poor thing,' I muttered, patting her. 'I know you don't want to go. But we have to! We have to go and find …' I paused and licked my lips. 'Find Sarah and Harry.'

The trumpets of protest continued, but with a curious little question mark at the end.

'You see, there's another dimension poking into this one. And it has taken Sarah and Harry. You like them, don't you – even though Harry leaves his towels on the floor.'

Do go on, the engines said.

'Well, we can always get some new companions later. If we must. But let's get the old ones back first. No sense in leaving companions lying around. They'll only get up to mischief. And, we have to seal up that realm. Energy is seeping through – making itself at home here. Behaving very badly. At first I thought it was nanites, or a virus – but no. Nanites are charming things. Whatever this is, it creeps around twisting everything it touches. Idiots would call it magic, but it's worse. Why, look at you – it's trying to infect you. It's even had a go at me…' I lifted up a leg and plonked it on the console, rolling back my sock. A scratch ran down my shin, the wound glowing gently. 'We're lucky. We're resilient. But not poor Sarah and Harry. Went down like skittles. And that's what's going to happen to all creation if we don't seal it up.'

The ship protested.

'Yes, I know. It's far easier to call for help, get the Time Lords to seal it from the outside. Taking a TARDIS inside that dimension is just going to push that gap wider, build a bridge across a chasm. But we have to, don't we? Because of Sarah and Harry.'

The ship supposed so.

'And, well, because …' I broke into a tired grin. 'Because it's going to be fun.'

The ship's engines chuckled. I'd got her!

I twisted a dial and felt it respond a touch more adroitly. 'Ah, now we're talking.'

The TARDIS jumped away from the island, the plucky blue box throwing itself into a livid scar that hung over the horizon.

The pucker in reality was no bigger than a tear in an envelope, but after the TARDIS had pushed its way through, it was that little bit larger. It floated on the sky like a mote of dust in the eye. You could see around it with perfect ease. You barely even noticed it, unless you tried.

But it was getting bigger.

The ship plunged down through the tear, and I clung to the controls.

Both my ship and I were putting on a brave face. Both of us were infected, which gave us passports into that nightmare realm, but not without a cost. I could feel the infection spreading, creeping, nibbling through my brain.

As the engines of the ship rose and fell, a light seeped from the heart of the ship – a sickly, dirty orange glow that stuck to the air. The poor old girl was very ill, but, oh, she was a fighter.

The closer we got to our destination (I blinked – where were we going again? Why were we going?) the more the infection tightened its grip on us both.

A crack like a snapping femur recalled me to my senses. One of the walls, my lovely walls, had split down the middle, and brambles spilled out, thorns scraping at the panels. There was a darkness behind the walls, one that glowed that same unhealthy ochre.

'We'll get there,' I thought. 'But in how many pieces? And can we get back?'

The machine gave another roar, one of danger and distress.

'We'll get there,' I repeated, holding her like a sick old hound. 'We'll get there even if it kills us ...'

The TARDIS landed, and I stepped out onto a blasted heath.

'Hello,' I said. 'I'm the ... I'm ... Oh dear.'

I rubbed the back of my head, marvelling at the lovely tangled curls of hair everywhere. Well, that was something. I pushed my fingers into my face – strong forehead, sharp nose – and tapped a finger across my teeth. Well, there were a lot of them squeezed in there somehow. Obviously wonderful for eating apples.

I rummaged in my pockets and produced an apple, along with a promising bit of string and a lolly stick. Whoever I was, I had a very useful coat.

I suffered a moment's confusion about why I appeared to be wearing such a long scarf. Was it cold here? It didn't seem that cold.

I peered at my surroundings.

Well, they weren't promising.

I was standing in a gully, tall, black mountains rearing up on either side of me, their peaks belching sulphur into a dirty butter sky.

The narrow path stretched in either direction, meandering between lumps of coal the size of boulders. Rivulets of lava trickled down the slopes, soaking the air with smuts and fumes, pooling in a slow-crawling river that burnt its way through the valley.

A smell lingered at the back of my throat. The heady whiff of petrol station, mixed with the choking fat of an abattoir fire.

'Charming place.'

Vast and rumbling as this emptiness was, it felt claustrophobic. Hardly space to think, let alone to breathe, not in this choking air.

I wondered if the area in which I'd landed was as good as this place got. Perhaps this was just a quarry or something and around the corner, it was quite nice, actually. Maybe there'd be a tea shop.

I peeped over the side of the path. Scree spilt from under my shoe, and I looked at the lava hissing as it snaked its poisonous way along the bottom of the valley. Well. Not promising.

I turned back to my ship, and groaned.

The TARDIS's outside was normally a cheery, incongruous blue box, battered by countless scrapes we'd dragged each other through. The overall look of it was friendly and absurd. What even was a police box? (I was sure I'd known at some point, but I couldn't put my finger on it at the moment.) Whatever a police box was, it was equally at home anywhere in the universe, a dogged little blot on the landscape with its friendly message on the door and a cheery little lamp on top.

What I saw now was a battered remnant. The blue surface was burned by the fires they'd been through, and the woodwork had blistered and buckled as those strange, thorny creepers pushed their way out, scouring the surface.

As I watched, the briars wrapped themselves around the box, enclosed it completely, and squeezed.

There was a terrible splintering sound, and the glass in the doors shattered. More creepers poured out.

The light on the top went dark. The friendly message on the door fell off.

I stood there, bereft.

'What have I done?'

I turned and edged my way along the path. 'I've a long way to go, and even longer before I can go home.'

I slouched on for a bit. Really, if I'd wanted to visit a painting, it wouldn't have been by Turner or Hieronymus Bosch. There was a watercolour by Monet I could have happily holidayed in, or a living amber by Tarrant-9 I wouldn't have minded a weekend cottage in. But no, I thought as I kicked sulphurous pumice over the side of the narrow path, here I was trapped in some art school temper tantrum.

I reached the summit of the peak. To the left and the right of me were more dismal mountains. I looked back. The only vegetation was that awful black vine, spreading out of the ruin of my ship. There was no other life, just an endless smoky horizon of cinders and a constant volcanic grumble.

'I have no idea where I'm going,' I lamented. 'Which is tiresome.'

I leaned against a boulder. It was disagreeably sharp.

My leg throbbed. I tugged at my trouser leg and a mark that glowed the same vile amber as the lava trickling past me. Had I known it was there? There was something crawling and wriggling underneath the wound, and just looking at it was making me feel worse.

'Well, that's not good,' I said, hastily tucking my trousers into my socks. If I could forget my name, I could certainly forget about a small scar, couldn't I?

I readied myself to trudge on further, but the path suddenly gave way beneath me, rumbling and shaking as lava bubbled its way up through it.

'This place is not welcoming,' I sighed, scrambling hastily up onto one boulder and then, as that began to sink into the lava, leaping across to another. As the lava hissed and surged about me, I realised I was playing hopscotch in hell, using lumps of clinker like stepping stones, picking my way across the ridge as it flowed and shifted around me.

The last boulder stranded me eight feet from solid ground. Around me, a stream of lava glomped and puddled, hissing and splashing and just daring me to fall in.

'I have had better days, haven't I?' I lamented to the lava, wondering if that was true.

Gathering my scarf and my wits about me, I leapt through the air, landing in a winding belly flop on some gravel.

Breathless, miserable, choking on the vile air, I crawled my way up a narrow incline, wrapping the charred ends of my scarf around my hands to try to save them from the hot flints.

Finally I reached the side of a path, my head thumping in the diesel atmosphere.

I found myself completely at a loss. I couldn't remember for the life of me who I was, where I was or why I was here.

'What do I do now?' I bellowed, my voice echoing from the mountains. 'What do I do?'

Which was when I heard the noise.

A puttering.

A friendly, utterly incongruous puttering.

An old black cab lumbered into view, making its way obliviously along the mountain path.

The light at the top was on, which was the most hopeful thing I'd seen for a while.

I scrambled to my feet and stuck my thumb out, then threw all caution aside and windmilled my hands in the air.

'Taxi!'

CHAPTER SEVENTEEN

'I've had 'em all in here,' said the driver.

'Oh yes?' I was doing my best to make polite conversation, but finding it difficult with no idea of who I was, sat in the back of a black cab being driven through burning mountains.

'Had 'em all,' the driver repeated. His voice had worn itself out with use. 'Got a name, have you?'

'I appear to have mislaid it,' I confessed. 'I had it when I left the house today but ...'

'Don't you worry, it'll come back to you. Happens a lot when crossing the waters of Lethe,' the little man in the greasy peak cap tapped the side of his head. 'Wait a minute. I know who you are!' His eyes twinkled shrewdly.

'You do?'

'Yeah, I've had enough of your sort in here.'

'My sort?' I felt a moment's worry.

'Yer. Didn't you used to be the Doctor?'

'Oh! That's right. I'm the Doctor!' I exclaimed. He was right. How delightful. Wait a minute. My face fell. 'Wait – did you say "used to be"?'

The tiny, rat-faced man grinned triumphantly, showing off his remaining tooth. 'Course you were, we all were other people.' The man sniffed. 'I used to be a policeman. Had a lovely bicycle. But that was long ago.'

'Have we met?' Trying to cope with a sudden surge of memories, I had the oddest recollection. 'On a beach?'

'Maybe,' the driver gave a prodigious sniff. 'Back when you were the Doctor, perhaps.'

'I still am the Doctor!' I protested, and worried at how that sounded.

'Nah,' the driver seemed very certain. 'You used to be. All over now. That's what I was telling yer. Where was I?'

'Talking.'

'Yeah,' the driver considered. 'I'm Charon. This is my job – to transport the living to the Land of the Dead.'

'Am I dead?' This was a lot to take in.

'Well, you're here, ain't you?' Charon cleared his nose loudly, one nostril at a time. 'I collect lost souls. As I said, I've had 'em all in here. All your lot.'

'My lot?' I felt terribly confused and just wanted to be home, wherever that was.

'Oh yes. The white haired feller in the velvet. Had him not so long ago. Right good little natter we had. Course, he, ah, didn't leave me a tip.'

'Sadly no,' I commiserated. My previous self – I remembered him! He had been many things, but he was a terrible tipper. I was clutching at facts like a dizzy kitten at string. Had I somehow brought the TARDIS to the Land of the Dead? Why? Was there even such a place?

Charon the cab driver continued to drone on.

'Stretch out if you like. Have a nap. Properly sprung seats, those are. Cosy as a bed. Your predecessor had a lovely doze, one knee up, talking about daisies. Feller before, he insisted on mending the engine. Couldn't get it going again properly for weeks.'

It could all be a hoax, I mused. But I was beginning to doubt it.

'Am I really dead?' I asked. 'Forgive me, you must be being asked that all the time.'

'Don't you fret.' Charon gave a good-natured little chuckle and offered me a tin of boiled sweets. 'All part of the job.'

The taxi pottered along a winding path, past a slowly trickling river of lava. An uneasy silence settled between us. I still hadn't got an answer to my question. I wondered if I should find a delicate way of reframing my question.

'Yeah, you're dead, mate,' Charon blurted out. 'It's my job to ferry you to your forever home.'

'I see.' I was always wary of a euphemism.

'Job's got harder of course,' said Charon, readjusting his cap. 'This used to be a lovely road.'

At that point, the taxi lurched a little, one wheel skittering over the edge of the narrow pass. I grabbed for my hat.

'Close one,' said Charon.

'What would happen? If we fell in that? I mean, if I really am dead, wouldn't I just go back to the start? Like in snakes and ladders?'

'Tricky, as I've never tried it.' Charon sucked air through his teeth. 'I see the logic, when you put it like that, but no. That lava –' he indicated the bubbling mass the car was sliding towards – 'that's Lethe.' He swung the gears in reverse and the cab remounted the path. 'The river of oblivion.'

'Oh dear,' I said. 'It's not how they describe it in the books. It gets rather a gentler write-up.'

'True, true,' Charon nodded sagely. 'But times have changed, the land has changed. All this? Used to be Elysian fields.'

The cab puttered on through a tundra of burning mountains and I mused on what I was being told. I tried to keep an ear open to what the cab driver was saying, but I was finding it a little difficult to concentrate. My mind was trying to race, but kept finding chunks of itself were missing. The result was a hesitant tiptoe through my memories.

'… course, you're probably worried how things are going back home,' said Charon.

'Am I?'

'You look the sort,' Charon mused. 'And it's only natural. Had a Martian Warlord in here the other day, in a right state he was. Apparently he'd taken a sickle to the third spleen in the middle of a right set-to. Fretting that battle wouldn't go well without him. Demanding I turn the old bus around.'

'And could you?' I felt a surge of hope.

'No.'

'Ah. Of course not.'

'They all ask. No harm in it, don't apologise.' Charon steered us onto a swaying bridge over a perilous chasm. Looking down, I realised the planks were made out of the bones of some giant creature. 'Everyone's like that – whether it's a war, the office, or even the rose garden, everyone's got something they need to go back for.' Charon cleared his nostrils again. 'But don't you worry, the universe goes on tickety-boo without you.'

'Does it?' I wasn't entirely certain about that. 'You see, my line of work – well, and I hate to seem immodest, but, if the wind is in the right direction, I sometimes save the universe.'

'I'm sure you *did*,' said Charon politely, 'But don't worry. Some other chap's stepped into your shoes already.'

'Really?' I wondered. Was that really the case? I had so enjoyed being the Doctor.

'Oh yes. Lovely young feller.'

'Ah! Good!' I frowned. 'Young, you say. How young?'

'Head boy type,' Charon muttered, with just enough of a twist. 'Eager enough, I dare say. But, I tell them all – well, it's like when I had the grumpy old one in here. You remember him?'

'Oh, I do.'

'He was a one, I tell you, constantly asking me to turn the heating up. Ever so worried about the little chap who came after. Anyway, I told him, you're in safe hands, relax and have a rest.'

'That's some consolation, I suppose,' I said politely. 'It's just – I really feel I was only getting started. We were having such fun.' A sudden memory jabbed at my soul – I'd not been travelling alone. How could I have forgotten them? 'Sarah, Harry and I. What fun we had! Shame it's all ended.' I couldn't remember saying goodbye to them, but, ah well, I hoped they were doing well. A miserable thought struck me – they were probably doing very well indeed without me.

'They'll be all right,' said Charon. The taxi started up another blasted hill, and the driver turned to me with a confidential air. 'It may all be over for you, but I'll tell you this, if I may, sir. You were always my Doctor, Doctor.'

'Thank you, that's very nice of you to say,' I said, feeling my head sink back into the cushions of the seat, sink and keep going. I was so tired, and perhaps, perhaps I could just, just once, have a rest.

The taxi jerked to a stop, startling me out of my reverie.

'Uh-oh, here comes trouble,' remarked Charon, sounding sourly annoyed.

I blinked, wondering, just for a moment, where I was, how I'd ended up here and what was happening. I was aware I'd been about to drift off into a sleep, and had the oddest sensation that that would have been a bad thing.

The cab's engine was idling.

Ahead of us, blocking the path, was a single silver figure.

'What's a Cyberman doing here?' I said, staring at it in alarm.

It was a Cyberleader, skull wired into its metal head. It was standing in the middle of the road, bringing its weapon to bear.

I leapt forward, trying to grab the steering wheel, but the partition wouldn't let me.

'What yer doing?' asked Charon, slapping my hand out of the tray where he kept his sixpences.

'Drive! Get away!' I yelled, but the first blast from the gun hit the cab. The windscreen shattered. Another blast and one of the lights went up in flames. A third shot dinged off the roof, tearing a sizzling strip out of it.

'My cab!' wailed the driver.

'Get us out of here!' I shouted.

'On this path, you must be joking,' snorted the cab driver. Another explosion rocked the car.

'Then open the door!' I demanded.

With a sniff of bad grace, the driver released the lock on my door.

I threw it open, and crouched behind it as a shield. I popped up behind it and waved to the Cyberleader.

'Hello there!'

A shot impacted the door. I popped up again, a little to the left. Another shot severed the door from its hinges.

This was exactly what I had planned. Seizing the loosened door, I rushed towards the Cyberleader, feeling the metal grow hot in my grasp as it took the brunt of shot after shot from his gun.

Cab doors are built to withstand many things – a small collision, the hob-nailed boot of a governess – but cannot sustain themselves for long against concentrated energy weapons. I had to be quick – I rushed forward, charging into the Cyberman. It plunged its fist into the door, releasing a lethal blast of electrical energy, which fizzed over the surface.

I felt it crackle in a kind of cage about me and realised that my hunch about the door's upholstery acting as an insulator had paid off. I raised myself up from my crouch, peeping up through the window to find myself eye to empty eye with the Cyberleader, the barren sockets of its skull glaring at me balefully through its helmet.

With some awkwardness, I cranked a handle, winding down the car door's window.

'Hello!' I said. 'Haven't we met before?'

The Cyberleader did not reply.

'I do think we have,' I continued. 'But what puzzles me is what you're doing here. Besides, of course, attacking public transport. Care to offer an explanation?'

The Cyberleader's skull continued to stare at me, a sickly light glowing deep inside it.

'You're looking blank. More so than usual, I'd say.' I risked a sympathetic cluck. 'Either you have a plan that is so complicated and audacious that a mere flesh-and-blood organism like me wouldn't understand it, or you're just as baffled to find yourself here as I am. Which is very interesting, don't you think? Should we compare notes? Hmm?'

There was a pause.

'I must fight you,' said the Cyberleader.

My mind was properly racing once again. Oh how I'd missed that feeling! Right now, standing on the side of a burning mountain in what may or may not have been the afterlife, squaring up to a Cyberman and not entirely sure why any of us were here, my thoughts were spinning around like mountain goats on a merry-go-round. And they were beginning to form a nasty suspicion, one which kept refusing to focus itself.

The Cyberleader reached around the door and grabbed my hand, crushing it like a vice. Clearly its power packs were drained, otherwise I'd have been lit up like a Christingle, but that was really very little comfort when I could feel the bones of my wrist sliding over themselves in a desperate hurry to get out of each other's way.

I wrenched my hand free with a gasp and stared up at the Cyberleader through the car window.

'Would you mind not doing that?' I said, trying to ignore the pain. 'Your actions are not logical. They are motivated by emotions – confusion and fear.'

The Leader's skull glowed an angry red.

'I will say this, though,' I remarked. 'You've got my mind working again. I've not just remembered who I am – but how I do what I do.'

The metal fist pulled back from the door ready to plunge forward into my face. But I'd been hoping for exactly this. I wound up the toughened-glass window, trapping the creature's fist in the door. Then I stepped rapidly away.

'We'll pick this up later,' I said, blowing on my fingers and diving back into the cab.

Charon took a moment to consider the Cyberleader with its arm trapped in the disembodied door. He watched the creature smashing the door against the ground, then looked back at me accusingly. 'Well, what do you want me to do about all this then?'

'Drive, please.' I grinned suddenly. 'I do hope you're insured.'

The cab started up, and moved away.

As it accelerated, I risked a glance back. Freed from the door, the Cyberleader was now racing towards us. It reached in through the open space, grabbing me by the shoulder.

'Drive faster!' I cried, desperate to be free of the creature. It was yanking me half out of the doorway, and the razor-sharp gravel was whipping beneath my face.

'On it, guv,' said Charon, and the car put on a welcome spurt of speed. I wrenched myself free and back inside the car, and watched the Cyberleader slow down and come to a stop, staring after us.

'I wonder what you're doing here?' I mused, rubbing my shoulder.

Charon drove us on, reaching a curious dead end in the road caused by a yawning abyss.

'We'll have to go through the Sallows,' Charon announced, and indicated left.

'Not the Sallows!' I exclaimed. 'Why? What are the Sallows?'

'You'll see,' Charon muttered, and turned us off onto a side road, bumping down a disreputable slope.

We emerged in a valley that was, by comparison, lush and verdant. Occasional plants struggled to exist among the pumice. Traipsing among them were odd, crouched figures.

'These would be the Sallows?'

'You've got it,' Charon acknowledged.

I looked keenly at the figures: they were – no had been – humanoid. They were bent over. At first I thought it was by the sheer effort of their work, but then realised their postures were deformed – these people scuttled. Some of them had a different number of limbs, or an extra head. Many were covered in dirty grey carapaces, the surface of the shell pitted with impacts from tumbling lava. Scattered among them were scarecrows. Some toiled beside them. Others hung from poles on the crests of hills, sentinels.

'Are these the natives of this place?'

'They're more the remains of them, poor blighters,' said Charon. 'If you disappoint, you end among 'em fairly sharpish.'

'Disappoint?' This was a new development, and not a welcome one.

Charon spat through the shattered windscreen, his spittle hissing as it landed on the hot bonnet of his cab. 'This place has laws, you know. Not many. But one of them is to keep his nibs entertained. These sad souls gave up – and just look at them.'

I watched as one of them crawled forward. Part of the face was human, but the nose and mouth and jaw all extruded into a long beak. It picked up a lump of rock in its teeth and mournfully munched at it. It gave me a look of utter despair.

'The poor things,' I said, already working out what to do.

Charon nodded. 'I can't stand the sight of them. Plus, from time to time, they think the cab's food. Normally, I can keep them off—'

'But today you're missing a few bits. Sorry about that,' I said.

Charon shrugged. 'Making a living in the Land of the Dead is getting harder.'

We drove on, and the ground began to slope upwards again. I looked back at the thousands of toiling creatures scrubbing away at the charcoal and gravel. 'I want to help them,' I said.

'Newcomers do.' Charon sniffed his disapproval. 'You'll grow out of it.'

'I hope not,' I proclaimed. Seeing the Cyberleader had tugged at a rumpled rug in the living room of my soul. Dead or not, I *was* the Doctor. I solved problems. 'I'm good with lost souls.'

'We'll see,' sniffed Charon. He looked ahead and ignored my next few attempts at conversation.

We crested another hill and swept onto an unwelcoming plateau. Large boulders lay around us – only, as we passed, I realised they were the broken heads of giant statues, lying scattered around, their sightless stone eyes gazing emptily back at me.

'What are they?'

'Eternal rulers,' Charon grunted. 'All that remains of them.'

A glum feeling slunk around my boots. 'I've disappointed you, haven't I?' I suggested.

Charon shrugged. 'Doesn't matter to me one way or the other, guv.'

'What have I done?'

'The others noticed it sooner. That's all.'

'Noticed what?'

'Exactly.' Another sniff. 'I guess there comes an age when you stop looking up. Anyway, we're nearly there.'

The cab pulled up and I got out, looking around. 'Here does not seem to be anywhere.'

Charon considered this remark philosophically, all the while letting his sturdy old engine putter away. 'Fair enough.'

I suddenly realised what I'd forgotten to do. Hastily I patted down my pockets. 'Ah,' I announced. 'Your fare. And the damage to your cab. I'm most terribly sorry, but I haven't the money on me right now.'

'That so?' Charon cleared his throat, hawking a small ember into the dirt. 'Last one said much the same thing.'

'Well, add it to my account and get the next one to pay.' I grinned and produced a bag of sweets. They always helped. 'Have a jelly baby?'

Pleased, Charon took one. 'Thank you, Doctor, that'll do nicely,' he said, smiling with both of his teeth. He popped the sweet in his mouth, turned in a tight circle and drove away.

As I watched the little black cab vanish, the bizarreness of the situation steadily crept up on me. 'I hope this isn't all a dream,' I remarked. 'Or a holographic simulation – that'd be tedious. Maybe it's my addled brain, but I just can't put my finger on what's going on here.'

I kicked at a few lumps of rock. It didn't help.

One rock went sailing into the face of one of the carved heads.

It opened a great stone eye, gazed at me in silent reproach, and then shut it again.

'I do beg your pardon.' I bowed and turned away. 'How did I let Charon down?' I mused. 'Something about not looking up.' At least, I thought, this was as strange as it was going to get.

Which was when I noticed the castle floating in the sky.

FEAR OF LIES

I could tell my assembled audience of Time Lords was getting restless.

'Flying castles! Giant insects!' The muttering had become a hubbub and was nudging towards a brouhaha.

One revered Time Lord took to his feet, trembling with rage. He said the first words anyone had heard him say in four centuries: 'The Doctor is a charlatan!'

There was a scattering of applause.

'The Doctor has made this whole story up, just to frighten us!' The old duffer was finding his voice again. 'He's invented it out of whole cloth, just to shake us down. I say we wipe him out now!'

There were cheers at that, and the beam of light intensified around me.

I struggled to keep to my feet. I looked up at them all, jeering away, at the Sword of Never crackling as it sliced down towards me, and, of course, at the inevitably solicitous face of the Zero Nun.

'Surely my esteemed colleague is mistaken.' Her smile was silken. 'You haven't made all this up, have you?'

'You could check yourselves,' I said. 'Who would dare try and pull the wool over your omnipotent eyes, mmm?'

'We could check,' the Zero Nun averred.

'You could,' I repeated. 'So, why don't you?'

The crowd fell silent.

'Because you're afraid that you'll find out it's all true.' I grinned at them all. 'And that would be far more comforting to you, far less frightening than knowing that it's all real.'

The treacle-tongued Nun glided forwards. 'That's not what anyone wants to think, Doctor, let me assure you.' She stretched out a claw as if to reach through the brilliant light that held me pinned, to pat me on the arm. 'All of us want only to reach the truth of what happened. And I'm sure that you'll be able to provide us all with a convincing account of your actions, one that clears you completely.' I wouldn't have blamed her if she'd thrown in a wink at the crowd.

They all got her drift. 'Quite so,' a few of them harrumphed. Some thumped their perigosto sticks on the floor. Even geriatric sharks can sense blood in the water.

'I'll admit my story is outlandish,' I said. 'An entire world that exists only to mock me?' I favoured them all with a severe expression. 'The very idea. How absurd.'

That gave them pause.

'Shall we continue?'

CHAPTER EIGHTEEN

The castle hovered in the air. It didn't look like a fairy tale, pink turrets hovering neatly at the top of a beanstalk. Instead this castle was ugly – torn roughly out of the ground like a weed and suspended in space. Its floating was more an insult, somehow making it even uglier – hanging there. Had it been built or carved from the rock, or had it grown like a crenelated tumour? Hard to tell. But at some point it had become a castle and now hovered above the plateau.

'Oh, I don't like that,' I thought, all the while working out how to get inside. It was most definitely a baited trap, absolutely the most dangerous place I could be, so immediately the most interesting.

Creatures appeared on the edge of the plateau, revolting things that looked like someone had cross-bred an ape with a lobster and then, hating the result, ground it under heel. They scuttled and clattered, a swarm of them. They picked up rocks from among the statues and hurled them up at the castle.

'Excuse me, are you the Resistance?' I approached them hopefully, but they just threw rocks at me as well.

At the same time a nearby volcano belched into action, sending torrents of hot pumice up into the air, battering against the sides of the castle. I realised that some of the carbuncles on the fortress were old missiles that had embedded themselves into the edifice.

As the castle drifted overhead, the entire planet reacted to it with a primal rage. Even the stone heads opened their mouths to scream at it. Apologising, I clambered onto one of them, hoping to find a way into the castle and out of this mess. It was still a good twenty feet above me and, even had I been able to jump, I'd have been left clinging to the underside like a limpet, which was never a good thing to be. There didn't seem to be any handy hatchway in the base of it.

I essayed a jump – just in case the fortress had a gravity induction field around it or some other handy little device. Instead, the action drew the fire of the squashed lobster-apes, and I had to fling myself flat against the surface of the giant stone head. Peeping from under my hat, I watched projectiles arc over me, some of them clattering against the base of the castle and then falling back.

Things started to drop from the castle. Things which fell struggling, burst into flame and exploded across the plain. The more they fell, the higher the castle drifted. The bombardment drove the creatures wild, and they scattered, screaming and howling in terror and rage.

At the same time, a portal opened in the side of the castle, and a vast wind began to suck at the air. As I watched, several angry lobster-apes were hoovered up, spinning in an angry tornado, vanishing howling inside the castle.

Clinging to the side of the giant stone head, I considered my situation. If I let go, I could allow myself to be swept up into the castle, but I didn't really fancy my chances inside a giant vacuum cleaner.

It was at that point that a drawbridge lowered in the front of the castle and something shot out, a narrow rectangle.

Squinting through the wind, I watched it drift down towards me.

It looked like a giant playing card. I really hoped it wasn't. It was one thing to be staring up at a giant symbol of feudalism; playing cards with one was quite another.

'Excuse me,' said the card. 'Are you the Doctor?'

'Yes.'

'I'm your invitation.' The card's voice dripped in the air like honey off a spoon.

'Oh, dear,' I thought. This was worse than a playing card. Now I looked at it, I could see the gilt edges and my name embossed on the underside. How embarrassing.

'Would you care to come inside?' the invitation extended itself.

I clambered onto the card and it soared up, past the maelstrom of angry, flailing creatures still drifting up through the air.

'What's happening to them? Will they be all right?'

'Oh yes.' The card sounded politely bored. 'We always need new resources.'

The card flew inside the castle drawbridge, which closed behind them like a jaw.

'Inside the beast,' I said. 'Well, I'm fortunate that I'm a valued guest.'

'You are valued,' said the card prissily, and I didn't like its meaning.

We were drifting along narrow rock corridors, carved with no sense of grace or beauty. The card pulled up at a door, and I stepped off.

'Am I expected?'

'Yes.'

'By whoever is in charge?' I indicated the door. 'Are they behind there?'

'Oh, gracious no,' the card's voice sneered. 'But you'd better go in.'

Taking that ominously, I knocked.

'Come in!'

So, I entered.

'Ah, there you are,' the lizard said. He indicated a plush leather chair. 'Come in. Take a seat.'

169

The room contained a couch, a chair, and a good deal of clutter. The lizard was splayed out across the large velvet couch. He was wearing pyjamas and a neatly tied dressing gown that looked like a waistcoat with ideas above its station. He had delicate, aesthetic features – everything about him was long and pointed. Exquisite green claws were pushed to his temples in a demonstration of artistic anguish.

I was trying to take it all in. 'Are you the ruler here?'

'Sit down, do!' the lizard screeched, and then winced. 'You're not going to be tiresome, are you?'

I promised solemnly that I would not be, whilst wondering what was going on. I settled into the chair, marvelling at how little comfort it offered.

'Don't fidget,' the lizard wailed. 'Please don't squirm. It affects my senses.'

I made an effort to sit still, but the chair seemed dead set against this. It was almost as though it was arranging its atoms against me in a series of tiny jabs and nips. I supposed that, if cards and lizards and scarecrows were sentient here, then so, appallingly, were chairs.

'I'm the Doctor,' I announced, shifting my weight uneasily.

'I suppose that's a confession.' The lizard gave a wriggling yawn, stretched like a cat, and made to get up from the couch. 'I'm Mr Tembel. Really, this is terribly inconvenient – I feel too wretched today and of course you have to turn up.'

Mr Tembel made his weary way over to a tantalus and filled himself a tumbler. 'Ginger pop,' he announced, sipping it. 'Some days it really is all that keeps me going.'

'Oh, I do agree,' I said sincerely.

'Want some?' Tembel offered.

'If you wouldn't mind.'

'Well, I *wouldn't*, but I'm afraid I can't let you have any. Wretched, isn't it?' Mr Tembel sat down on the edge of his couch, as though afraid it might bite him. 'You see, that's my job.'

'Not offering me ginger beer?'

'In a nutshell.' The lizard pressed a claw to his forehead and sank back against an arm rest. He took a sip from his glass. 'Oh, that is better, a little better. The tiniest improvement. Some days I fear I may just stop all together.'

I'd had enough. 'Well, this has been lovely, but, you know how it is – places to go …' I made to get up, and realised I was firmly fixed in the chair. Was it some kind of force field? 'Oh dear. I appear to be stuck to this chair. We weren't getting along well to begin with, and now it won't let me go.'

Tembel nodded without any great interest. 'That's how the chair works. Stasis field. I fear it leaks. It's what I attribute my terrible condition to.'

'Your terrible condition?'

'This awful, absolute abject lethargy,' Mr Tembel wailed. 'Oh, I know, I probably strike you as the soul of activity, but inside I am wretched. Some days it takes all my effort just to reach my ginger beer. I would move the table closer but I just haven't the strength. Can't muster it.'

'I've an idea,' I said brightly. 'You could let me out of this chair and I could shift the table for you.'

'The idea!' exclaimed Mr Tembel, then fell silent.

I wondered if there was a way I could walk out of the room with the chair stuck to my seat.

'It has been the worst of weeks, the very worst, but perhaps next week will be better,' Mr Tembel sighed. 'I have that hope.'

'Don't we all?' I was trying to inch my fingers into my jacket to find my sonic screwdriver. If I could get the old fellow to access setting 12 I could maybe disrupt the chair's stasis field and escape.

'Look.' Tembel balled his hands into his eyes, and yawned. 'I'm really not in any state for it, but I suppose I should press on with torturing you.'

I blinked.

'It's embarrassing really,' Mr Tembel sighed. 'Here I am, Inquisitor of the Realm, and it's completely draining.' He staggered to his feet and pushed at a sprung-loaded drawer, and a set of wickedly sharp instruments and saws slid slowly out. 'Just look at this lot.'

'I'd rather not,' I said.

'But do,' Mr Tembel groaned, leaning against the cabinet. 'I've barely the strength to lift them, let alone wield them with any effort.' He somehow managed to raise a small drill. It whirred menacingly. 'What is to be done?'

'I know!' I suggested brightly. 'If you freed my arms from the field, I could do the best I can to torture myself. That drill, for instance.' I glanced down at the chair, working out how quickly I could drill through the armrest. 'Or maybe a saw? I'm sure I could do a lot of damage to myself before I talked.'

'That's very kind of you, but I couldn't.' Tembel shuddered with self-disgust. He advanced on me, the drill whirring, fast and nasty.

'What would you like me to tell you?' I asked, trying not to flinch.

'Oh, well …' Mr Tembel paused, turning the drill off. 'Nothing really. Mostly I interrogate people just to break the spirit.'

'Consider it broken,' I vowed.

'Very good, very good.' The lizard tapped the side of his nose with the drill. 'After all, it's doubtful you know anything important, isn't it?'

'Highly doubtful,' I promised, and sucked at my lip, thoughtfully. For some reason saying that stung me.

'I say, what lovely teeth you have. Shall we start on those?' Mr Tembel leaned forward, the drill flashing wickedly away.

I braced myself. Having to say goodbye to my smile, that would be a terrible thing.

I felt the drill scrape against one of my teeth. It bit into the enamel, sputtered and died.

'Oh, isn't that just my luck?' Mr Tembel gave a heartfelt groan. 'I forgot to charge it.' He staggered wearily over to a corner, and plugged the drill in. 'What am I to do now?' he wailed.

'We could go for a walk? Have a chat?' I suggested, running my tongue against the rough surface of my tooth. 'You have questions. I have answers. We could just work through them and then we'd be done.'

'It's a kind thought – but no, it's no use,' Mr Tembel groaned. 'I've so much to be done and I can't even get the basics right. It's just crushing me.' He flopped onto the sofa, flinging his arms over his eyes. 'Sweet Morpheus take me!'

A few moments later he began to snore.

Well, I'd never been tortured like that before.

Stuck in a chair, unable to get out, I really took against that snoring. Worse, I felt something unusual creeping up on me. A sense of despair.

A long time passed. The chair was very uncomfortable. The sound of the lizard's snoring was utterly horrible. A creeping boredom settled over me and became stifling. I suspected this was the most effective torture I'd ever endured.

'Excuse me!' I called. 'Excuse me! I'm in a bit of a hurry here.'

The lizard ignored me, and I had to wait unendurably until it finally woke up, yawned extravagantly, and sprang off the chaise. 'I really feel it's a fresh start, don't you?' Mr Tembel pottered over to the drill. 'And this has recharged too. Some luck at last. Shall we get to it?'

'Absolutely,' I agreed, without much joy.

'Mind you,' Mr Tembel eyed the tantalus. 'I could murder another drink, but I seem to be out. I could go and get some more, but alas –' he turned to me, dolorous – 'I find myself a little embarrassed for funds.'

'Oh … dear?' I ventured.

'Yes, absolutely. Things have been a little slow. But one has to live, doesn't one?'

'Well, unless one gets tortured to death,' I thought.

Mr Tembel made his way over to me, tapping the drill thoughtfully. 'I don't suppose you could see your way clear to lending me a little something?'

I blinked. I'd never been asked to lend money to a torturer before. 'Ah …' I began.

'I promise I won't go any easier on you if you do lend me money. Anything less would be unprofessional.'

'Wouldn't it?'

'Just a little something?' Mr Tembel pressed. 'And maybe I could go easy with the pliers.'

I shrugged as much as the chair would allow. 'Let me see,' I said. 'I am a little restrained. Unless …?'

Mr Tembel pointed with a buzzer, and I found I could move my arms. I reached into my coat pocket and pulled out some string, some elastic bands and a paper bag.

'Is that money?' asked Mr Tembel eagerly.

'Afraid not,' I apologised, 'they are jelly babies. Would you like one?'

'That's very kind of you but I couldn't possibly,' Mr Tembel said, reaching down to take a sweet. He chewed it thoughtfully and then pocketed the bag. He wandered away, peering out of the narrow window. 'What is to become of me?' he wailed.

'I don't know,' I muttered sourly, missing my sweets.

Mr Tembel yawned magnificently. 'If it wasn't for being able to hibernate, I don't know what I'd do. I might just slip off for the rest of this week and then we'll pick it up the next.'

'Wait, wait, wait!' I yelled, aghast at the prospect of spending any longer in that chair. 'What do you want to know?'

Mr Tembel opened a sly eyelid. 'You're just trying to humour me.'

'I'm not,' I protested. 'I'll tell you anything.'

'Why are you here?'

'Well – I think I died,' I began. 'The details are hazy. I was probably doing something heroic. That's normally how I die. Funny thing is, I can't remember. Is that usual?'

'Happens quite often.' Mr Tembel waved it away, clearly uninterested. 'Delusions of heroism ...' he muttered to himself.

'But ...' and I couldn't hide my frown, 'if people turn up without any memory, what is the point of interrogating them?'

Mildly abashed, Tembel shifted uncomfortably on the chaise. 'Some truths don't require facts. Tell me, what are your fears?'

'If I could remember what I died of that'd help. I'm probably afraid of *that*. By the way, is this place really the Land of the Dead?'

'That is one name for the realm.'

'It sort of reminds me a little bit of Dante, but jumbled up with other stuff. For instance, the creatures toiling away among all that lava – the Sallows and the Scarecrows – they were once new arrivals like me?'

'Well, yes, but—'

'And did they confide their fears in you?'

'Once ...'

'And then, at some other point, you sent them out into the world? When they were no longer of use – and they're living off the rocks?'

'Well, not me personally, but yes, more or less ...'

'And the dead come here and end up munching gravel? You're not selling me on your eschatology.'

'They find peace. Of sorts.'

'And yet you need to know my fears? How does that fit in? Why does the lord of this realm need to know those?'

'Well ...'

'Because I'm wondering quite a bit.' I broke into a grin. 'Ask me another – I'm rather enjoying this.'

Mr Tembel did not seem to be enjoying it as much me, poor thing. 'Our lord needs to know the things that you hate.'

'So he can exploit them? Oh, that's easy.' I laughed for the first time in ages. 'Weak tea, cold porridge, seaside landladies – things which are drab, mediocre, joy-sapping. It's one thing to be no good at rounders, it's quite another to make everyone else like rounders a little bit less. Rounders. Why did I think about that?'

'I have no idea,' said Mr Tembel evenly. 'But what do you fear?'

'Such probing questions!' I carried on smiling. 'I have a friend who you'd get on with like a mouse on fire.' And then I slapped my thigh. 'Of course. Sarah Jane Smith and Harry Sullivan!' Invigorated, I strained against the chair.

Mr Tembel observed me with vague, malicious interest. 'You'll get nowhere by struggling.'

I leant back and laughed. 'That's the only way you get anywhere,' I said and stood up.

The lizard stared at me appalled.

'I've worked out what you're doing,' I said, dusting myself off. 'You were trying to bore me to death! To make me feel insignificant. That I no longer mattered. But then I remembered my friends. Oh, how could I have forgotten them again? That's how I escaped from your chair, by the way – what is a man but the summary of his friends? And my friends are truly wonderful. Sarah and Harry – they think the world of me! What lethargy field could cope with that? So it gave up.'

'You!' the lizard snarled with surprising energy. 'You're an egomaniac!'

'Maybe I am,' I conceded. 'But then again, I am the Doctor. That's going to go to anyone's head.' I gestured to the door. 'Is that the way out? I do hope so. Yes, it has been lovely being tortured by you. I barely screamed, it was so informative. You've helped, you really have. I've realised I'm not dead and that I have to rescue my friends and nothing, nothing's going to stop me now. Bye-bye!'

With a cheery wave, I sailed out of the door.

'We'll see,' said Mr Tembel, and smiled a nasty little smile. The wretched creature helped itself to another biscuit, and then faded away.

CHAPTER NINETEEN

I hadn't been expecting a party.

I'd followed the sounds of merriment down the narrowing rock corridors, beginning to wonder if I was hallucinating. The ghosts of clinking glasses and the mild babble of polite conversation drifted towards me.

Unexpected or not, I'd figured a party was a good place to learn things, to meet people, to find out what was going on, to make friends, to put my foot down, to start a rebellion, to make a scene ... and perhaps there would be cake. Would a fruitcake be too much to hope for?

I emerged into a large cavern. It had been painted silver and a picture window had been hacked into it. People clustered around the window, looking down at the rivers of fire, the belching volcanoes, the pathetic creatures skittering around the barren fields. The view was awe-inspiring.

The people were an eclectic mix, some dressed in fancy dress (at least, I presumed it was fancy dress) as elephants and alligators and clowns and princesses. Suits were sharply pressed, ball gowns flowed and trailed, and everyone's hair sparkled with diamonds. Everyone wore masks, those little half-mask things that remind one of ghosts or owls. Oddly, as they spoke, the lips on the masks moved. The effect was disturbing.

I moved among them, doffing my hat and sizing up the room. Yes. This was a big and impressive place and these were big and impressive people, used to show and spectacle – after all, they were standing in a ballroom in a castle floating over a sea of fire – not for them the quiet word in the ear and the careful suggestion. I could bend the odd ear but I doubted it would work. No, these people would appreciate a bit of spectacle.

I leapt onto a podium, taking someone's glass. I sniffed it. No, alas, not ginger pop. It really wasn't my day. Still, I tapped the glass loudly.

'Everyone! Good evening, I'm the Doctor and if I could have a moment of your time …?'

I pride myself on my voice, I'm sorry, but I do. My voice could restart a car. It boomed, it resonated, it made an impression. Except—

This time, no one noticed. No one reacted. Everyone carried on talking among themselves. Conversation flowed, wine sparkled, laughter tinkled.

I tried again. 'Everyone! We are all in terrible danger.'

Someone maybe halted just a little in the act of raising their glass. The tiniest of pauses.

'We are trapped in a realm of darkness!'

Did someone's fork hover while scraping a plate?

'Not to be immodest, but I could be your last hope.'

Was someone turning towards me? Just a little? No.

I gave it one final go. 'Please, you have to listen to me,' I bleated, and then stopped, abashed. Aside from when I was chatting to sheep, I never bleated.

These people could not hear me, could not react to me. The solution hit me – of course, how silly! They were projections of some sort – a hologram or another variety of light show. Day-trippers would be easily fooled, but not me, no. I reached out a finger, proving my theory by poking it through the shoulder of one of the revellers. Hologram!

Only it didn't go through.

The woman turned minutely, and threw a freezing glance at me.

'I'm most dreadfully sorry,' I apologised, 'but now I know that you're real and I have your attention—'

She turned away.

I repeated the experiment a couple of times, prodding different guests, and even once tried to cut in on the dancefloor. In every instance I was rebuffed, which left me feeling hurt and discombobulated.

'I've been sent to Coventry! It's not that I don't exist … it's that I don't matter to them.'

Sarah had once made me travel on the Underground at rush hour; being here felt like that, only worse. I took refuge in the canapes, successfully helping myself to a vol-au-vent. It's quite something when only the profiteroles believe in you. I was used to being the most important person in the room – unlike despots and megalomaniacs, this wasn't a position I'd ever sought, it just sort of got handed to me on a regular basis. Call it my charm. Turn up, say a few outrageous things, pass round the jelly babies, handily remember you won against an old king's cousin at croquet, and eventually all eyes will be on you and whatever looming disaster or unavoidable catastrophe there's been will soon be averted and there'll be happy endings all round. (Well, that's cutting a long story short and leaving out all the dungeons and ray guns, but they're really just punctuation.)

No, I reflected as I consoled myself with the queen olives, this was serious. I was in a room full of people who did not care a fig about me, and I did not like it one bit. How was I to find out what was going on? How was I to save the day?

The fog was descending on my brain again. I focused and remembered my mission. I had come to find my friends; I had to stick to that thought as their memory kept slipping around like eggs in a frying pan. Sarah and Harry. Were they in the crowd? Were they even now several inches away from me, mingling among the rich and famous, staring down at the breathtaking desolation beneath?

I decided to investigate. I began by sneaking around the room, then remembered that no one cared. I sauntered through the crowd, eavesdropping, peering at faces, and popping candied fruit into my mouth. The people pressed in around me, completely oblivious to me, yet utterly in my way.

Two sensations crept up on me and neither of them crept welcomingly. One was that my friends were somewhere in here. The other was that, for the first time in my lives, I was utterly irrelevant.

My path was blocked by a whirl of masked dancers spinning past, and I wondered what it was that was uncanny about them. I found one standing near a pillar, and bowed to it. 'Excuse the impropriety,' I said. The figure blanked me. 'I know you won't even notice. I was just being polite,' I said, and removed the mask.

Underneath the mask was nothing. There was just a gap in the face, porcelain filled with sawdust, which now spilled out and trickled to the floor.

'I do beg your pardon,' I said, and slid the mask back into place.

The creature did not even seem to notice. It waved at someone who wasn't there, and went away to dance.

'I know your secret, I know your game,' I announced to the room. If anything, the room ignored me even harder. I took savage comfort in this. The whole party had been designed simply to provoke me. Well, no such luck. I wasn't born tomorrow.

'I just need to find my friends, and then I'll go. Have you seen Sarah and Harry?'

The room made it perfectly clear that they did not care, one way or the other.

A figure ran into the room. A young man in a hurry and a pinstripe suit. 'Sarah, Harry!' the man shouted. 'Brilliant! We're needed.'

Two figures at the far end of the room put down their glasses and ran excitedly after him. 'Yes Doctor!' they called and bounded from the room.

The room broke into a scattering of applause. There was excited muttering.

'Is that the Doctor?'

'Doesn't he look young?'

'Now the Doctor's here, we're safe.'

Well, I hadn't been expecting that.

I leaned against a wall very hard.

'If that's the Doctor, then who am I?'

I left the ballroom and no one noticed me go.

I sulked down a narrow stone corridor. I sniffed the air – something was missing. I realised it was the sound of distant alarms and feet thundering towards me.

I no longer mattered. As the realisation hit me, a pain stabbed at the end of my fingertips. I held them up, marvelling at them. They were joining together, the fingers running over each other like molten candlewax.

My ears pounded, and I doubled over in pain as my spine twisted. I could feel stubby shafts of cartilage poking up through the skin of my back. My skull was pinching like a new pair of shoes. The skin of my arm was coarsening, turning first to wood and then to stone.

'I'm becoming a Sallow!' I gasped.

So that was it, I thought. My weakness had been found and now I was being broken down and discarded. Like those other poor lost souls. I rallied, tried to fight off the change, but the pain as my jaw dislocated overwhelmed me. I fell against the rock wall, marvelling at how deliciously cool it was. I could just sink into it and forget myself forever. No more struggle, no more fight, no more impossible odds, no more Doctor.

Someone tapped me on the shoulder. 'Excuse me!'

Now someone wanted to speak to me? 'What?' I turned away, feeling desperately self-conscious.

'It's just … Don't I know you?' It was a woman's voice. Jaunty, assertive.

Not now! I was becoming an insect. I didn't have time for an autograph.

'It's you, isn't it? It absolutely is!'

'Is it?' Ordinarily, I would have been happy to be recognised, but right now I was plunging into misery and just wanted to be left to get on with it.

'Oh, brilliant! I do know you! I definitely do!' The woman had a northern accent which, if I hadn't been trying to scream, I would have found quite charming; like the rainbow stripes on her blouse.

'You must excuse me,' I said. 'Now is not a good time, I'm turning into a beetle.'

'Oh, fair play,' she said.

'I'm not sure that's got much to do with it,' I growled. Or, at least, I tried to growl, but the metamorphosis was tugging at my face, pulling my nose into a proboscis.

The infuriating woman bent over me, and I was fairly sure I'd glimpsed her at the party. Had I? Was she really here? Was she a figment of my imagination? One final hallucination caused by my brain cells popping like bubble wrap?

'It's not really on, that's all.' The woman slouched against the wall, jamming her hands in her coat pockets and rubbing her boots against each other. 'You know, meeting one of your heroes and finding he's pretending to be a fly.'

'I'm not pretending,' I said petulantly, finding my voice. 'I really am growing a chitinous epidermis. It affects the mood.'

'I can imagine it would.' Her attention seemed to be wandering from my plight.

'I'm sorry, did you say I was a hero of yours?'

The woman nudged me in the ribs. 'That's better.' I noticed how kind her eyes were. She smiled at me, blowing aside a couple of strands of blonde hair. 'Look at you! I think you're pulling yourself together. About time.'

I held out a hand in greeting, and then marvelled to see it was back to normal. 'How did that happen?'

'That is so brilliant!' The woman shook my hand delightedly, pumping it up and down. 'Pleased to meet you. Didn't you used to be the Doctor?'

'Used to be?' I smiled. 'And I am again. No getting rid of me.'

'No, there never is!' the woman agreed, laughing.

'Thank you for the distraction,' I told her sincerely. 'I really was crumbling under psychic attack. The seeds of doubt had been planted and were starting to hatch. A bit like … moths! Feeding on my weaknesses.'

'Oh, that's all right,' the woman nodded, taking my nonsense seriously, which I always liked. 'And what were those weaknesses again?'

'They don't matter now,' I said, pulling myself together and brushing my problems away. 'How many arms do I have? Just the two?'

'Just the two,' the woman confirmed just a shade too gravely. 'A left and a right.'

'Much the best,' I said, checking they were on the right way round. I gestured down the corridor. 'Well then … I should probably find my friends.'

'Oh, I know the feeling,' the woman said. She looked back over her shoulder. 'I've a party to get back to. Might be fun. Then again, might not. Sure I can't tempt you?'

'Oh no.' I shook my head ruefully. 'That party wasn't my cup of tea. Anyway … it was nice to have met you.'

'Absolutely yes!' the woman announced and headed off with a cheery wave.

Whoever she was, I made a mental note to thank her, the next time we met. And I was sure we would.

I came to a narrow slit in the wall, staring out of it at the landscape burning below.

Everything that had happened since I'd arrived (if I had arrived) had been designed to confound me. Someone had reached into my memories, even the ones I hadn't had yet, and given them a good squeeze until the pips squeaked.

I moved away from the bleak view, and continued my way down the corridor. I noticed how uneven it was – at first I assumed it was scoured by the tools that had made the corridor, but then I looked again. The marks were carvings – ancient carvings. There were just the vaguest traces of what had once been elaborate bas reliefs. Oh, how I loved a bas relief.

I stepped back as far as the narrow passage would allow and devoted myself to reading the history of the castle. It was a mystery to solve, and it distracted me from my own problems, of which I'd had quite enough.

Although the details were sketchy, I read a tale of lands who knew only war, an endless war which had raged, without regard for the endless slaughter. Creatures had fought across the stars until the entire dimension had seemed on the point of collapse. The survivors had been gathered together, offered peace and stability by … well, it was hard to describe. It sort of appeared in some of the carvings, but had been erased – not scrubbed out by a censor, but the details had been rubbed away by aeons of fingertips caressing the stone. So, this place had been in trouble, there'd been unstoppable war, and then someone had turned up and, with an unconventional solution, had stopped it. Well, there we go. Something I could identify with.

I carried on walking until I came to a door. I knocked.

There was no answer.

Shiftily, I looked left and right and tried to open the door.
It was locked.

I produced my sonic screwdriver. I waved it across the lock, and the door swung open. I gaped into the room beyond.

'Ah, Doctor, come in,' said the Devil.

FEAR OF THE DEVIL

'The Devil, though?' My audience was jeering. 'The Devil!'

I could sense that this latest serving of barley water was a touch strong for them.

'The Devil!' The Zero Nun threw back her veil and glared at me with affected disappointment. 'You expect us to believe that the creature you're about to meet is the Devil?'

I was all innocence. 'Would I lie to you?'

'Doctor, I've done my best to advocate on your behalf,' the Nun simpered. 'But the Devil!'

'Well, these things happen,' I protested. 'And believe me, they're just as distracting for me as they are for you. It's all explained.'

'Is it, though?' I recognised my old Paradox Declension Tutor in the audience, glaring at me with the dusty weariness of a forgotten garden shed. 'It had better be, Doctor, though I doubt it, I doubt it. But then, my friends –' playing to the crowd a little bit, the old rascal – 'that's the Doctor all over, isn't it? The Doctor is nothing without his fiendish enemies.'

'That's not fair,' I protested. 'There was a time when I didn't have enemies. My evenings were a lot quieter. Enemies are like books: one day you look around and think, "Gosh, I've suddenly got so many. How did that happen?" And, as we all know, the real answer – whether we're talking about dastardly masterminds or tatty paperbacks – is that you'll get around to them all eventually. It's just a question of being patient.'

That silenced them a bit. Time Lords have infinite shelves and all the arcane wisdom of the universe to get through, some of it quite dense. A guilty pile of unread tomes totters beside every Gallifreyan bedside. (It doesn't help that we don't really sleep.)

'There's a thing none of you realise,' I pressed on. 'Villains are a matter of perspective. Why, ask the Daleks about the catastrophes they've unleashed on the universe and they'll swear it's all my fault! They may even say that we're the villains in their drama. Imagine that!'

There were cries of heresy. Others urged the Sword of Never be activated right now. They'd had enough of my fantasies and my morals, and they'd had enough of me.

The Zero Nun urged them all to caution. 'Perhaps the end of the Doctor's story will justify the telling of it,' her lips said while her eyes clearly finished with '… but I doubt it.'

I tried to explain. 'As I was saying, it's all a matter of perspective. Harry Sullivan – now, he's properly brought up, went to the right school, never got caught with his fingers in the pick 'n' mix – he simply views villains as The Wrong Sort. The Opposing Team. In his dear little head they're the kind of people who drop litter, never stand a round, and won't stop at the side of the road to change a hapless driver's blown-out tyre.

'If you ask Sarah Jane, her idea of villainy is more subtle. After a life interviewing politicians, she feels that evil is to say one thing and mean the other. To never lie, but to bend the truth until it can't look itself in the face.

'Which brings us to the Devil, as he's sometimes known. Is he one of Harry's cads? Is he one of Sarah's word-twisters? Or, is he all a matter of perspective? Well, I assure you the creature waiting for me in that room really was the Devil. He exists. And you should be afraid of him. But there's also a very good explanation for him. One that I don't care for one bit.'

CHAPTER TWENTY

I entered the room warily. It was long and panelled with wood. Most of it was taken up with a large meeting table. Portraits hung on the wall. Somewhere a clock ticked. It was all so very ordinary.

Sitting in a pool of light at the end of the table was a figure in a suit. What was remarkable about the figure was its head. The head was a globe of pure white fire, blinding me if I tried to look at it directly.

'Hello!' the figure waved, its voice rich and sprightly. 'Don't stand on ceremony! Come in! Come in!'

My eyes drifted across to the paintings – a dozen of them, all of the same figure. A man in a suit with a burning globe for a head.

'Family portraits?' I asked.

The figure simply responded with another cheery wave, flapping me towards a chair. 'We're so pleased to see you!' he said.

'We?'

More figures sprang into light. A dozen of them, sat around the table. All of them in business suits, all of them with glowing spherical heads of fire. Identical to the one at the head of the desk, but also all somehow smaller and weaker, like photocopies.

'Ah, I take it this is a family business.'

'This is the whole board.'

'A board? How exciting. I adore a meeting,' My tone was summer dry. I made my way up the table, shaking everyone's hands and exchanging meaningless pleasantries. None of them replied, which made me try even harder.

'Hello, how are you, did you have a decent journey, how were the trains, you're looking good, have you lost weight, what about the weather, eh?'

Finally, small talk exhausted, I turned insolently back to the figure at the head of the table. 'And you are?'

Not at all put out, the figure leaned back in his chair, and plonked his legs on the table. As he did so, he pushed out a chair for me. 'I have the privilege to rule here.'

'And very nicely you do too,' I enthused, ignoring the chair. 'Why, who hasn't looked at a sunset and thought, "All that's missing is a flying castle"? Well done, you.'

The figure placed his hands behind his head, and I marvelled that the cuffs of his suit did not burst into flames. 'True,' he said, sounding delighted. 'My name is Scratchman.'

'Oh.' I was sufficiently impressed. 'As in …?'

'The Devil, yes.'

'Ah.' I sat down.

'I've had many other names, over the years. But that's what you'd understand me as. And there's no sense in a list.'

'Not at all.' I hated lists.

'I'm so glad you agree.' The burning globe seemed to be smiling. How did it do that? I shuddered, feeling a great and terrible desire to get to my feet and flee. There was something about the faceless urbanity of the creature. It surveyed me with a blank malevolence, as though it was reading my soul and giving nothing back except a polite curiosity. Was this really the Devil? It couldn't be. Could it?

'My friends call me Scratch, and I hope you will too. After all, we have so much in common.'

Despite myself, I sat bolt upright at that. 'I beg your pardon?'

Scratch chuckled, and made a wafting motion with his hands. 'Don't worry! I'm just talking broadly. Have a cigar.' Scratch pushed a box towards me.

I took a cigar and examined it carefully. 'I don't, really …'

'Go on, be a devil.' The burning globe seemed to wink.

I took the cigar, hunted around for matches and then held it to Scratch's face. I watched the tip glow, and then sat back, puffing away. 'Haven't done this for years, very odd habit. But there were some nuns in Cuba who were terribly insistent,' I remarked. 'Takes years off your life.' I blew out a smoke ring. 'Why, I might not make it to a thousand.'

'Hush now.' Scratch held a finger to his total lack of lips. 'Not in my realm. Here you can have whatever you like without consequence.'

'Really?' I gasped, tossing the cigar into a bin. 'Then I shall have a ginger beer!'

Scratch sprang up, crossed to a decanter and poured me a glass of quite marvellously chilled ginger beer. Finally! I took a fizzy sip, grinned appreciatively, and observed Scratch over the rim of my glass. He was becoming expansive.

'Doctor, I have ruled this realm for millions of years. Recently – over the last thousand or so years – a small rip has appeared, allowing me the tiniest peep into your dimension. A little influence here, a few scarecrows there … You remember the scarecrows?'

I frowned. 'It's a little hazy. Recent events are.'

'Doesn't matter. Details never do.' Scratch drummed his fingers happily on the table. 'I'm explaining myself to you – so that we can work together.'

'We can what?'

'Oh I know what you're thinking – an alliance with the Devil. It sounds bad on paper. But hear me out. Why, this whole dimension would be dead now if it wasn't for my actions. If I'd played by the rules, it would all have been snuffed out. I've saved this universe. Surely you can see the similarity between us?'

'How?' I felt a creeping itch in my brain.

Scratch tapped his non-existent burning nose. 'I'm a lord of anarchy. My methods are unorthodox, yes, but I've saved so many people and achieved a blissful stability here. Order out of chaos.'

'An order of anarchy?' I couldn't help smiling.

'You appreciate the irony. When I peek through that tiny tear into your reality I see so much chaos, so much disorder, so much terrible death – and who do I see, nipping back and forth, trying to hold back the flood? You!'

'I'm touched.'

'And it is remarkable. You're the me of your universe!'

'I'm the Devil?' I spluttered on my ginger beer.

'You're certainly a lord of anarchy! Why, how many gods have you bumped off?'

I blinked.

'And I can help you, my dear Doctor. Just as I brought stability to my realm, if we work together we can bring order to yours.'

'Ah …' I demurred. 'I think you have a misconception. You may lord it over this dimension, but I'm afraid I have no ambitions to become the ruler of my universe. For one thing, I hear the hours are shocking.'

Scratch burst out laughing, a warm sound that I couldn't help grinning at.

'No more do I rule here. I obey the niceties, but really, the idea of responsibility …' Scratch gave a long and mocking groan. 'The beauty of this system is that it runs itself. So I can pop off on holiday.'

'How terribly efficient.'

'Well …' Scratch seemed abashed. 'I like holidays. Don't you?'

I conceded the point, and couldn't help thinking of that time I'd landed a prize trout in Loch Lomond back in the sixth century.

If only there was more time for angling. But things kept getting in the way.

'We must go fishing some time!' Scratch exclaimed, plucking the thought from my mind. 'It sounds a wonderful hobby. Sadly, we don't have many fish here ...'

'What with the sea being lava?'

'Yes.' Scratch nodded his absurd burning head. 'But we make the best of things, as you do, Doctor. We could be so good for each other.'

'Could we?' I contemplated my ginger beer. It really was excellent.

'Absolutely,' Scratch assured me. 'And it could be our little secret. No one else need know. All you'd have to do is pop back through the rift – your ship would widen the gap and I could follow through and start helping. You could have all the credit – not that you'd take it.'

'No, no,' I said. I'd always shunned the limelight.

'But word would get around like gossip, and everyone would look at you and go, "There Goes The Doctor! Do you know what he did? Did you ever doubt him? Not me!"'

I found myself nodding along.

I became aware that the other figures at the table had all turned to look at me. As one, they nodded.

'Let me just put it to the board!' said Scratch and gestured to the others. 'Fellers! Do you approve?'

Each figure lifted up a football rattle and whirled it around their heads. The room filled with a deafening clacker.

'Well, looks like the team's all on board. What do you say?'

'A deal with the Devil?' I smiled. 'I'm imagining the Master's face right now. He'd just die of jealousy, poor lamb. This would absolutely kill him.'

'Oh it would! It would!' Scratch had clearly heard of my nemesis. 'Some people try too hard, don't they?' He laughed fondly. 'I can tell you're tempted. Oh, do say you'll agree.' Scratch reached out his hand.

'Well, of course,' I said. 'We're on opposite sides of the coin. Negative energy can translate into something positive in another realm. And you are right. There's only so many times one can arrive on a planet too late. Only so many deaths one can see. Only so many noble sacrifices.'

I reached for Scratch's hand.

CHAPTER TWENTY-ONE

I reached for Scratch's hand.

'Only …' I paused, fingertips hovering. 'The thing is, a funny thing happened to me on my way here tonight. Three funny things.'

'The journey through the realm can be perilous and strange.'

'Can't it!' I nodded. 'First there was the ferryman, then a lazy lizard, then a party.'

'Doesn't sound too bad.'

'Three different encounters. Three different niggles, looking for weaknesses. The ferryman took my memories, the lizard bored me, the party ignored me—'

'Did it? How shocking.'

'A woolly little thread ran through them. Making me feel insignificant, unimportant, that my time as the Doctor was over.'

'Surely not!' Scratch protested.

'Finding my weak spots, softening me up, so that when I got some attention I'd be flattered.'

'The very idea!'

'Why, if it hadn't been for that Cyberleader turning up—'

'A Cyberleader? Dear, dear!' Scratch's tone was that of a waiter apologising for a mouse in the soup.

'Yes. I wonder how he ended up here? Still, if it hadn't been for him jogging my memory, I might have been lost.'

'Lost! I am appalled,' gasped Scratch and then burst out laughing.

I laughed too.

The figures around the table all burst out laughing – ha, ha and ha – and then fell silent.

'The board like you,' said Scratch.

'I like me too,' I agreed.

A stillness settled over the room. The globed figures of the board all stared at me. Scratch tapped a restless finger on the table. The board all tapped their fingers at the same time. They were all waiting for me to speak.

'So,' I asked, 'what's in it for you?'

Scratch glowed bashfully, and gestured around the room. 'I'm proud of what I do. I find out what people want, what they're lacking, and I give it to them.'

I nudged the board member next to me.

'Nicely done, didn't you think?' I said. 'He didn't answer the question, but he said some pretty things, and that's almost as good.'

My smile snapped off, and I turned back to Scratch. 'I repeat. What's in it for you?'

'A mere bagatelle.' Scratch brushed a burning smut from his suit. 'The link between our realms would remain open and stable. I could pass through from time to time. As you can see – my world here flourishes, but it is limited. I could feed on more. Just a little – just a few stray thoughts that wander through. The odd wish here, the occasional unfulfilled longing there.' He inclined his glowing head. 'Nibbling at the plankton of the soul.'

'I see,' I nodded. 'Lots of little Faustian pacts.'

'Exactly. I like making my deals. They're very misunderstood. Why, Faust and I had such fun together!' Scratch leaned on the table, resting his globe on the palms of his hands. 'I reach out to a few souls, give them what they want in life, and, when they expire, I bring them here. It's simply a way of establishing an energy exchange between two dimensions.'

'You make it sound almost boring.' I sprang up and paced the room. 'You've gone to enormous lengths to make this whole set-up mundane. Anarchy? Why, you've a meeting room, you've got yes-men, you've got a jotter and inkpots and ...'

'I've a system, that's all. I've mellowed in my old age. Haven't you?'

'I've barely started,' I beamed.

'What do you want? Actually –' Scratch flapped a hand – 'Let me tell you. I'll let you be this Doctor forever.'

'What?' I stopped pacing.

'You liked being the others, but you love being you. And you don't want to give that up, do you? Who would?'

'It's certainly tempting,' I couldn't help admitting. His words struck me. I tried being facetious. 'I'd miss the teeth ...'

'But? I can sense a but.' Scratch wagged a finger. 'I do find them boring.'

'You tell me that you'll bring peace to the universe. And I'm almost persuaded. Only, I can just remember a very charming lady who once lived on an island. Her name was Sophonisba and I found her utterly splendid. And because of you, she died.'

The members of the board leaned forward, twelve identical little creaks.

'Ah.' Scratch stood, and the light in his globe dimmed dangerously.

'Ah, indeed,' I scowled. 'An immortality of me – but an eternity of looking the other way? How many times would I blink and find my paradise was missing a planet or two ...?'

'You've got me, there,' Scratch shrugged. 'Planets are so moreish. I'm helpless.'

'And then …' I strode up to Scratch and stared at his face, burning like a sun. There were pits on the surface, tiny pockets of flame that glowed and danced and shifted under my gaze. 'You were asking about fishing earlier. Well, I'll tell you how it works. You stole my friends. Bait to lure me here. And it worked. You hooked me, you reeled me in, you're about to land me. But, and this is just the problem with how my brain works, I can't worry about myself while I'm worrying about my friends. Wipe my memory and I'll still not forget them. So. Where are they? Can I see them?'

'It's a no, isn't it?

'Yes. It's a no.'

Scratch sighed. He leaned back against an oak-panelled wall and it started to smoulder. He slouched, shoving his hands in his pockets. 'I do so hate a no. Don't I hate a no, fellows?' he asked the board, and they all nodded in grim unison. Their globes all began to glow the same angry amber.

'One final push, Doctor. If you join me, you can have your companions back, of course you can. You can have anything you want – friends, jam, a Teasmade.'

'But you know I'm not going to agree.'

'I do,' Scratch nodded, and his globe flushed a deep and fiery scarlet. 'But that's all right. Because there's an alternative, one that's more fun. Tell you what! Let's have a fight!'

The members of the board burst into applause. The same clap, over and over, perfectly in time. The clap of a hungry crowd.

I took a step back. 'I won't fight you,' I vowed. 'I can't fight the Devil. I'd never win.'

Scratch silenced the board with a sweeping gesture. 'You'll fight me,' he promised, sneering. 'And, if you lose – which you will –' the figures around the table all nodded – 'then I'll get to keep you and your friends and your universe.'

The glowing head burst into flame.

'Oh dear,' he said. 'I can't keep my excitement in.'

The flames spilled from Scratch's head, shooting up the walls and dripping onto the carpet. They devoured the walls, mushroomed up and spread over the ceiling in a canopy. The oil paintings went up like firecrackers.

I remained standing there, calm in the inferno. I watched as the table reached flashpoint. The board members remained seated, burning brightly as the table flared around them. Some of them were clapping again as they burned. I watched as burning oil paintings slid from the walls. I watched as the flaming debris ignited the carpet around me. I didn't even cough. I stood there, staring at Scratch. When a Time Lord needs to be serious, he can be very serious indeed.

'Join me or fight me, Doctor.'

'You know my answer.'

'I do,' smiled Scratch.

CHAPTER TWENTY-TWO

I was running, running through a vast darkness. There was no direction, there was no up or down, there was just blackness. Was this the plan, I wondered? To be forever running through the darkness with the terrible feeling of something at my back? Was this the price I'd pay for standing up to Scratchman?

I had been running for most of my life. Running from explosions, from monsters, from routine. Always heading to the next catastrophe, the next adventure.

A nasty thought snuck into my soul and wriggled around. What if Scratch wanted me to run? What if I was like a gerbil on a wheel now, feeding that man's desires?

I stopped running, forced myself to take a calming breath, looked around. Nothing. Absolute nothing. Nothing with a floor. Yes. I could stand still. Yes. I could stay here.

I counted to ten. Counted off another ten seconds. Perhaps, yes, I would make it to a whole minute. I felt my hearts beating too fast and I concentrated on slowing down first one and then the other.

Come on, Doctor, stay calm. You can do it.

What was this darkness? What did it mean? Why couldn't I stop my own panic?

Unable to stay still a moment longer, I ran on further, tripped over my own feet and fell, tumbling down into unnerving nothing.

I woke and realised there were two points of light glaring balefully at me in the distance, like eyes.

I picked myself up painfully, dusted myself down (out of habit) and lurched towards the light. 'Scratch!' I called. 'Call this a fight? It's just mind games with menaces.'

There was no answer. To be fair, I hadn't really expected one. I looked around for a stone to kick angrily.

'No pebbles.'

I began a trot. From a bit closer, I could see that the glowing eyes had pupils, pupils that squirmed and wriggled and waved and called out my name. I pulled up, baffled.

'Doctor!'

I heard the cry on the wind and broke into a grin. It had been a long time since I'd heard my name called like that. Music to my ears.

My vision cleared. Standing ahead of me in spotlights were the figures of Sarah and Harry.

Laughing with delight, I ran towards them, shouting out their names. As I reached them, they stopped calling out, their delight paused, sheepish.

'Sarah? Harry?' I squinted doubtfully. These looked like my two dear friends, very much like. Imprisoned in Gubbage Cone light-prisons. But my friends. And yet there was every chance that they were imaginings, fakes, duplicates.

The figures of Sarah and Harry looked back at me, and then their eyes sank down to the ground, dubious.

'I say,' Harry began, and I realised how much I'd missed that lovable fool's ability to tell you what he was about to do. 'It's jolly nice to see you and all that, but, and not wanting to look a gift horse in the mouth, just …'

He faltered, and Sarah piped up. 'What Harry's failing to say is how do we know it's you, Doctor?'

'Yes, you could be a robot clone or something. Sorry, Doctor, but you could be.'

'Oh.' For some reason their suspicion hurt. 'Have you, by any chance, met any other Doctors while you've been here?'

'No, of course not!' Harry said. 'We've just been sat in the dark.'

This was splendid news. 'I'm sorry about that. But I can assure you I'm very much me.'

'You would say that,' countered Sarah. 'And Harry and I have been stuck here for hours and we'd believe almost anything.'

'Haven't we just,' enthused Harry. 'Why, if it wasn't for me doing all I could to keep our spirits up—'

'Yes, please be the real Doctor and get us out of here,' Sarah cut him off. I gave her a sympathetic look. There had been songs, hadn't there?

I approached the spotlights and reached for them. 'You're trapped by a simple belief field,' I said.

'What's one of those?' asked Sarah

'Because you believe there's a restraint around you, there is a restraint around you.' I grinned. '*Cogito ergo* prison.' I reached out a hand. 'Take my hand, Sarah Jane.'

'Really?' said Sarah dubiously.

'Oh yes.' I gave her my very best wink. 'Believe that you can do that more than anything else and you'll be fine.'

Sarah reached out, screwing her eyes shut, and her fingertips brushed against mine. With a yank, I pulled her out of the pool of light.

'Crikey,' whistled Harry. 'I see the trick.' He stepped forward, and the lights around him buzzed, shoving him back.

'Believe harder, Harry,' I admonished him. 'You've a small, polite mind. You obey rules, you keep off the grass, and this is how it repays you. Trapped in a pool of light because you can't think beyond it. Very limited imagination. Well, Harry, I'm telling you now, for once in your life, think big! Where's your maddening overconfidence when I need it?'

Harry strode angrily out of the light. 'I say –' he raised his voice and squared up to me – 'that was a trifle harsh, if you don't mind me saying so and … Oh.' Harry realised he was out of his prison.

I patted him fondly on the shoulder. 'Good work!'

'Got any jelly babies?' asked Sarah. 'I'm starving.'

'Alas no,' I apologised. 'I gave them to a lizard.'

'Of course you did,' Sarah nodded. 'So, where are we and what are we up against?'

'Well,' I began, then yodelled.

The noise caught my friends by surprise.

'I was just trying to work out how large this void is.'

'Sounds pretty large.' Harry listened to the dying echoes, swinging his arms around. 'Pretty chilly too.'

'That's the lack of energy,' I told him. 'We're being bled like batteries. This whole realm feeds off people.'

'Feeds off people?' Harry looked alarmed.

'Yes. It feeds off dreams, souls and, failing that, gristle, tissue and bone marrow.'

Sarah made a face.

'Sounds unpleasant,' Harry said.

'Yes. It'll eat you up and then transform the remains. But don't take it to heart. In this realm you should never take anything to heart. Because this place takes your heart and comes back for your soul. You've got to keep your spirits up and keep moving.'

'Transformed? Like the scarecrows?' We had been walking for a few minutes and Sarah had lots of questions.

'Oh yes. They were an experiment. An utterly alien form of energy taking baby steps into our universe. A form of energy that calls himself Scratchman.' I paused, brooding. 'You'd think of him as the Devil.'

'I would, would I?' Sarah made a face.

Harry was having none of it. 'The Devil? With horns and so on?'

'More or less, yes.' I considered giving Harry a lecture on how many human representations of the Devil were actually race memories inspired by entirely different species of wandering scientists who just so happened to have horns, and gargoyles for lab assistants. It had led to some mildly objectionable acts of cultural appropriation. 'Scratchman is a creature of another dimension that feeds off the emotional vulnerabilities of others in return for giving them a little power.'

'Like Mephistopheles coming to Dr Faustus in the old play?' Sarah suggested. 'And there's always a price to pay in the end.'

'Quite. Up until now Scratch's power in our universe has been limited, through a pinhole between his realm and ours. But the scarecrows were a bridgehead. I think they were a gift for the Cybermen.'

'A gift?' Harry looked alarmed.

'Sort of setting himself up in a *pied à terre* on Earth?' asked Sarah.

'Or a beach hut,' Harry suggested. 'Hot and cold running souls.'

'You're both being facetious,' I intoned solemnly, adoring them. It really was very cold here. I could almost feel the neurons slipping out of my fingertips. 'Despite his claims to the contrary, I think Scratch has pretty much exhausted this realm. He's devoured this dimension – he wants ours next. And he wants me to take him there.'

'Oh,' said Harry. 'But we're going to stop him, aren't we?'

'Of course we are!' I boomed, and then lowered my voice, confiding. 'It's just that I don't have the faintest idea how.'

'Oh dear,' said Harry.

'You know, I'm supposed to fight him in order to win you back.' I paused. Scratchman was watching us, planning his next move. When was the fight going to begin?

'You're going to fight the Devil? Really?' Sarah smiled up at me. 'That's very kind of you.'

'My only problem is that Scratchman is a pan-dimensional entity and I'm just a sunny optimist relying on my wits. But we'll pull through.' I had my doubts, but it didn't do to let on.

'Are you really sure you should fight him, though, Doctor?' asked Harry, dubiously, adding to my misgivings.

'Harry's right,' said Sarah. '*He* should fight Old Harry.'

'I'm sorry?' said Harry.

I stuck my hands in my pockets and roared with good-natured laughter.

'We're in limbo here. Nothingness. But the world outside is a different matter.' I briefly laid out the outlandish landscape beneath the flying castle. 'My suspicion is that everything here has been created from the leftover imaginations of his previous victims.'

'Hell really is other people?'

'Very good.' I patted Sarah on the shoulder. 'Psychic energy is a rich fuel. Imagination, strong feelings, fear. He's been trying to get inside my head ever since I arrived.'

'What happens when he does?'

'Once he knows what my deepest fears are, then I'm afraid we're sunk,' I said. 'I can feel him prowling around the cat flap in my mind. He'll get in. But, in the meantime, with nothing solid to feed on, we're simply in limbo, which gives us time to plan.'

In the darkness came a rumbling.

'Doctor …' Sarah whispered. 'Has Scratchman found a way through the cat flap?'

'No, no,' I assured her. 'We should be fine. Just so long as we keep our imaginations in check. Sarah, it's vitally important you keep your mind blank.'

'What about Harry?' asked Sarah.

'Mind blank? You just told me to think big!' Harry protested. 'Very limited imagination, you said, but …' The rumbling came again. 'Er, what is that?'

'A monster?' said Sarah.

The rumbling grew louder.

'It sounds just like …' Harry shook his head. 'No honestly, it sounds like … but it's really odd, as I was just thinking about …'

'Harry, what have you done?' demanded Sarah.

I had grabbed their arms and we were already running. Something was coming at us out of the darkness – a huge, shimmering reflection of the three of us, distorting and fluttering as it got closer and closer, and the noise it made, that terrible rumbling noise getting louder and louder.

'But it can't be …' protested Harry, looking over his shoulder. 'I was just, I mean—'

'Harry …' growled Sarah.

'Keep running!' I shouted as the noise got louder.

'What were you thinking about?' yelled Sarah.

'Pinball,' finished Harry, meekly.

CHAPTER TWENTY-THREE

Sarah Jane Smith had run away from a lot of things in her time with me. She'd run from Daleks, Sontarans, no end of robots, even the Loch Ness Monster. Running was second nature to her, the same way that some people hold doors open or put on a posh voice when answering the phone.

Now she was being chased by giant ball bearings.

At first the thunder of their arrival made it seem like they were everywhere in the darkness. But then the neon lights started to come on. Of course they did.

We were trapped inside a vast pinball table. An infinity of polished steel and baize slid before us. Steel walls reared up around us. Huge bumpers flipped back and forth, and everywhere, with a grinding of gears and the groaning of giant, hidden springs, vast steel balls thundered at us. Above us was a canopy of smoky glass, over which the shadow of something huge moved, as though a giant creature was playing the game.

Hanging in mid air was a series of neon signs. Some of them were the usual suspects, TILT and JACKPOT and BONUS, but one or two could only have come from the mind of Harry Sullivan. Such as the one which read OH DEAR.

As we ran, Sarah racked her brain to remember all she knew about pinball. It wasn't much. The pub opposite *Metropolitan* magazine had had a pinball game and Sarah had enjoyed watching colleagues throw their wages into it. The principle was easy enough – balls would be shot out of the innards of the machine. Players had access to a series of flippers which they could use to steer the course of a ball, bouncing it against various obstacles and bumpers, each of which would raise the score … before the ball inevitably got caught somewhere and tumbled out of sight back into the machine. A sort of metaphor for life, and equally a neat demonstration of why Roddy Jones was always short of a round before pay day.

Pinball had seemed jolly, harmless fun, and hadn't claimed much of her attention. It was just something that was there, like cricket and racing pigeons.

Then she'd met me and away we'd gone, giving up any thoughts of pinball in favour of the far more interesting challenges of ancient cities that were trying to kill you, or the gentle art of befriending alien squid.

And here she was now, trapped inside a game of pinball. All because of …

'Harry, how could you?' She had ducked behind a bumper. Three giant silver balls whipped past.

'I don't know, old girl,' Harry protested. 'It just sort of popped into my head. You know, the Doctor and Mr Scratch, I just imagined the two of them plonking it out over a game of pinball while we sat at a table with a half of best and some salt and vinegar crisps.'

'Cheese and onion, Harry.'

'Steady on, old girl, I'll buy both,' Harry smiled. 'Anyway, I'm awfully sorry, but I just thought it'd be nice to sit back and relax for a change while the Doctor got on with it. It was a very small idea, really, just tucked away at the back of my head.' Harry winced miserably as another giant ball whizzed past. Shimmering inside it was a screaming face.

'I see,' said Sarah tightly. I'd got ahead of them, and was trying to avoid a giant metal flipper. 'How would you say it's going?'

'Well, the Doctor hasn't been crushed yet, so I don't think we're losing.'

More ball bearings thundered past.

'Crikey,' sighed Harry. 'Is there any way of stopping this?'

Sarah contemplated her scarf for a moment. 'Harry,' she said. 'This is supposed to be a fight, isn't it? And yet, can you actually win at pinball?'

'Well, now,' Harry gathered up some of his scattered confidence and tried to fold it neatly. 'It's jolly simple, actually. Balls come flying out, you bat them around a bit, try to avoid getting hemmed in by some pins and so on and so forth until the balls sink out of sight. You take it in turns and the object is to beat the high score.'

As he said this, a chorus of wickedly sharp needles slashed through the air around them, embedding themselves in the floor to form a wicket of pins. Someone was clearly still listening in to Harry's thoughts.

'I've got all that,' Sarah sighed. 'My point was that it's not really a two-player game, is it?'

'Well, not really in a turn-based sense. I mean, that'd be chess, or darts, or skittles – now, skittles, now, that is a game ...'

'Harry, no!' yelled Sarah.

But the damage had been done. She could feel the bumper they were hiding behind shift and change. It twisted into the dimensions of a large chess piece – a bishop. It slid away from them, exposing them to a fresh volley of balls. As they ran, she saw the pintable altering. The shiny surface split into a black and white chequerboard. The bollards were all changing into chess pieces, marching slowly across the board in a stately gavotte, ignoring the chaotic pinging of balls around them.

A large neon sign lit up saying CHECK. Another said THAT'S NOT RIGHT, IS IT? SORRY.

A knight plucked one of the pins from the floor and, using it as a sword, swiped it at them. Harry and Sarah ducked back.

'What have I done?' gasped Harry as a giant lead weight swooped over their heads, scattering some equally giant pawns.

'The game's tuned into you, Harry. Don't conjure any more nightmares – try to think about how we win!'

Harry flung himself to the ground, dragging Sarah with him as a cascade of giant cannonballs smashed into a rook. 'You've got to admit that's a bit tricky!'

A few yards ahead, I was trying to get my head around the game, and the game was trying to get around my head. My chief delight was working out the rules of a situation and then bending them a little. The problem, as far as I could see it, was that, right now, the rules were constantly shifting, and never in my favour.

If it was pinball, then, perhaps, I was supposed to stop Scratch from hitting a high score, but the whole situation was grotesque. Not helped that the whole set-up was using Harry Sullivan's brain as a 9 volt battery.

'Never expect a fair fight from the Devil,' I muttered, throwing myself out of the path of another steel sphere. I caught a flash of something twisting inside the silver – had Scratch found a demented use for those poor Cybermen? Rendered down and turned into ball bearings. It almost made one feel sorry for them.

Perhaps I could do something with that – only, again, the board seemed to keep shifting, a strange jumble of different pintables, like someone had run through a Soho bar, gathering up the best bits. I ran over a gaudily-painted '500' picked out in cheery end-of-pier colours, dashing towards a flipper, wondering if I could just get the cover off it – perhaps underneath the housing was some circuitry, and if there was circuitry then there was a way in with the sonic screwdriver, a way to take control and fight back.

I reached the flipper, and crouched down, snatching at the metal casing. It was live, and, if I was going to get inside it, I was going to have to proceed very gingerly.

As I worked, I got an instinct. I hate being watched when I'm working. A shadow fell over me, and I scrambled out of the way. As I did so a sceptre smashed into the metal, sending a shower of sparks arcing across the board.

I sprang up and stared in amazement at the giant ebony Queen towering over me.

I had never reasoned with a giant chess piece before, but I gave it my best shot. 'Your majesty,' I began, 'this must be terribly confusing for you. I'd ask you to try and remember who you really are, and pause and consider your position before taking any hasty action.'

The Black Queen regarded me, her chiselled face cruel and impassive.

'This is not who you are,' I insisted. 'You're being manipulated. And that, your majesty, will never do. After all, you're a queen, not a pawn.'

The Queen stood completely still. The maelstrom of the pintable roared and banged and sparked around us, but for a few precious moments, there was just the Black Queen and me. And then she reached down, plucked me up and threw me against the metal flipper.

I was engulfed in a cascade of sparks. I cried out, and fell to the ground. I'm afraid to say, I passed out at that point, the flipper battering against my prone body, lighting it up.

A neon sign appeared. It read ONE DOWN.

'The Doctor!' screamed Sarah. 'We have to get to him.'

The two fought their way towards me across a drunken fury of living chess pieces that glided backwards and forwards, smashing into each other and fighting to the death. Occasionally a pinball would crash into a piece, either knocking it flat or tumbling it into one of the many holes in the board. The pieces, normally silent, would fall with a ghastly, all too living scream.

Sarah glanced towards one of the holes, but couldn't quite see what was inside it.

They ducked and dived, but the going was lethal. Harry whisked them behind a bishop, using its stately progress as a shield, carrying them nearer and nearer to my sparking form.

A few yards across the board, their luck gave out, and the bishop was smashed away by another swipe of the ball-on-a-string.

'Harry! Skittles?' yelled Sarah.

'Sorry,' Harry shrugged. 'We should probably run for—' but Sarah had already hared off.

She made it to me, dragging me away from the sparks by my ankles.

'Look out, Sarah!'

As Harry's cry reached her, she realised something was looming over her. She turned. The blessed figure of the Black Queen slid up, grabbing for her with a murderous claw. Sarah's eyes widened.

Harry threw himself against the Queen, but was flung back against an advancing pawn for his troubles. He sprang up and dashed back towards the Queen. 'Excuse me!' he called.

Again, the Queen was diverted from Sarah and me, turning to pummel Harry against a wall and then sliding up to crush him.

The diversion gave Sarah the time she needed to drag me out of harm's way behind a barrier of frightened black pawns. She caught her breath and observed the lethal chaos of the board.

The situation was bad, and not helped by a neon sign that said EVERYONE IS GOING TO DIE.

Sarah Jane Smith had a fiercely logical mind that, paradoxically, refused to take no for an answer, even from me. It was at its best when fighting her corner, and at its even-better when the corner was a tight spot.

On the one hand, they were supposed to be fighting back against Scratchman. On the other hand, she'd realised it was impossible to win at a game when you were trapped inside it, unless there was some way to use the game against the player.

'There has to be a way to stop this,' she thought. 'There has to.'

While Sarah was working out how to fight back, Harry Sullivan was working out how to continue breathing. He was having the life squeezed out of him by the Black Queen. She was staring at him with her fine, cold features, a cruel smile stretched over her face as her stone hand crushed his chest.

His vision was blurring, his heart was pounding in his head, and he really could see the final curtains drawing … when all of a sudden, the Queen was knocked aside.

Rearing over her was a white knight. Clinging to its back was Sarah Jane, laughing. Furious, the Queen righted herself, rallied, and returned to the fight, but the Knight swiped at her while she was still off balance. With a look of sheer fury, the Queen toppled, falling down one of the holes in the board.

'Well done, Sarah!' gasped Harry.

Sarah peered into the hole and realised why the Queen was screaming. A long way beneath the hole was a vast lake of fire. The Queen's body tumbled over and over, lost in the heat haze, exploding before she touched the surface of the burning lake.

The knight abruptly swerved, throwing Sarah Jane off. It was obeying its rules and trying to avoid the hole. It bowed to her regretfully. As it did so, a pinball smacked into it, knocking it flat. Before Sarah could react, she found herself tumbling backwards, scrabbling for a purchase as the section of floor she was on tilted up, turning into a ramp. Helpless, she started to slide. She pushed down on the tiles, bringing herself to a tentative stop, and looked behind her. Her head was lolling over the side of a hole.

Two pawns, one black, one white, tumbled squealing past her into the pit. They were still fighting as they fell. She watched them both shimmer and melt, hitting the surface of the lake as balls of fire.

Sarah scrabbled around for something better to cling on to and failed. The ramp carried on tilting, and Sarah found herself sliding headfirst into the pit. Her fingernails slapped uselessly at the surface of the ramp, seeking any tiny divot on which to find purchase. Finally she stopped, upside down, her head tipped back over the chasm at that peculiarly unnatural angle that comes when a hairdresser is shampooing you in a basin. Her eyes were watering from the heat haze and the smuts choking the air.

The ramp tilted even more and Sarah, helpless, slid slowly into the hole.

As she vanished over the lip, a hand grabbed her. She looked up. It was Harry Sullivan, swinging her up to safety. 'Let's get you out of there, old girl.'

'Yes let's,' said Sarah, doing her best not to let too much anguish and gratitude show in her tone. Harry heaved her out, and they lay there for a moment. 'Oh Harry,' she said, 'Am I glad to see you.'

'Likewise,' said Harry, and didn't even tease her a little. 'What do we do now?'

Sarah pointed to a pile of cowering pawns. 'Over there,' she said. 'I left the Doctor lying behind those giant pawns.' Bless Harry, he didn't even blink at that nonsense.

They sprang up and ran for the barricade. A series of pinballs shot out of nowhere towards them. Harry shoved Sarah rudely out of the way, and she went flying. She felt a cannonball whizz past her face, and she fell to the floor.

She turned over to see Harry lying a few feet behind her. 'Come on, Harry!' she urged, springing up and taking refuge behind the pawns.

Harry knelt up, and then winced. 'No good, old girl,' he sighed. 'One went over my ankle.'

'Then crawl. It's not far.'

'Fair enough.' Harry thought Sarah could be a little unsympathetic at times.

Harry started crawling towards her, and was, all things considered, doing a reasonably good job of it ... until a silver flash swung down from above and hoiked Harry up by his trousers.

Sarah stared at this, aghast. Harry was dangling from a seaside amusement arcade claw. He was waving.

'Harry!' she called.

'Don't mind me!' he called. 'I'll be fi—'

And he was whipped up and out of sight.

Sarah watched him for a moment, and realised she was waving. Poor Harry. Brilliant Harry. Bless Harry.

She scurried over to me. I had one eye open and looked confused.

'Sarah ... did you just see Harry flying? And why is a giant ebony bishop grappling with an oversized pinball?'

'Doctor ...'

I focused. 'Right,' I said. 'It never ends, does it? Is this all down to Harry's imagination? I really have underestimated him. The one time he does some thinking and this is what we get.'

I sprang to my feet, shaking myself down from head to toe like a dog bounding out of Highbury Ponds. I spied a passing rook and, grabbing Sarah's hand, dashed over to it, sticking out my thumb.

'What are you doing?' squeaked Sarah.

'Thumbing a lift!' I yelled. Revitalised, I leapt into the air, grabbed one of the crenellations, and, in one movement, scrambled up, dragging Sarah Jane behind me.

We perched in the Rook's turret, surveying the chaos we were crossing. I pulled a telescope from my pocket and swept the territory like a general.

'You say Harry unleashed this mess from his brain?'

Sarah nodded.

'And you were wondering how we win this game from inside it?'

Sarah nodded again, and grinned. My head sometimes goes at $33^{1/3}$ rpm. Sometimes at 45. But this was definitely a 78 moment.

'I think,' I announced, 'that I have a plan.'

Chapter Twenty-Four

The skies glowed and fizzed and more lights snapped on. Digital numbers danced, and insane messages flashed up in neon and then burned out. Phrases plucked from Harry's neurons glowed pinkly – I'M FRIGHTFULLY SORRY and OH DEAR and WILL YOU LOOK AT THAT? hung over them.

'We're trapped in polite Blackpool,' Sarah said.

The neon horizon was now lit up with a vast high score; we'd done well to stay alive against that lot. In front of the scoreboard stood Scratch, positively glowing.

'Is that Scratchman?' asked Sarah.

I nodded.

'The Devil is a lightbulb in a smart suit?'

'Lucifer means "bringing light".'

'Well, there's a thing,' she said. 'How do we stop him?'

I just returned her smile.

Scratch saw us and waved, a terribly friendly wave.

'He's quite jolly,' ventured Sarah.

'It comes from having all the best tunes,' I remarked. 'Hold on tight.' I reached over the turret and slapped the side of the Rook. 'Giddy-up!'

As I said this, three more pinballs surged out from chutes and charged across the board towards the Rook. It took the impacts, throwing us about dreadfully.

The scoreboard lit up. JOLLY GOOD SHOW flared a neon sign.

I nodded, approvingly. 'So the chess pieces are still the scoring pins. This is fascinating. There's still some logic to all this.'

'There is?'

'Oh yes.' I crossed my fingers and hoped I wasn't fibbing. 'I just need to learn how to talk properly with this Rook. It's just a matter of finding the right vibration.'

'It is?'

'Oh yes. The psychic equivalent of checking its teeth and giving it a slice of apple. The Barbara Woodhouse stuff.'[1]

I held on to the side of the Rook and emitted a series of long, guttural notes.

Sarah Jane Smith stared at me as if I were a dotty relative making a scene in a supermarket aisle. Oh well, it comes to us all.

'Are you trying to talk to a castle in Whale Song?'

Meanwhile, and a long way above, Harry Sullivan found himself dangling inside a cage. Scratchman was standing on the gantry next to him. The heat from the neon display was searing.

Scratch leaned down, and Harry got the oddest feeling that that burning globe was grinning.

'We built all this together, you and me,' Scratchman said. 'From your imagination, we made this.'

'I do rather wish you hadn't,' Harry replied.

'It's fun!' roared Scratch.

'My friends are dying down there,' said Harry.

---

[1] Barbara Woodhouse (1910–1988) was a television personality adept at training dogs, horses and chat-show hosts. All three were programmed to give her unquestioning obedience and devotion. Among her many legacies are the formidable commands 'Walkies!' and 'Sit!'

'And isn't it marvellous!'

Harry looked at Scratch and hated him. Before travelling with me, Harry had hated very few people and been afraid of even fewer. One thing about having his horizons broadened, he reflected ruefully, was that he got to be terrified on a regular basis.

He looked sourly at the thing leaning into his cage. It was absurd. A pillar of flame in a suit. It was also absolutely terrifying. Was this really the Devil? He felt a primal instinct to back away from it screaming, to throw rocks at it, to revile it. And yet, the terrible thing with its glowing head just leaned closer and closer, that blank burning globe of a face somehow seeming to grin and grin and grin.

'You know I can hear all of this?' said Scratch, taunting. 'I can read your every thought.' He pointed to a sign which said I AM TERRIFIED.

Even Harry thought it looked embarrassing. 'Still true, though,' he muttered sourly.

Scratch reached out and grabbed Harry's hand. Harry flinched, feeling the skin on his hand twist and burn in the creature's grasp.

'Are you going to cry out?' asked Scratch calmly and politely.

Harry just made a hissing noise between his teeth.

'You're not, are you?' continued Scratch, disinterestedly

Harry counted off every terrible second of agony. His whole body was trying to snatch his hand back, but the creature wouldn't let go. It just held on to him, its grasp gentle but inescapable.

'Still not a peep,' Scratch continued.

Half mad with pain, Harry let out a whimper.

'There we are,' said Scratch and let go.

Harry stared at his hand. It was unharmed.

Scratch's burning arm slithered back through the bars of the cage. The creature looked satisfied. It pointed, pointed with that terrible hand, up to a sign in the air.

It said DEATH MATCH.

*

The Devil and Harry Sullivan watched the carnage down below. Sarah and I looked so small to Harry, huddled up in our tiny Rook, edging our way across the board. Around us battle raged, as pawns battered back against pinballs, and cannonballs occasionally carried pieces screaming into one of the pits, dropping them down to the lava below. A barrage of pinballs smashed against the side of the Rook, shaking its base. Harry saw Sarah cry out, but her voice did not carry.

The neon above him changed, the score going up, up and ever up. Harry squinted, trying to read the figures so close up. 'How is the Doctor supposed to win?' he enquired.

'He's not.' Scratchman leaned over, wrapping a fond arm around the cage. 'I know, I know, it's most unfair.' Well, of course he'd rigged the game.

'The Doctor has a plan. He will stop you!' Harry regretted how childish his voice sounded.

'I'm sure he has,' Scratch affirmed happily. 'And we're going to make it more interesting for him.'

Scratch snapped his fingers, and the giant claw winched Harry's cage up and out, hoisting him over the battlefield.

As his weight shifted, Harry fell forward onto his face. He felt the floor give slightly, horribly. He realised the base of it was hinged, like a conjuror's cage. At any moment it could spring open and drop him out. He felt terribly unsafe, and scrabbled around to brace himself against the sides of his prison.

He realised the claw was swinging him over the pitch, across the battle, and out over one of the holes in the ground.

'This really isn't good,' said Harry Sullivan.

A neon sign lit up. HELP! it said.

Down below, Sarah had grasped what I was doing and had taken charge. My plan was simple and straightforward, and, she quickly realised, needed to be in her hands. She knew I couldn't resist complicating it.

'Leave it to me, Doctor,' she said. 'Can we go left a bit? Thank you!'

'Oh, but—' I began and then caught her look. 'Left a bit. Certainly.'

Sarah used the Rook to start rounding up the other chess pieces, driving them across the board like a sheepdog hounding sheep. As the herd moved, the pinballs smacked against them, still pushing the score up higher and higher.

ULTIMATE HIGH SCORE read a sign.

'Not a problem?' said Sarah.

'Not a problem,' I replied. 'This is about ending the game.'

'Did you hear something?'

'No. What?'

'Nothing. Over to that corner.'

The Rook's course marshalled the various chess pieces into a rough circle around one of the holes in the board. More and more ball bearings shot across the table, smacking across the table and striking against the pieces.

'I'm sure I heard something,' said Sarah.

'It's just the sound of a plan working marvellously,' I laughed.

Having formed a barrier, the circle began to close around the pinballs pouring into it, trapping them. The score soared, but the balls had nowhere to go but into the chute. We were emptying the board. With no pieces left in the game, it'd have to stop.

A small drift of sparks rained down from somewhere above.

'Sarah?'

'Yes, Doctor?'

'I think you did hear something. I just heard it too. It said, "Look up!"'

We looked up. Dangling a long way over us was Harry in his cage. Each time a pinball smacked against the pieces, the cage lit up with sparks and Harry whimpered.

In the distance, the figure of Scratch waved at us.

'Our plan!' gasped Sarah. 'Scratchman knows what we're doing.'

'Of course he does,' I agreed. 'If we finish it, we could kill Harry.'

Another pinball entered our trap. Another shower of sparks and a cry from Harry.

'But now we've set it in motion, how do we stop it?' asked Sarah.

Three more strikes. The cage lit up. Harry gave an agonised howl.

'I'm not sure we can.'

'But Doctor, he's going to go up like the guy on a bonfire!'

The circle closed.

Harry Sullivan was rattling around his cage. It was live with electricity, and there was no getting away from it.

'Please,' he shouted, 'stop ...'

The vast chess pieces moved together, stone edifices slamming against each other. Trapped within the cordon, the remaining spheres smashed fruitlessly against the chess pieces. Overhead the score soared with each impact.

Sarah tried to drown out Harry's cries. 'Doctor, you've got to find a way to stop it. You must!' she begged.

'Hold on, Harry, just a little longer,' I muttered, gently stroking the side of the Rook as the air filled with sparks.

Overhead, the cage crackled and sizzled as the pinballs smacked and pinged off barrier. One rolled back, dropping down the hole in the floor, then another. My plan was working – we'd built a drain.

Soon the score stopped increasing, and the barricade thudded with fewer impacts. The last of the ball bearings trickled off down the chute, and the board was empty of them.

Silence fell across the battlefield. The air was filled with ozone and the smell of sulphur.

Sarah realised she was crouching. She straightened up, standing and surveying the empty arena. It looked like a disco after hours – lights still glowing away, but all the dancers had long since gone home.

I threw my hat into the air and boomed, 'Scratchman! I may not be able to win, but I've stopped you from scoring.'

In the distance, Scratch applauded slowly and loudly. 'Well done, Doctor. Very well done.'

I accepted the compliment. 'I don't care for the theatrics. Release Harry.'

With a clunk, the vast grabbed swung towards us, lowering the crate with a dazed Harry scrabbling around inside like a haunted guinea pig.

'He's all yours!' called Scratch.

The cage came lower and lower and then, suddenly, the floor of it sprang open and Harry tumbled through, vanishing down one of the chutes in the floor.

'Harry!' screamed Sarah.

'Oops,' said Scratch.

FEAR AND FRIENDS

Harry's terrible demise got to my Time Lord audience, I'll tell you that. They were on the edges of their seats, roaring with anger and dismay. I imagined Harry's face if I'd told him that he'd won over the most powerful race in the universe.

'I say,' he'd have said. 'That's nice.'

But they really were most put out.

'You let your companion die?' The Zero Nun was back on her feet.

Lord Bardakajak glared at me. 'How could you, sir? How could you?'

I put up my hands in protest. 'My friends.' I risked it, I did. 'My friends, earlier this evening you were all for killing me simply for interfering. Then you were impelling me to sacrifice the entire planet Earth in order to stop Scratchman. Now I've let just one Harry Sullivan go to his doom and you're up in arms.'

'Well yes!' Lord Bardakajak waved this away. If he was learning a lesson about how the universe really functioned, he wasn't going to let it get in the way of his fury. 'But Harry Sullivan. Next thing you'll be saying ...' He leaned forward, concern etched into his skin, mottled like old geraniums. 'Sarah Jane Smith – she will be all right, won't she?'

I hid my smile. What am I saying? Of course I couldn't hide my smile.

'Ah, Sarah,' I said. 'Doesn't she tell you everything you need to know about friendship? Time Lords don't really do friends, do we? And yet, when you go out into the universe, you acquire friends, like a dog picks up fleas. It could happen to any of you.'

They were horrified at this heresy.

'Having friends is nothing to be afraid of,' I reassured them. 'They're there for the small things in life – laughing at your jokes, drinking your tea, rescuing you from dungeons. Friends remember you how you'd like to be remembered, and forget the rest. Friends turn up at the last moment, friends tell you to keep running.'

I was hitting my stride now, perhaps a little too vigorously.

'The thing about friends that I've never got the hang of is saying goodbye to them, and humans live such mayfly lives. I fear for them every moment they're with me, and fear the loss of them like an ache. Some friends make us kinder, some friends make us sharper. But – and this is the point –' I paused again, just to see if they were sharpening up – 'with friends around, there's always someone to tell you when you're wrong … and sometimes they're right! That's what I'd like you Time Lords to think about. Who's around to tell you when you're wrong? Who are you afraid for? Who are your friends?'

There was a shuffling silence.

'Shall I continue?' I suggested.

CHAPTER TWENTY-FIVE

Harry Sullivan failed to die. He'd got so good at this he was wondering about popping 'surprisingly immortal' on his *Curriculum Vitae*. Lady Luck was, as ever, looking over his shoulder. Sometimes she applauded, sometimes she peeped through her fingers.

Startled, Harry tumbled out of the cage and was through the floor before he'd even had a chance to scream properly. He missed the sharper protuberances of the shaft (any of which would have dashed his brains out) and landed abruptly on a ledge. Winded, he looked around, blinking.

Up? The distant shimmer of neon, the sound of Scratch's laughter.

Down? He wished he hadn't glanced. Distant lava bubbled away.

'Right,' he said to himself. 'Right. I'm over a volcanic lake. Of course I am.' He sighed. 'I've had better days.'

He essayed climbing back up. After all – he hadn't fallen that far, had he? He managed to find a few promising footholds and began a steady crawl back up the shaft.

'Doctor, Sarah,' he muttered, 'Don't worry, I'm coming.'

He grabbed hold of a nub of rock which turned out to be horribly sharp; he lost his hold and slid back down. He twisted, desperate to avoid toppling into the inferno below, and landed awkwardly on the ledge. For a few moments Harry pitched giddily over the side. An insane amount of scrabbling and swearing, and he regained the ledge, choking on the sulphurous air.

Harry breathed out, breathed in, breathed out again.

The good news was that he wasn't dead yet. The bad thing was that he couldn't climb back up. He regarded his hands. They were beginning to blister. They were badly cut. Everything hurt.

He contemplated curling up in a ball and then harrumphed. Sullivans were made of sterner stuff.

Besides, he'd learned something really quite surprising about the ledge he was lying on.

Scratchman cupped his hands in front of his face and called across the battlefield to me. 'How's it going, Doctor?'

'Can't complain.' I waved back from my turret. 'Sarah and I have beaten you, you know.'

'What about Harry?' squeaked Sarah.

I waved this away like a lost postal order. 'Yes, well, we lost the odd piece, but still.'

'Harry!' repeated Sarah.

I gave her a look that silenced her.

'You think you've won?' Scratch hemmed, and gestured up to the neon signs above him. Above the scoreboard with its hundreds of digits, a sign plucked from his thoughts. It read I DON'T MEAN TO GLOAT.

'Ah, that's just the final score, a small inconvenience. That's all people like you ever look at. But –' and I began to prowl the castle wall – 'I realised something …'

Sarah kicked my ankle.

'We realised something. This fight of yours was rigged. There was no way we could win – hurling boulders at us, what kind of competition is that? I've attended prize marrow competitions that were less rigged. But – and this is the important bit – we stopped the game. Which is all we had to do.' I clambered over the Rook's ramparts and slid down its side. 'This is over. Now! Would you care to discuss terms?'

'Terms?'

'Yes, the terms of your surrender,' I grinned. 'Surrender. That's what the losing side does.'

'But I have not lost.'

I turned back to help Sarah down. 'Come on, I'm bored of shouting, let's go over and have a word with the old Devil. I can't stand a bad loser.'

Harry leaned out into the pit again to confirm his suspicions.

He was right. The ledge had formed on top of a hatch. A proper, solid metal hatch built into the side of the shaft below. This was not without its difficulties. For instance, where did the door lead? Where was the handle? Was it locked? If so, could he find a key or pick the lock? That was the tricky thing about life with the Doctor, poor Harry reflected. It was always that tiny bit harder than it needed to be.

He swung himself out over the chasm. He'd hooked his feet under a ridge in the rock, and was sort of hoping that wishes and a stout pair of socks would keep him there. He dangled, trying to get a clear idea of the hatch.

Well – it was definitely a hatch. There did not seem to be a handle, or a button, or a helpful little label. Clearly it had not been designed as a last-resort escape for plucky naval medics with a promising life and lots of great-grandchildren ahead of them.

Harry realised there was a seam running between the hatch and the steel surround. He tried prising it with his fingertips, but they really had been through a lot, and fairly soon he was forced to give up and just dangle for a bit, a grown man upside down over a pit of fire, sucking his fingers and mourning the loss of a thumbnail.

It was very warm here. And he was wearing a duffel coat. His good old friend on several unpromisingly misty planets, his cushioning on a few rough landings, his saviour in an electrified cage, it had been through a lot, but it wasn't the best thing to be wearing in a chimney. He toyed with trying to take the poor thing off, but that wasn't going to work. He then remembered that it had a goodly number of pockets.

Harry patted down his pockets (or, since he was upside down, patted up his pockets), and discovered a penknife. He figured if I had a sonic screwdriver, this was the next best thing.

He selected a blade (again, not that easy upside down with ruined thumbs, so points for effort, please) and wedged it behind the hatch. He felt the hatch give slightly. Not much – after all, a penknife isn't much of a lever to use against a metal hatch, but he only needed to prise it open sightly. He tried harder. The blade snapped.

Harry Sullivan thought about luck. He thought about life. He thought about career progression and whether the Naval Board would consider giving him one of those nice postings on an island with a beach full of hammocks and coconuts.

He selected another blade on his penknife. It was a bit smaller, and actually he wouldn't miss it as much. It was theoretically a small saw, but he'd never tried sawing through anything with it. He guessed it might just about manage the inside of a roll of toilet paper.

Harry went to work on the door. The teeth of the saw found purchase against something inside the hatch. There was actual and definite and marvellous progress. So much progress that he even saw the door move, just a little. He was clearly digging into some kind of mechanism. Harry jabbed a bit harder.

All of a miserable sudden, he realised he had leant out too far. Panicked, he let go of the penknife, flailed a little and got his balance back. Breathing deeply, Harry reached out for the penknife, still wedged in the hatch, and was about to grab hold of it again when a falling bishop struck him a glancing blow.

Meanwhile, Sarah and I made our way across the pitch. A glowing neon stairway appeared ('It's a bit disco, isn't it?' muttered Sarah in my ear), and we climbed it up onto Scratch's platform. Harry's empty cage still hung there, swinging ghoulishly.

Above it dangled a sign: I'VE WON I'VE WON I'VE WON.

Scratch gallantly offered Sarah his hand to help her up the last few steps, but she shrugged it aside. The three of us stood side by side looking out at the desolation.

'I've always loved this sight,' said Scratchman.

'I've always hated battlefields,' I replied.

'And yet, you can't look away.'

Scratch pulled a cigar from his pocket. A man made of flame smoking was, I thought, the most absurd thing I'd ever seen. Worse was the smell – it was one of those cheap cigars that made you think of wet dogs and dirty pub ashtrays. Scratch puffed a series of smoke shapes which drifted lazily out into the plains before them.

'As you can see, all your pieces are gone,' I told him, 'And most of mine are still standing. You've taken an island, my ship and poor Harry and still I've got more than you.'

'And therefore you've won?'

'If you like.'

'I do not like. Let's even the score.' Scratch pointed with his cigar, every inch the mogul. He snapped his burning fingers and the remaining chess pieces rolled away down the hole into the chasm. 'There. The board is swept clean.'

The giant chess piece tumbled down the shaft past Harry. As it fell, the bishop shifted and changed, becoming a strange, forlorn chittering creature. It flailed briefly and then burst into flame.

Harry, stunned, heaved himself back onto the ledge, narrowly avoiding being minced as several more chess pieces tumbled past him. He flattened himself back against the wall, watching them change into those pathetic, scrabbling, howling insects as they went. Harry wondered if the changes upstairs boded well for Sarah and me, and whether or not he should be attempting some last-minute rescue of some sort. From the ledge. That he was trapped on.

Realising that defeatism would not do, Harry made sure the coast was clear, and leant back out over the gap, reaching down to grab the penknife still jimmied into the hatch. Trying to grasp it, he knocked it loose and sent it into the void.

'Goodbye, old friend,' said Harry. He dangled there, definitely and absolutely not feeling the crushing misery of defeat. 'Something will turn up,' he said at last, and repeated that out loud a few times.

The hatch opened from the inside, swinging wide with an industrial hiss and knocking Harry out of the way.

Harry fought to keep his hold on the ledge, but it was fruitless. He found himself dragged off it and, draped over the door like a shirt over a radiator, he sailed out over the chasm.

Harry could hear something coming out of the hatchway. It was scuttling. Scuttling could not be good. Not fancying being devoured from the legs up, Harry twisted his head round to see what was heading for him.

It was another of those insect creatures. As it hurtled towards him it kept repeating to itself, 'For Scratchman, for Scratchman, for Scratchman!' with little enthusiasm.

Harry ducked as the creature brushed past him and launched itself into the air, plunging down towards the fires beneath with a pitiful shriek.

'Poor blighter,' Harry muttered.

A second creature scuttled past and hurled itself to its doom. And then a third. By the time Harry had hoisted his way up to sit on the hatch, a fourth insect was approaching, still muttering under its breath.

'Excuse me!' Harry called.

The insect stopped, and so did the chanting of its miserable mantra.

'Why are you doing this?' asked Harry.

'Because Scratchman orders us to,' the insect said sadly. 'We are of no further use to him, and this, our last service, is the greatest we can perform.'

'But—'

'Once it is over, we are finally released.'

'You are?'

The insect paused, contemplating the dreadful fall to a terrible death. 'When I first entered Scratchman's service, long, long ago, I was promised so much. The more I dreamed, the more he gave me. But when I ran out of dreams and nightmares, I pleased him less. Finally I bored him, and he changed me into this. For many centuries I have toiled for him, in the fields and then in the castle. But now I no longer even dream of freedom. When that last dream is gone, that is when I must end.' The insect consulted its spindly legs sadly. 'Our master's energy is running low.' It regarded Harry sourly. 'You're one of the new arrivals, aren't you? You've caused much damage. You have cost the lives of many of us.'

'I'm dreadfully sorry about that,' said Harry sincerely.

'Don't feel too bad,' the creature said, but clearly didn't mean it. 'We are just the memories of life, twisted into something to amuse our master. You're thinking of fighting back, of escaping – but really, you'll just cost more lives and you'll end up like one of us – sooner or later. Sooner, in your case.'

'Thank you,' said Harry.

'And then nothing awaits you but millennia of service as one of us, and finally, as fuel for him.'

'Fuel?'

'We must keep his dreams aloft.' The creature nodded miserably. 'If I were you, I'd save myself the torment and jump now.'

'Will it be quick?' asked Harry.

'No,' the creature said. 'But it will at least be over.'

And it launched itself into the air, dived down into the sulphurous air, gave a single cry, and burst into flame.

Harry had some thinking to do. The beetle had told him a lot of intriguing things, but he was also aware that the hatch was slowly swinging closed again. Realising he was about to be crushed, Harry swung up his legs with the last of his energy, and went tumbling into the pipe.

'Good grief.'

Harry had emerged in a vast chamber that felt like a boiler room. Lines of the weird beetle-thing were being herded by scarecrows and large, angry-looking crabs into the tubes. Well, except for the tube Harry had come from.

A large crab hovered over him clicking menacingly. 'What are you?' it cried. It had two miserable-looking human heads waving on its tendrils. 'No one's ever come back from the chute before. No one would dare!'

Harry sensed growing attention from the other guards and beetles.

The creature's claws snapped forward to push Harry back into the shaft.

Harry could really have done with a rest. Instead he scrambled out of the chute, hands out in front of him. 'Excuse me, sir!' he said, politely.

The guard crab glared at Harry with its several eyes. 'Why do you look like that?'

'Well, sir …' Harry's eyes took another turn around the room while his brain tried to reach a reasonable speed. 'The thing is …'

The crab had a suspicious turn of mandible. 'Yes?'

'Scratchman has given me my old body back!' exclaimed Harry brightly.

The room full of creatures fell still. He had their complete attention.

'He did this …' Harry dried momentarily, before inspiration struck. 'As a sign!'

The room was so quiet you could hear a claw click.

'You see –' Harry hit his stride, and hit it at a saunter – 'he wants the sacrifices to stop. Right now.'

'I'm sorry?' said the crab, its two human heads banging in consternation. The TARDIS's translation inside Harry's head seemed a good deal more polite than the anguished, chittering it made.

'You heard,' Harry rallied. 'Scratchman has ordered me to tell you that he wants no more sacrifices. You are all free.'

'But how will we power the engines of his great castle in the sky?' the guard asked.

'Do you question Scratchman?' Harry thundered, getting into the swing of things. 'No. He tells you that you are free. Leave here – go, be free!'

This was greeted with a short, anguished hush, and then a massive tide of beetles swept Harry up as they scattered through the citadel.

Upstairs, I stared at the empty battlefield.

'All gone,' I sighed. 'I can't stand pettiness.' The outrageous fib cheered Sarah up no end. 'And now I know what you're up to, Scratch. You're definitely the master of this domain. But boring people love to run incredible properties into the ground. Which brings us to you.'

'Boring?' Scratchman huffed. 'I am a little offended.'

'Yes, you're the Devil and you're *boring*.' I thundered. 'This is your universe – but you've reduced it to nothing more than a dying rock. How large was this space before, hmm? How many galaxies have you burned through, until all that's left are ashes and clinker? You say you've saved this place? You've burnt it all.'

Scratch's face flushed a sullen amber. 'That is harsh.'

'And now the cupboards are bare, you're planning to sneak into the universe next door, start stealing from their fridge. How long before that's all gone? How many other universes have you munched through before this one, eh?'

Scratch examined his fingernails, dropping his cigar and grinding it into the gantry.

'I thought so!' I do like being right.

'But as you've pointed out, I rule this universe,' retorted Scratch. 'It's mine to do with what I choose.'

'Eating a universe is not the same as ruling it.'

Scratch's head glowed sullenly. 'That is not what I do. I'm vital to the running of this place. The conservation of energy is a delicate art that would be impossible without me.'

'Bosh!' I thundered. 'You think you're important? Turn yourself off, no one would miss you. Even your boardroom full of 40-watt copies wouldn't even flicker. You've never considered what it's like to actually live here in your service. That's the problem with your sort, you're all about fights between kings. People with castles in the air always forget about the pawns.'

'The pawns?' enquired Scratch.

I nodded and winked at Sarah. 'Or a forgotten knight in shining armour.'

There was a loud explosion and the chamber lurched.

'Harry!' exclaimed Sarah.

There was another explosion and a sickening sensation as the castle plummeted.

'Definitely Harry!' I laughed. 'Grab hold of something, Sarah, we're falling out of the sky!'

Chapter Twenty-Six

Harry found himself tipped into a ballroom by a surging tide of beetles. Sitting on the marble floor, he took in his surroundings and rewarded himself with a very solid blink before noticing the loud consternation as the partygoers swatted and screamed at the creatures swarming through them and out of the room.

'Goodness me, I am sorry,' he apologised, in case anyone was listening. Harry straightened himself and had a good look around the room. All the partygoers were staring at him, and the Sullivans did not enjoy being the centre of attention.

'Hello,' he said, nervously. 'I am awfully sorry about those beetles. They're a nice sort, really. My name's Harry Sullivan.'

The masked revellers all leaned forwards, just slightly, like they were on tiptoe, and then as one, they sucked at the air.

Something beyond the sheer oddness of the movement struck him. Then he realised. The plaster lips on their carved masks were puckering as they tasted the air.

'I say,' Harry began. 'That's a little ... isn't it?'

Without him noticing them changing, some of the blank masks had faces now. He was surrounded by half a dozen Sarah Jane Smiths.

'Sarah? What's going on?' he asked, thoroughly confused.

'Oh, Harry,' one of the Sarahs sighed. 'You are an idiot.'

The other Sarahs laughed.

'Listen,' Harry said. 'There's something you should know'

'What is it?' asked another Sarah, her hands on her hips. 'Knowing you, you'll have messed up somehow.'

'That's not fair! This is all some kind of illusion,' protested Harry. 'I'm not messing up! Not always.'

'Of course you're not.' A Sarah arched an eyebrow.

At which point, the room lurched alarmingly, and a lot of alarms went off.

'Although,' admitted Harry, 'I am rather afraid I'm crashing the castle.'

I was hanging on to a neon sign. It read FRIGHTFULLY SORRY.

'That's how I knew Harry was still with us,' I was saying conversationally. As the room fell apart around us, I tried to keep my grip. 'Messages like that were still appearing.'

'And if Harry's alive,' Sarah was dangling from a railing, 'well, there's bound to be an explosion, sooner or later, isn't there?'

'Quite,' I said, reaching out to hold on to her.

'Look, could you pass me your scarf?' she asked. 'It might work as a rope and I can get us onto that walkway.'

I tossed a length of scarf across the chasm, and Sarah, with a frantic wriggle, managed to loop it round the railing. With a terrified squeak, she managed to climb up then threw the scarf back to me. Swinging her legs, she hoisted herself up onto the platform.

'What's happening?' she shouted. 'Is Harry doing this?'

'Of course.' I pulled myself up behind her. 'A closed system is one that becomes solipsistically reliant on its rules. Scratchman sustains himself by feeding off the souls of others. I rather imagine that something has interrupted his supply chain.'

'Harry?'

'Always Harry. This entire illusion was conjured from Harry's imagination, remember? Scratchman's got none of his own. And since the illusion didn't vanish when Harry dropped from sight, *Pinball erat demonstrandum* – and a little hand up onto the platform? Thank you.'

Sarah and I edged along the platform. All around us was ominous creaking darkness, lit only by apologetic neon.

'Where's Scratchman?' asked Sarah.

'Probably gone to try and sort out the chaos.' I smiled. 'Poor Devil. Look, there's a doorway over there.'

The ballroom lurched again, and Harry found himself hurled against the picture window. Several of the revellers thudded alongside him, and he felt the glass crack.

He picked himself up onto his knees, and realised that several of the guests now wore my face.

'You really are an imbecile, Harry Sullivan,' one of the fake Doctors snarled.

'I get it,' Harry said, shuffling on his knees over the glass, trying not to notice the dizzying landscape swirling below. 'This is the whole world having a go at me, isn't it? You've all been conjured up by Scratchman, haven't you?'

'I shouldn't have to tell you that, Harry,' scowled another me.

Another Doctor sprang to its feet, ignoring the web of cracks spidering beneath his feet. 'It's obvious to even pond algae that that's what's happening, Harry Sullivan.'

'Quite, sorry, Doctor,' mumbled Harry automatically and took another ginger shuffle forward. 'So you've all been created to make me feel insecure?'

'Absolutely!' one of the fake Doctors was jumping up and down on the glass. 'Tensile strength, friability, excellently tempered!' it cried as the glass cracked. 'Am I talking about you, me, or the glass, eh?'

'Very good, Doctor,' muttered Harry, and took another tiny creep.

'Why, with six of us Doctors, we should have your psyche open as easily as a can of corned beef.'

'Totally,' Harry vowed solemnly, and shuffled a little bit more. 'Of course, if only I was more intelligent.'

'Oh, Harry, if only you were,' one agreed. As it said this, the castle took another plunging lurch, adding to the chaos in the room.

'Why,' said Harry carefully, 'if I was as clever as you, I'd be able to work out a way to stop this castle from crashing.'

'That's true,' a fake Doctor nodded, springing to its feet, dancing across the splintering glass, and tearing apart a control panel. 'You don't have a clue, do you? You've not even tried to access the mainframe.'

'He hasn't even tapped into the neutron flow,' another fake sneered cruelly, pulling a sonic screwdriver from the ball gown it was still wearing. 'By working out a vibration field, you can then feed that back into the system and counteract the engine failure.'

'Crikey, Doctors, you are clever,' exclaimed Harry brightly. He watched as a dozen ersatz Doctors all raced across the wrecked picture window, each engaged in some scheme or other.

'Well, of course we're cleverer than you,' the group of impostors chorused. 'Mind you, there are several of us and only one of you.'

'I don't stand a chance,' Harry said, edging to safety as the fakes dashed back and forth across the splintering window.

'It's a wonder you breathe,' a Doctor snapped, 'You've as much cunning as tapioca!'

'I can't argue with that.' Harry grasped at the wall and took his first solid breath. 'I'm just not sure you should be so cavalier about that glass.'

'Nonsense,' a Doctor cried, jumping up and down on it. 'This stuff is so solid you could serve it with custard. That's your problem, Sullivan. Too cautious. See?' The pitching of the room stabilised under the whirr of half a dozen sonic screwdrivers.

'There we are!' one of the fake Doctors announced, booming his delight around the room. 'We're bringing this under control splendidly.'

'Well done, Doctor!' Harry was pulling himself onto a ledge.

'It's easy enough when you're a genius,' a Doctor laughed. 'I do believe we're not going to crash after all!'

'No?' Harry looked down at the ground whizzing towards them.

'No!' a Doctor leaned over him. 'Just stabilising the artificial gravity!' He took a jump. 'Splendid!' He landed, his full weight planting on the glass. It made a terrible cracking noise The Doctor gave Harry an anguished look. 'Sullivan, I do believe you're not so stupid after all.'

The glass shattered.

'Oh dear,' said a dozen ersatz versions of me, falling through the window. One can't feel sorry for them.

Harry, knocked back by the howling rush of air, barely had time to cry out as the castle nosedived.

In another part of the castle, Sarah was clinging to the battlements. It gave her the kind of view normally only afforded to the wheels of a plane as they made an emergency landing.

'Doctor! Do something!' she called.

'Don't worry!' I replied. 'It's all under control!' I was hanging on to a flagpole for dear life. 'If I can just access the engines, I should be able to even us out at any moment. As this realm is powered by thought, it should just be a matter of thinking good thoughts very hard.'

'So, if I think we're not going to crash, we won't crash?' Sarah sounded dubious.

'Shade more conviction, Sarah,' I encouraged. 'But you're quite right. There's absolutely no chance that we'll—'

We crashed.

CHAPTER TWENTY-SEVEN

I've fallen out of many things, but a flying castle was a first. For a moment I had the most glorious hallucination – as though there were a dozen copies of me, all falling past, all exploding like fireworks.

Falling's fine, but landing's always been a problem. Sooner or later, gravity's going to catch up with me.

This time I landed on a slope, and rolled down the scree, tumbling helplessly. The air was knocked out of me, and it took a few heartbeats before I realised where I was and what was happening. Opening my eyes, I was startled to see a lake of fire rolling up towards me.

'I'm going to die doing roly-polies!' was my magnificent thought. I scrabbled, frantically trying to stop, but nothing could slow down my Dervish whirl into the hissing pool of lava. I flew over the edge and then cried out, but my scream was choked off. Choked off by my scarf, which suddenly pulled taut and yanked me to a stop.

I found myself dangling over a lake of fire. I could feel the soles of my shoes melting even as I was strangled by my own scarf.

'Help,' I croaked, feeling the scarf tighten mercilessly. I tried to reach up, desperate to gain a handhold.

'Stop struggling!' shouted a voice.

'Sarah?' I gasped. 'Are you ... by any chance ... holding on ... to my scarf?'

'Why are you so heavy?' she shouted back. 'I seem to be spending the entire day holding on to you.'

Sarah was dragged into view over the edge of the cliff, holding on desperately to the end of my scarf.

'Sarah Jane, I quite see your problem,' I informed her in an agonised whisper. I flailed like a Christmas tree ornament under attack from a cat.

She slipped a few inches further forward, small black stones skittering over the edge, hitting me and then sliding down to explode on contact with the lake.

'Pull me up and I'll give you a hand!' I promised hoarsely. The tip of my shoe struck the lake, and burst into flame. I yelped, jerked and sank a little further.

'You're not helping!' Sarah yelled. And then she yelled again in surprise and terror.

'Sarah!' I cried.

Sarah continued to yell, words like 'No!', 'Get off!' and 'Stop that!', and yet, strangely, I found myself yanked up over the ledge.

'Sarah! I'm coming!' I hissed, trying to work out if I had any larynx left.

The sight that met me was peculiar. Sarah was standing to one side, looking thoroughly angry and perplexed, raining ineffectual blows on a Cyberman, who was holding the other end of my scarf.

I stared.

'Well—' I croaked, and then my voice gave out completely.

At which point, Harry Sullivan appeared from behind the Cyberman. 'I can explain,' he said.

FEAR OF DEATH

My audience was getting restless yet again.

'Preposterous!' thundered Lord Bardakajak, echoed by some young wags from Temporal Incursions. 'This is all preposterous!' he repeated, pleased to be getting a bit of attention.

'How so?' I asked.

The Zero Nun came forward once more, sanctimony dripping from her wimple. 'Surely you can see my colleagues' point?' she simpered. 'When we started, your story was all scarecrows and so on, and that was harmless enough if you like that sort of thing.' She favoured the room with a beneficent mien that showed that naturally, she did not include any of them in that group. They beamed back. 'But now here we are, plunged into this fantasy universe of yours, woven from the nightmares of you and your companions, with all those monsters, and explosions, and endless jeopardy ... Come now, Doctor, surely you can agree it's a bit much to take in?'

'Can I?' I asked politely.

'I'll be blunt.' She proceeded not to be. 'Time Lords have a unique relationship with death. We progress from one series of bodies to the next and ultimately pass into the Matrix, where our souls can observe the infinity of our race. Put simply, forgive me, we do not die. The only Time Lord here with anything to fear from death is you.'

She pointed up to the Sword of Never.

'So,' she continued, 'why this need to pepper your fable with constant scrapes and brushes with death?'

'Well,' I said, resisting the urge to list the beings I knew who'd laugh at the Time Lords' notion of immortality like a supercomputer giggling at a slide rule. 'You learn a lot about people from how they deal with jeopardy. Are they afraid and yet still run towards the fire? Humans have only one life, and it's so short – but they'll throw themselves in the path of danger if they think the outcome is worth it. Isn't that fascinating? Especially when you compare it with us – why, the sands of our time would make beaches, and yet we hoard our lives like we're down to the last grains. Doesn't that interest you? Who do you really think is afraid of death? The humans, or us?'

They went silent. The kind of angry silence that told me I'd scored a palpable hit.

'Speaking personally,' I discoursed, 'Sarah once asked me why I was afraid of dying as I'd just wake up as someone else. "It's the someone else bit that gets me," I told her. "Being the Doctor suits me. And, it's selfish of me, I know, but I just can't stand the idea of someone else getting to do what I do. I'm a comfy pair of shoes – I fit the Doctor just right. The Doctor's had other shoes before, and will have many more – some brogues, some stilettoes, but like all shoes, they take a bit of wearing in, whereas, look at me. I'm sturdy and there's quite a bit of mileage left in me. See? Being the Doctor comes down to having a good sole." I don't think she appreciated the pun – so few people do. But that's my point. My fear of death is simply because I'd miss this life.'

'Perhaps you are wise to be afraid,' the Nun gave me a silken smile, and the light above me glowed with the keenness of a rapier.

Regardless, I pressed home my final point, and I knew they'd hate it.

'Despite all your protestations to the contrary, despite it being irrational, the Time Lords of Gallifrey are afraid of death. Death is practically impossible for us, and yet that makes us fear it all the more. Isn't that curious?'

CHAPTER TWENTY-EIGHT

I stood recovering on the cliff edge with the Cyberleader. 'This is unexpected,' I began.

The Cyberman did not reply. Hardly surprising. They're not chatty at the best of times.

'Thank you for saving Harry. And for bringing him to me,' I tried again. 'And for saving my life.'

The Cyberleader stared ahead, the empty skull glowing inside its metal head.

I looked over at Sarah and Harry, bickering fondly at a distance, and I had a thought.

'You didn't enjoy saving my life, did you?'

The Cyberleader shook its head, just slightly.

I risked a smile. 'That's it, isn't it? This place is Hell, and what is Hell for a Cyberman other than being nice?' I threw back my head and laughed. 'Ha! When you attacked my taxi earlier, you were trying to rescue me from the driver!'

The Cyberleader made a sound which might have been a hiss of despair.

'Scratchman tortures his victims by finding what they fear the most. Spiders! Loneliness! And, for you, it's little acts of kindness. How wonderfully absurd!'

Another silence.

'Don't let it get you down,' I patted the Cyberman's steel shoulder.

'We were misled.' The Cyberleader turned its head to me, the empty skull miserable. 'We were offered power. We were offered bodies. We were offered an endless army.'

'Yes. I bet you were. So you made a bargain with Scratchman and gave him a first foothold in our universe. Wasn't it logical to check the small print?'

The Cyberleader's head snapped away. 'Emotions,' it announced with something like disgust. 'We began to ... feel ... again ...'

I felt pity for the creature. Several hundred years as a living corpse, walking around in a tin coffin. What had it done in that time? What horrors had it committed? Circuits were stitched into the husks that stopped emotion, that blocked memory. Scratch just had to pick away at them. Turn a few back on.

'Memories returned. And with them ... feelings.'

Who'd have thought the Cyberman's weakness was guilt?

The Cyberleader nodded. 'We were brought here, we were promised a cure. Instead the condition became worse.'

'Of course it did,' I thought.

The crimson sky reflected angrily on its faceplate. 'I am the last of my unit. They have all succumbed. I am the remainder. It is probable that I am the last of my species.'

I doubted it, but couldn't bring myself to offer the creature consolation.

'How does it make you feel?' I asked gently.

The Cyberman hissed, jerking its head around to face me, the skull rattling against the helmet. The blank dark holes of its eye sockets stared blankly at me. 'I regret their loss. I dislike being alone. I feel ... sad.'

I jumped in surprise. 'Poor tin toes!' I said.

The Cyberleader, a fearsome creature with the power to crush rock in its fists, emitted a mournful wet clicking from inside its throat. 'What is there for me to do now?' it asked. 'My continued function is pain. My processors are overwhelmed with negative feedback about previous actions.'

'Your processors?' I stepped back, saddened and appalled. For a moment, just a moment, I'd felt for it. 'It's called a brain. It's still in there. Dried and shrivelled and overrun with wiring, but it's still a brain. It's doing what it was built for – learning and thinking and growing and feeling. Scratch has offered you a strength – feeling bad about our mistakes is how we learn from them. You've a chance, to learn from this. You can stomp around this hell, doing good deeds and feeling miserable about them, or you could come with us, nail down Scratchman's coffin, and then find the rest of the Cybermen and help them grow. What do you think of that, eh?'

The blank eye sockets bored into mine. Then the Cyberleader turned and walked away.

'Ah well, I tried.' I slid across the slope and re-joined Sarah and Harry. They watched the silver shape slink away. 'That was possibly the last chance the Cybermen had of recovering their souls.'

Sarah shuddered. 'That thing fills me with horror.'

'It feels the same about itself,' I remarked. 'That's its problem.'

'He was very nice to me,' Harry put in, seeing the best in everyone. 'Dragged me from the wreckage, found you and Sarah, saved your life.'

'Exactly,' I said. 'Forced to do these things by Scratch. A torture. He finds the weakness in all of us.'

'For Harry that's pinball.'

'Well, actually,' sighed Harry. 'Sometimes it's—'

'No! Harry! Don't!' Sarah clamped a hand over his mouth and quickly asked a question. 'What do we do now, Doctor?'

I appreciated how fast she'd moved. 'We'll just have to finish Scratchman by ourselves, seal this dimension, find the TARDIS, make our way home.'

I set off towards the ruins of the castle.

'Oh,' said Sarah, and then called out. 'Doctor, there's something you should know.'

'About the TARDIS? Yes. You've left it in a bit of a mess, I know,' I boomed, waving back at her. My every gesture was one of confidence and calm. But inside, let me tell you, it was quite another matter.

As we picked our way along the side of the valley, the castle cracked and split before us. Something dark leaked out of it. It looked like the carcase of a vast felled leviathan.

'What's happening to it?' asked Sarah, as the beast started to dissolve.

'It looks revolting,' said Harry.

'It must be down to Scratchman,' I suggested. 'He's feeding off the remains of the castle.'

'Feeding off the castle?' asked Harry.

'This whole realm is made of the dreams of ghosts,' I sighed. How many souls went into a mountain, how many had been used to paint the sky?

A distant screaming filled the air. The air darkened, choking with soot. The darkness puddling at the base of the valley gathered itself up into a giant shadow, a shadow in which tiny shapes writhed and wriggled helplessly before vanishing. Claws reached out from the shadows, claws which snatched and plucked creatures from their cowering shelter among the rocks, sucking them all into itself.

'Hell is having a closing down sale,' said Harry.

'Scratchman is rallying.' I was grim. 'He's coming for us. One last desperate push. The final battle.'

The darkness swept over us.

At first we were all running through an endless night, sometimes stumbling, sometimes falling, but I somehow kept us going. I made Sarah and Harry hold onto the ends of my scarf, I ordered them to keep upright, I even made them clamp the wool over their mouths, to keep the choking, sooty air out.

Gradually our eyes adjusted to the maelstrom. There was no sun, and the lakes of lava had cooled, but there was still light, a sluggish reluctant thing – it seeped and crept over the landscape. As the world was wrapped in shadow, objects no longer had shadows of their own. Dark grey stone stood out starkly against a black sky.

Sarah's skin had the marble sheen of a statue, but her hand still felt warm in mine. I glanced at my own arm, and was distressed to see it looked as pitted and weathered as old stone.

Harry's normally rugged features were haggard, his eyes blazing darkly.

There were scraps of colour in the wasteland. Sarah's cagoule grubbed up a sullen yellow, patches of red and green on my scarf rubbed at the eyes. But beyond them was stark, dead emptiness – the world held up like a terminal X-ray.

The silence was haunting. The world was so dead the crunch of our footsteps thundered through it. We reached a plateau.

There was a whispering on the wind, a murmur of voices singing 'Auld Lang Syne'.

Should auld acquaintance be forgot ...

'I thought everything here was dead,' said Harry.

'Everything is,' I replied.

'Is that so?' said a voice, soft and forlorn.

Shapes materialised out of the darkness before us. Heartbreaking ones.

'Oh,' said Sarah.

Miss Sophonisba Mowat took a few steps forward, and then held out her hand, marvelling at it. 'That's me,' she said. 'It's my hand.'

She looked up at me and then back at the villagers on either side of her. 'I thought …' she began.

'You are,' I said sadly. 'You died, Sophonisba. I'm terribly sorry.'

'Then how …?' She examined her hand again. 'This isn't quite right, is it? It seems fragile.' She reached out and tugged at one of her fingers. It snapped, a brittle crack. She gave a little cry, as though stifling pain and then stopped. 'That didn't hurt,' she exclaimed.

'No,' I said, and wanted to be anywhere else. The expression on her face could have ended a world.

'I'm still twigs and rags, aren't I?' Sophonisba tugged at her hair. Strands of straw and cobweb fell out of it. 'I'm still dead.'

'You all are,' I apologised. The villagers looked at each other in silent consternation.

'Then why am I here?'

'To mock me, I'm afraid.' I plunged my hands deep into my pockets, unable to think of anything else to do with them. 'Scratchman wants to remind me of the people I've failed to save. He thinks he is confronting me with my deepest fear. It's not. It's just my shame.'

Sophonisba reached out to the scarecrow of the man next to her, a tiny, bewildered old man. He had started to cry, sawdust dribbling down his mahogany cheeks.

'We're all lost, aren't we?' she said, hugging the man.

'Yes,' I agreed. 'Just spirits. I have no problems looking you in the eye. I try not to forget any of you, not ever. But I won't let your cost be added to my account by Scratch or anyone else. You didn't die because of me. And I'll do all I can to keep the toll from rising.'

'You'll forgive me,' said Sophonisba with a touch of Morningside ice in her voice, 'but that's scant consolation right now.'

'I know,' I agreed. 'You've been conjured up as a cruel trick by a being of infinite cruelty. It's my job to stop him. You're …' and my voice faltered.

'A distraction?' Sophonisba raised an eyebrow.

I looked sheepishly at my boots.

Harry stepped forward. 'I'm sorry about what happened to you, but it's not fair to blame the Doctor. He doesn't forget about people.'

'No, indeed?' Sophonisba indicated the man she was holding, so frail he looked little more than a bag of kindling. 'Then what's this man's name?'

I looked up, my eyes weary. 'Were we introduced? In the church? In all that madness?'

'You've forgotten.' The man's voice had a dry paper rustle, like old tobacco rubbing in a tin.

'Your name, yes, I've forgotten that,' I admitted. 'But not who you were. You stood up for me and lost your life. You helped operate the generator that powered my silly little machine that helped to protect your world. Yes, your world ... You fished off those islands all your life in a boat built for you by your father, the last boat he ever built. Every winter you hauled it up onto the beach and gave it a fresh coat of green paint while drinking a flask of cold tea and watched by the gulls. I'm truly sorry I can't remember your name, but I can remember everything else about you.'

The man nodded, a look of stern acceptance, and a slightly mollified Sophonisba took my hand gently in hers. I tried not to flinch at how it felt like holding a skeleton's. 'So we're just a tormenting distraction?' Her smile was ironic.

'As I said,' I repeated, hating every little word, 'Scratchman has burnt his empire of souls, all for a glut of power to throw at me. And it won't be enough.'

'I actually meant,' Sophonisba coughed delicately, 'we're just a distraction from *those*.'

I turned to where she was pointing. Something stirred among the rocks. Creatures scuttled out from behind the boulders, black, hairy, hungry shapes crawling towards them.

'I say, Doctor!' shouted Harry. 'Giant spiders!'

Sometimes, I reflected, Harry did not make the world easier just by naming everything in it.

There was something odd about the spiders. They were built out of twigs and scraps of rag – they were scarecrows too.

'And what about those?' demanded Sarah. Behind the spiders crawled monstrous wicker slugs. And robots glided, robots of woven thorns. Some she recognised, many she did not – a strange pile of bramble hexagons, a crawling tree-stump crab.

All of them came rushing, gliding, crawling across the vast plain towards us.

'What is all this?' Harry asked.

'The Final Battle,' I said, and despite everything I couldn't resist turning to Sophonisba and laughing. 'Having failed with you, he's plundering my memories!' I roared, and my laughter clapped the skies. 'I don't have time for museums!'

'These are from your life?' Sophonisba remarked. 'That's hardly encouraging.'

More creatures flooded the plain, running towards us. Not all were scarecrows. Some seemed to have grown out of leftover organs. Horrid things like wetsuits made out of liver flopped towards us. Vast wobbling tumours that screamed slowly.

'Is that a giant robot?' asked Harry. 'Should it be covered with maggots?'

'If I start screaming, I shall never stop,' Sarah announced.

'Curious, isn't it?' I said as the vast army sloughed towards us. I raised my voice. 'Hello! If this is supposed to intimidate me, perhaps you've forgotten that I've beaten you all. That kind of thing can slip the mind, I know, but really, it shouldn't. My dance card is full of victories.'

I looked at Sarah Jane and Harry, and then back at the islanders, who were all staring in horror at the advancing tide.

'You're not even a little bit concerned about them?' asked Harry.

I winked. 'The art is not to let it show,' I whispered as the army thundered towards us. 'That's the difficult bit. But you'll get the hang of it.'

'You really think so?' said Sophonisba archly.

I acknowledged her barb.

'She has a point,' said Sarah. 'There are a lot of them, and they're heading our way. We can't fight them all!'

'True,' I admitted. 'But if the best that Scratch can offer is a bunch of beaten has-beens, he's really not trying hard enough.'

'I know!' Harry joined in, chuckling. 'I mean, really, who are those three supposed to be?'

Harry was pointing at three scarecrows who had appeared in front of me.

'I mean, they're absurd.'

'Harry, no,' Sarah grabbed for his arm.

'Honestly, Doctor,' Harry sailed on like the *Titanic*. 'What did you fight those three old codgers for? A raffle ticket?'

The three scarecrows advanced towards me.

My tone was sombre. 'Those, Harry, are my former selves.'

CHAPTER TWENTY-NINE

'They used to be *you*?'

'Well, Scratchman's idea of my past selves, Harry, yes.' I felt truly discomfited by the sight.

Harry had only met one of my past selves briefly, and it was really just a nodding acquaintance, but even he could recognise the scarecrow with a sackcloth cape and straw hair as my third self. The little fellow with the bird's nest hair and the shabby trousers was clearly my second incarnation. And the forbidding creature with the skull of a giant crow? Well, that'd just have to do for the original me.

I strode towards the mockeries of my past selves. I pointed to my third body, and grinned. 'You, you look particularly good as a scarecrow. You should keep it.'

'Now look here, there's no need to be facetious, there's a good fellow,' the Third Me retorted. (Sarah told me later she realised how fond she'd been of the prissy old thing.)

'Oh dear, we're as baffled as you are,' lamented the Second Me. (Sarah thought he looked quite smart for a scarecrow.)

'Your only problem is what you're going to do about our predicament, isn't it? Hmm?' the First Me announced. I marvelled how it even had crow's claws, clutching a hawthorn walking stick, and the way the creature paced back and forth, as though it were edging up and down a branch.

The three scarecrows turned to each other. 'You know, I don't think he has a clue,' muttered the Third.

'Sad to see how we've grown up,' said the Second.

'I worry I've gone senile,' the First announced.

The ghastly creatures turned back to me and shook their solemn heads.

I couldn't help but laugh at them. 'What's this supposed to be, Scratchman? First those I failed to save, then an army of monsters, now funfair mirrors?'

'Well, my boy,' the First tugged at his dusty lapels. 'There is *the* great secret of your past, isn't there?'

'Oh dear,' said the Second, twanging at string braces. 'We tend not to talk about that.' One of his eyes fell out, and he hastily scooped it up, squinted at it, then popped it back in.

'Quite so, quite so,' the Third shook his muddy head. 'Bad form.'

Sarah looked up at me with sudden foreboding. 'Secret?'

Every man must have his secrets. Every man must have a corner of his brain with a locked door and a KEEP OUT sign. But even so, for these three impostors to hint at what they knew. Ah. The impertinence!

I barked with laughter. 'Dark secret? Scratchman is just plucking ideas from the surface of my mind, like picking peas out of stew. I wouldn't worry about any of it.'

And then, with slow deliberation, I gave one last look at the approaching horde, at the three scarecrows of my former selves, and dramatically turned my back on them all.

'Is that how you propose to deal with your problems?' enquired Sophonisba. 'By sulking at them?'

'Don't worry,' Harry reassured her. 'The Doctor has a plan. Don't you?'

I insouciantly waggled my fingers in the air, strumming an invisible ukulele. Then I neatened my scarf and practised my yo-yo.

'Doctor,' prompted Harry.

I ignored him too and began to hum.

'Is that "Yes, We Have No Bananas"?' Sarah piped up.

'No it isn't,' I smiled.

'What are you going to do about the monsters?' Sophonisba asked.

'Yes, young man!' called the First Me, his beak clacking. I could tell he was furious at being ignored. Serve him right. 'What are you going to do, eh?'

The rampaging army drew closer.

'It's beginning to look a trifle urgent,' the Second Me called nervously.

And closer still.

'Something needs to be done, old chap,' counselled the Third Me, always fancying himself the grown-up in any conversation.

When I spoke, it was with a low and steady intonation. 'Scratchman is running out of energy. This is all a distraction.'

'A very deadly one,' Sarah put in.

'True,' I admitted. 'But it's a last gamble.'

'We still need to fight them.'

'I'll come up with something,' I promised. 'Perhaps.'

The three scarecrow versions of me marched forward.

The Third tapped me politely on the shoulder. 'I say,' he began.

I half turned. 'What do you lot want?' asked. 'Yo-yo tuition? I can teach you the Three-Leaf Clover?'

'Actually, no,' said the Second, sheepishly. 'We have to take a stand. Awfully sorry,' he continued, as he grabbed my arm.

'You're needed elsewhere, my boy,' commanded the First. The strange, crow skull snapped back and cawed. As it did so, the three scarecrows vanished, snatching me away with them.

Sarah and Harry rushed forward, and then ground to a halt.

I had vanished. And there was nothing between them and that mass of monsters.

Sarah and Harry turned to each other, and then back to the clutch of villagers.

'What are we going to do?' asked Sophonisba.

I found myself being manhandled towards the gates of a vast and shining palace by three scarecrow impostors of me.

'Kidnapped by a tribute act!' I tried laughing it off, but I couldn't contain my fury. 'You've left my friends at the mercy of those creatures.'

The three stepped away from me. Were they perhaps a trifle ashamed? I should hope so.

'Well, aren't you going to open these gates?' I demanded.

There was a sheepish pause between the three humbugs.

'Our master would ah, very much like you to do it,' harrumphed the Second Me.

'Your master?' I poked the little fellow's carrot nose. 'That's not how any real Doctor would talk.'

'A little manners never hurt anyone,' clucked the Third Me reprovingly and I wondered I'd got through life as him without being clouted more.

'You should show some respect for your betters,' snapped the First Me, which would have been impressive if he'd not been sharpening his beak on a little pebble he'd pulled from his pocket.

I blew them all a long, slow raspberry.

'Just go away,' I dismissed them. 'You've been put together by someone rummaging in the attic of my soul. And it's a hopeless jumble. You're supposed to frighten me, to make me worried about who I am ... On the contrary, you're making me feel very self-confident.'

'Well, really,' they chorused, all in different tones of grievance.

'If you really were the Doctor, you'd go back and help my friends, those villagers. But no. You're nothing,' I scolded. 'Don't tell me how to be the Doctor until you've learned it for yourselves. It's not about fighting armies, it's not about dark secrets, it's not even about being clever. It's about looking at a big door and never ever being afraid to open it.'

I threw the gates of the palace open and strode through without giving them so much as a backward glance.

'Well!' huffed the Third Me.

'Some people,' sighed the Second Me.

The First Me held up a claw, peremptorily. 'I think, you know,' and there was the ghost of a twinkle in the old crow's eye, 'that there are times when wiser heads can learn from an apprentice . . .'

I smiled, and vanished into the castle.

Sarah and Harry stood on a plain watching the monsters heading towards them.

'The Doctor will be back at any moment,' said Harry with no conviction at all.

Sarah turned to the villagers. This was not the first time I'd landed her in the soup, and she was excellent at swimming not sinking. 'We're going to have to fight, one final time,' she said.

'What with?' Sophonisba exploded with consternation.

The creatures were solidifying, becoming more real and horrible.

'I think that's our fault,' said Harry glumly, watching as a squirming tree-trunk formed into a large alien wasp. 'Feeding off of our fear.'

'We've plenty to go round,' said Sophonisba.

'We're going to be torn apart!' one of the villagers found his voice. The others nodded their terrified agreement.

'Stop that!' Sarah snapped. 'We've all got to stay calm.'

The front runners among the crowd were close now – the flying creatures, the fastest crawlers, those with the swiftest talons. A stench came from them, the smell of an abattoir, of burning car tyres.

'The Devil feeds on fear,' said Harry. 'That's how he keeps going. We need to stop.'

'You can't just stop being afraid!' said Sophonisba. 'Not just because some smart man tells me to. We've got nothing.'

A giant octopoid creature reared up over them, tentacles whipping through the air towards them …

'It's why the Doctor was taken away,' Sarah realised. 'He was always there between us and the monsters.'

I strode through the palace, feet echoing through its empty marble hallways. Occasionally I'd try a side door, just to see what lay beyond, but all the doors were locked. I smiled quietly. If I was right, there were no other rooms. This whole palace was just for show – a set of flimsy walls held together by stage weights and wishes. A corridor going only in one direction.

I reached the gilded door at the end, and rapped against it, the knock of ancient power known across the universe.

Tom-tiddly-pom-pom … pom-pom.

The golden door slowly ground open.

Scratch was sitting on a vast gold throne, being fanned by a dozen versions of himself clutching ostrich feathers. He raised a languid arm in my general direction. 'Enter, do!' he purred.

I burst into applause, the giddy, delighted applause of a man who has watched a mouse play a concerto. This really was too much. 'All this gaudiness, so impressive – a palace! An army! A great big golden door.'

'Of course,' Scratchman sniffed. I'd caught him out. Good. No one likes being told they've no taste.

I strode onto the elaborately patterned floor tiles and essayed a few hopscotch steps across them.

'The fool's paradise, the statesman's scheme | The air-built castle and the golden dream,' I quoted as I skipped, and then stopped, nose-to-nose with Scratchman. 'Enough of finery and fairy tales. Time's running out for both of us. You don't fool me. Save your strength, eh?'

For a moment, the flames in Scratchman's head glowed Bunsen blue, and then the throne room melted away, and the palace beyond it, all dissolving back into a wood-panelled office. We were back in his boardroom.

'Behind every fable is an office, behind every theme park a cafeteria,' I said.

'I'm keeping the throne,' huffed Scratch.

'Of course you are.'

The room continued to shift and bubble, the clean and polished lines melting away, until all that was left were the smouldering remains of the boardroom. The burnt-out copies of Scratch sat around, their suits melted, their globes cracked and blistered. The wallpaper still burned.

'Well, that's not looking good.'

Scratch shifted uneasily on his throne. 'Merely a period of austerity before we rebuild.'

I leaned against the charcoal fragments of the table, feeling the cinders splinter and crack beneath my palms. 'What do you want?'

Scratch's glowing face beamed at me. 'You know. I want what you fear.'

'Well, if you don't know that by now, what are you for?' Forgive me if I sounded impatient, but really. 'Since I've arrived you've prodded, tortured and interrogated me. Surely you know my weaknesses? No? Then what kind of Devil are you?'

Scratch leaned forward. 'I think there's more. There's so much more.' Scratch steepled his hands and tapped the index fingers together. 'Come on Doctor, you're a Time Lord. I know that much about you. You're the most powerful race in your universe.'

'Are we? How flattering.'

'And again, the evasions.' Scratch gave all his attention to rubbing at an imagined smut on the side of his throne. He was trying to look diffident. Well, he was up against an expert in looking bored. 'What does a Time Lord fear, Doctor? If I only knew that … If I could only become that fear … well, I could feed on anything in your kingdom, anywhere, anywhen.'

I tugged one pocket inside out, then the other and pulled a dolorous expression. 'I have no kingdom. I just wander the universe. And you already know my fears.'

'Do I? I've just skimmed the surface.'

'You make me sound like a cold rice pudding.' I was hurt. 'The effort you've gone to! The lives you've burned through. I should feel flattered. But look at how little you've got left. What's your plan from here? To take all you've learned from me, barrel into my universe and consume it?'

Scratch rubbed the burning back of his head. 'That is what tends to happen.'

'And look what gets lost in the process – the dreams of millions of years of life on a billion worlds all consumed by your hunger.'

'Not all destroyed,' Scratch's head glowed. 'You can learn about a culture through its fears. All their art, all their achievements – it's about fear. Those fears remain with me.'

'Ah!' I said. 'They may be dead, but their nightmares live on. Fascinating!' My smile dropped like a stone. 'But I'm still not going to let you eat my universe.'

'You won't be able to stop me,' Scratch sprang forward in his throne, leaning across the table, so that his face met mine. 'You're going to tell me what you really fear.'

CHAPTER THIRTY

My eyes were empty and cold as time. I had a terrible feeling about this. 'You really want to know what I fear?'

'Yes, yes.' Scratch was so intent. 'Tell me!'

The monsters were finally upon my friends. The first of them, the vast roaring octopoid creature, poured down, tentacles opening up to expose suckers bristling with needles.

As Sarah got ready to die, she was shoved gently, firmly aside.

'No, I don't think we'll waste the last of ourselves on screaming,' said Sophonisba Mowat firmly, 'but on fighting.' She turned to the villagers. 'These two are still alive. We, sadly, are not. So, it is up to us to protect them. Are we all agreed?'

And, as one, the villagers stepped forward to meet the onslaught.

I closed my eyes and breathed deeply. When I spoke, my voice drifted through the ruin. 'Scratchman, I shall give you what you want ... What. I. Fear.'

All around the table, the shattered remains of Scratch's cohorts twitched, their burnt, broken frames tottering to their feet. They stood, they swivelled, their charred globes oozing.

Scratch stared at the figures and held up an admonishing finger. But they did not pause. They carried on moving.

'My friends!' he cried. 'What are you doing?'

The figures pushed back their chairs, stepped out from behind them, and all began to advance towards Scratchman's throne.

'What are you doing?' he repeated, curiously.

The figures continued to move towards him.

'Doctor—' called Scratchman, with a trace of alarm. 'Doctor, what have you done?'

'I always like it when they say that,' I muttered, giving my head the tiniest of shakes. 'I've given you what you wanted. But you won't like it.'

Scratch sprang from his throne. The creatures grew taller with every step. Scratch edged past them. He raced to the once grand and gilded door and tore it open, staggering out into the void beyond.

They fought the army of monsters as best they could. Sarah Jane Smith and Harry Sullivan and a bare dozen remnants of villagers. They had no weapons, nothing that could hold back an onslaught. But they stood their ground and they held hands, and they remained firm.

A clubbed tail smashed three villagers to matchwood. A claw crushed another. One was dragged from the line screaming and torn apart.

Sarah gripped Harry's hand and held it tightly. Harry, blisters and all, squeezed back.

As the villagers exploded around them, Harry gave Sarah his best, his friendliest smile. Then a tentacle wrapped itself around his shoulder and started to tear him away from her. She held on to him for his dear life.

'Harry!' she cried.

'Stay calm, Sarah,' he called back with an assurance he no longer felt as something dark and sharp closed around him.

I stood alone in the ruins of the office. The charred walls were crumbling. The very last oil painting burst into flames and slid to the floor. I bunched my hands into fists and pushed them into the table, grinding it into charcoal, and then I opened my eyes.

I breathed out.

'Finally! I do believe that'll do.'

I went and stood at the door, looking out at the darkness beyond.

Sarah tried to take it all in. The villagers dying all around her. The sight of Harry vanishing into a creature that was entirely mouth. And something grabbing hold of her, pulling her down, slithering up to meet her.

This was, Sarah realised, the end. An end she'd never imagined, never glimpsed in her future. An end where I wasn't by her side.

She tightened her grip on Harry's hand and vowed never to let go.

The hideous grey nothing that was wrapping itself around her shivered and twitched, almost as though it had smelt something on the wind.

A disturbance, a confusion moved through the army of monsters. The vast maw engulfing Harry paused in its engulfing, and turned, curious as a cat. Almost as an afterthought, it spat Harry out. As it turned, so too did the beast next to it, and the one next to that. All of them turning and looking in another direction. And then with a chorus of hungry roars, they went lumbering off towards it.

'Are they retreating?' asked Harry, hardly daring to breathe. 'Is the battle over?'

'It is for us,' Sarah agreed. 'But look ...'

The monsters were not retreating. Instead they were gathering pace, roaring and shouting and howling and screaming. They'd scented blood and they were after it ...

*

Scratch was running, running in fear. It was an unfamiliar sensation, all-consuming and totally exhilarating.

'This!' he yelled across the plain. 'This is terrifying. This, Doctor, this is what you fear! An unending fury and hatred. Unstoppable! It's magnificent!'

He looked back at the smouldering ruins of his office. I lounged in the doorway, watching. Some of Scratchman's cohorts fell forward, their broken frames collapsing. But even as they came apart, their splinters still staggered and crawled towards Scratchman.

'How does it feel?' I enquired.

'Beautiful!' Scratch exulted. 'My every instinct – I can't control any of it. I'm absolutely in the grip of this fear. You've made my creatures hate me so absolutely. It's overwhelming. It's really something. How do you cope against all this?'

'Mmm.'

The cohorts stepped closer.

Scratch rallied. 'But these are my creations. I can stop them at any moment.'

'Are you sure?'

'Oh, yes,' Scratch simpered. 'I summoned them up, I can dispel them when they bore me. See!' He snapped his fingers.

Nothing happened.

He snapped his fingers again.

'Perhaps you're running low on lighter fluid,' I suggested.

'No, wait, this is all part of the terror.' Scratch seemed to be licking his lips, despite not having lips. 'Oh beautiful! Very clever.'

'It is, isn't it?' I called.

The cohorts crawled closer.

Scratch took a deep breath. 'I can bear this, these are just a dozen.'

'I see.'

'Is this the worst you can do, Doctor?' Scratchman sneered. 'Turn a dozen of my servants against me? I had hoped for better.' He tutted.

'Sorry to disappoint you.' I fished around in my coat and was pleased to find some mints. I popped one into my mouth.

'Not at all.' Scratch marched towards the group. He looked the empty, cracked globes and the burnt suits up and down. He grabbed one and tore it apart. It ripped down the middle – an empty suit with nothing inside. 'See? These are nothing. Easily dealt with.'

'I'm sure.' I tossed another sweet in the air and caught it between my teeth. 'But, and I hate to say this, do look behind you.'

Scratch seemed to smile, and then turned, and the fire in his skull dimmed.

Stampeding, thundering, roaring over the plain were hundreds and hundreds of monsters, all my old nightmares that Scratch had conjured up.

'Doctor, no …' breathed Scratchman in appalled admiration, staring as the ravenous horde tore towards him. 'You shouldn't have. You really shouldn't.'

'The least I could do,' I said, and went back into the office. I gave him a jaunty wave as I closed the door. 'Bye-bye!'

Scratch waved back weakly, then took to his heels and ran.

Scratch was running. Hovering and burning in every direction, the massed army of nightmares he'd conjured up swooped and screamed all around him. He knew his land was burning up, devouring itself to produce all this. As he ran, more and more creatures from my past were conjured up – an endless stampede of invention, all now solid and terribly real. Two giant brains in jars blocked his path, so he ducked left, under some giant wasps, and scrambled up a slope to find himself confronted by an entire city of metal.

'This,' Scratch gasped. 'I can't afford all this!'

He tried to banish the metal city, reabsorbing the energy from it, but then the doors of the city opened, and its terrible, terrible owners swarmed out. An endless angry army of stainless steel and hate.

Scratch groaned, running across the narrow range, feeling the rock beneath him begin to crumble.

And still the monsters poured on out of every crack in creation. At first it seemed like there was just one, or three of everything, and then a dozen, and then more.

'Stop!' gasped Scratchman. 'Make it stop!'

As he ran, the last rivers of fire froze over, the last volcanoes shrank like frozen warts, and the black sky pressed closer and closer to the crumbling dirt.

The land shivered open, a chasm opening beneath it.

Scratch jumped, landing on the far side, but, as he did so, the ground tilted up. He grabbed at the scree, feeling it slide away beneath him, and hauled himself up, frantically up, desperate to reach the receding edge.

He risked a look behind him, and there, marching across the frozen lake, were thousands and thousands of creatures.

'What a grim lot, my boy,' said a voice.

Scratch turned around. Perched on the top of the ridge was the strange crow he'd made of the First Me. It was tapping its walking stick on the ground. Sat beside it was the skeletal version of the Second Me. The Third appeared over the side of the ridge, sauntering just a little.

'Sorry to keep you! Just surveying the land.'

'Not good, hmm?' asked the First.

'Not at all.'

'Oh dear,' said the Second.

'Help me!' Scratch reached up to them.

The three figures just stood there and didn't seem to hear him.

Third Me produced a set of opera glasses (of course he did!) and squinted through them. 'Quite an assembly.'

'Proof that you should be careful what you wish for, hmm!' admonished First Me.

'Help me!' pleaded Scratch. 'I can't stop them! There are so many of them, and I can't stop them!' He tried to raise himself up, but there was no longer the strength in his limbs. 'The Doctor! He's ruining everything.'

'Tends to happen,' First Me said.

The Second fished in his pockets and produced a packet of sandwiches. He unwrapped them and offered them around. 'Corned beef?' The other Doctors refused, so he presented one to Scratchman. 'Don't worry, I've gone easy on the pickle.'

'Talking of pickles,' Third Me said, 'what are you going to do about that lot?'

'Me?' Scratch staggered to his feet. 'Why me?'

'Well, we're not going to deal with it. We're not really the Doctor,' the Second said glumly.

'Speak for yourself,' the First harrumphed.

'He often does,' the Third remarked sourly, and helped himself to a sandwich. 'I say, dear fellow, you didn't happen to bring a flask of tea, did you?'

'Alas no,' the Second announced.

'Stop this! Stop it!' Scratch screamed, pressing his hands to his burning skull.

As he watched, the fast tide of monsters bent kaleidoscopically, the land breaking up and sliding towards him and over and above him, a wave preparing to crash down on him.

'Do something!' he begged.

'I've already told you we can't,' the First clucked at him tetchily, then absently plucked a grub from his pocket with his beak.

'Put us together and we just bicker,' the Third tutted. 'Good lord – is that a Birostrop? Thought they were extinct.'

'Nasty,' agreed the Second.

'Help me!'

The First leaned forward over a frantically scrabbling Scratchman. 'I'm very much afraid this is it for you, my boy.'

'You're "very much afraid"?' Scratch laughed, hysterically.

'I was being polite. I'm not very good at it.' The First jabbed at Scratch with a bony claw. He glanced up at the vast cloud of nightmares pouring towards them from all directions and then at the enormous chasm opening up beneath them. 'Goodness me, what a lot of monsters. And there's just one of you to deal with them.'

'No one man could!'

'One has.' The First turned away, dismissing him. 'But you're not him. And neither are we. Farewell.'

Scratch looked up at the avalanche sweeping down on him, and, with a horrified scream, dived into the chasm.

The vast swarm of horrors followed him. They all vanished into the void. The darkness swallowed them up.

Then the abyss itself vanished. The last embers of glowing lava went dark. The small hill started to fade away.

'I think this could be it for us,' remarked the Second, fading away.

'We all have our time,' announced the First, fading likewise.

'Excuse me, old chap, are there any of those corned beef sandwiches left?' asked the Third.

Then he, too, was gone.

CHAPTER THIRTY-ONE

For a while there were ruins. Then they too faded away. Harry and Sarah staggered across the flickering absence of a tundra.

'It's closedown, Sarah,' said Harry. 'They've played "Sailing By" and now it's lights out.' He was slapping his hands around his shoulders. It was getting chilly.

Sarah pulled him on. 'We are keeping going. Because it's what he'll want us to do.'

'But what if he's dead?'

'Don't say he's dead, Harry.' Sarah paused between one stride and the next. 'The Doctor's not dead.'

'Of course he's not.' Harry staggered on through the dirt, feeling it sift and wither away. 'All the same, we're going to be wandering through darkness forever.'

'We'll cope.'

'You've got me by your side.'

'Yes I have. But, as I said, we'll cope.'

'Harsh, Miss Smith, a little harsh.'

The two of them were crawling now, the ground shifting and sucking at them. Sarah gave a cry, and tumbled backwards, sinking.

Harry gritted his teeth against the storm and reached out to her, grabbing her hand. 'It's like quicksand!' he yelled.

'Help me,' she cried. 'It's crushing me.'

Harry pulled again, and saw the ground shivering around her, trying to seal up. Sarah yelped with pain, and sank lower. Harry gripped on to her tightly.

'I won't let go, I won't,' he vowed. Sarah looked up at him, her eyes full of fear. Her shoulders vanished – he knew then that there was no hope, but he kept holding on. The ground shifted and bubbled and with a gulp she was gone.

But Harry had not let go. He had promised. He was yanked after her – in up to his elbow, then his armpit. 'Hold on Sarah,' he called, 'I'll think of something.'

The lips of the earth parted and, for just a moment, he thought he stood a chance and heaved against the ground. He caught a brief glimpse of her agonised face, and then he was pulled in after her.

Plunged into darkness, the ground crushing his neck, Harry fought to keep his mouth clear of the grit pouring into it. His ears were full of the pounding of the ground.

'All I have to do,' an absurdly calm, well-brought up voice in his head said, 'is think calm, practical thoughts. After all, if Sarah can fight off an army I can probably think of …'

And that's where Harry Sullivan's imagination pulled up short. Slipping headlong into the ground, a continent pressing against his ribs, he had nothing. He tried crying out – perhaps for help, maybe just a scream of frustration, but his throat was clogged with ashes. Lost in darkness, buried alive, poor Harry started to choke.

His last act was a lie, but a nice one.

He gave Sarah's hand one final, hopeful squeeze.

Suddenly, Harry was seized with a terrible, burning pain in his ankle which spread to his leg. Harry's entire body was being torn apart. Something was pulling him up, but, at the same time, the ground was fighting back, refusing to let him go. But whatever was pulling Harry up out of the ground was very strong indeed.

Harry felt his legs and then his chest being dragged free. His lungs bursting, he tried to breathe too early and more clinker crammed in, wracking him with spasms – but then, with a yank and a squeeze absurdly like pulling on a tight pullover, his neck was out and then his head and he was suddenly up and out of the ground, dangling over it.

Such was his shock that he almost let go of Sarah's hand, and scrambled back for it. He dreamt the earth squeaked in alarm, but he clung on to her, and up she came, yellow cagoule and sensible trousers and wide, angry eyes, squeezed out of the earth like the last, most precious bit of toothpaste.

The two friends flopped down, gasping and choking on the ground, and only when his airways were clear did Harry appreciate who his rescuer was.

'That is the very last time I am committing such an act,' remarked the Cyberleader, before striding off into the darkness.

'It's all going awfully quiet.' Sophonisba Mowat was leaning over Sarah, who focused on her with some difficulty. 'No, don't get up,' she told her. 'You need to get your strength back. There's so little left here.' She looked around sadly, and drew the rags around her hickory shoulders. 'I'm the last, and I'm a ghost of a ghost. But we stopped them, didn't we?'

'We did,' said Sarah. 'Thank you.'

'We don't need the Doctor for everything,' Sophonisba said with a little smile. 'But it helps.'

'It does,' said Sarah, and closed her eyes.

When she opened them, Sophonisba had gone.

It took Sarah and Harry some time to get their strength back, time that the realm seemed reluctant to give them. Hell was freezing over, and they were both shivering in a land that was as dark as it was small. Where once they'd been staggering through a vast desert that would have made Lawrence of Arabia proud, now it felt like they were crawling through the corner of a room. The sky was black, the ground was hard and bitterly cold to the touch. Even the weird non-light was fading. Sarah could only see Harry's lovely, stupid face if she squinted.

'What do we do?' Harry asked.

'Keep crawling until the universe ends,' she shivered.

'I get the feeling that the party's over and they want us to go home.'

'I agree,' said Sarah, 'But we're waiting for our lift.'

'The Doctor?'

'The Doctor.'

'He … he is coming, isn't he?'

'Always,' said Sarah with more conviction than she felt.

They crawled on in mutually agreed silence for a bit. Then Sarah was on her feet, springing up and running, running forwards.

'Look, Harry!'

'What is it?'

'Over there, don't dawdle, you can see it!' And Sarah was dragging him, and, borrowing some energy from next week, he tottered behind her.

'I can't see – I'm sorry,' he peered into the murk. 'Oh. What is that?'

'Harry, can you see an office?'

The two of them staggered towards the odd, burnt-out wreck of an office. There was a door.

'Should we knock?' asked Sarah.

'Obviously,' said Harry, because he was very polite.

They knocked.

The door creaked open. They stepped inside.

Sat on the burnt charcoal of a desk, there I was: cross-legged and meditating.

'Om?' asked Sarah. She was resisting the urge to hug me, I just knew it.

'Ommm!' I agreed after a pause. My eyes flicked open. 'You two found your way here at last.'

'At last?' squeaked Sarah. 'That's not fair.'

'No it isn't!' exclaimed Harry. 'We had to fight quite a lot of monsters.'

'Time-consuming, isn't it.'

'I know it doesn't impress you, but ...'

'On the contrary.' I sprang off the desk and embraced Harry. 'I've always found you very impressive. You manage so very much. Considering ...'

Harry smiled and then his grin fell. 'But—'

'Take the compliment and don't go angling for seconds,' advised Sarah. She tugged at my sleeve. 'So, what's happening?'

I smiled. 'Scratchman is defeated.'

'How?' demanded Sarah.

'I taught him fear.' I looked bashful.

'You made the Devil afraid?' Harry boggled.

'One doesn't like to be immodest,' I grinned.

Having none of it, Sarah jabbed me in the ribs. 'What did you show him?'

'Doesn't matter,' I said, a shade too quickly. 'The important thing is that once that army scented that fear, they couldn't get enough of it. Worn out, he consumed this whole realm and then himself. All that's left is a burst balloon – the oblivion of a universe.'

'And we're stuck here forever?' Harry had a horrid sinking feeling in his boots. This was going to be it, wasn't it, just the three of them in this room, an infinity of waiting for a bus that would never come. 'We're trapped.'

'Well ...' I gave him a splendidly dolorous look, then burst into my toothiest smile. 'I did a little meditating. Reaching out to an old friend.'

'And?'

'Here she comes.'

With a loud, triumphant, have-you-missed-me roar, a solid blue box pushed its way out of thin air and smacked down onto the ravaged carpet.

'The TARDIS!' Harry smiled.

My lovely TARDIS. I threw the doors open and gestured inside. 'Shall we go home?'

Sarah and Harry looked at the last of the office, the walls fading away, the paintings black.

'This place is spent, isn't it?' Harry asked.

I agreed. 'Once we leave, there'll be nothing left to leak into our dimension. The universe is safe from Scratchman.'

Sarah bounded inside and gasped. 'Doctor! The console. It's made out of wicker.'

I winced. 'Don't tell her, Sarah, she's been through a lot. The infection'll take a while to work its way out of her systems.' I leaned over to Harry. 'I mean it – not a word, Harry, the TARDIS is terribly sensitive.'

Harry nodded solemnly and went in. He gasped. 'Good lord, it looks like my aunt's patio.'

I shook my head, smiled and stepped in after them.

With a good-riddance bellow, the TARDIS left behind the last of a dead realm.

Maybe, just maybe, the faintest traces of three figures watched us go. But then again, perhaps they didn't.

END OF FEAR

'Is that it?'

There was uproar in the great hall.

'Doctor, surely that can't be the end of it?' The Zero Nun came forward, wintry as a chilblain.

'Why ever not?' I laughed. 'I've rescued my friends, we've put to bed a whole army of nightmares, we've sealed an interdimensional rift, sent the Devil packing and saved the universe. What more could you want?'

That did not go down at all well with my audience.

'But there are loose ends!' the Zero Nun said patiently. 'Those poor villagers – is that it?'

'Oh, them,' I said.

The audience were outraged.

'You hadn't forgotten them!' Lord Bardakajak roared. 'Those poor noble innocents, swept up in this catastrophe, and yet still they fought back. How could they be out of your thoughts for a moment?'

'But they're not,' I assured him. 'They were among the finest humans that ever lived – and yet, there was a time when you'd have had me throw the whole planet to Scratchman, wouldn't you?'

My audience demurred, protesting that, well, while some of them, some unenlightened souls might, once, perhaps have suggested sacrificing the Earth, they certainly did not speak for Gallifrey.

'Good,' I told them. 'If I may dare say it, I'm pleased to see the Time Lords have learned something from anyone – even from humans, even from me.'

It was a bitter pill to swallow, and they had lots more questions to wash it down with.

'But if this is all the evidence you have to offer,' the Zero Nun pressed on, 'I find your story isn't complete. You said you would teach us about fear. And you promised Scratchman you'd tell him what you feared. And did you?'

'I did,' I promised.

'But you didn't tell Sarah and Harry the details. So what was it that you feared?' the Zero Nun demanded.

'That's for me to know,' I said.

They didn't like that at all.

'Come now, Doctor,' the Zero Nun remonstrated.

'Perhaps I fear the monsters. Perhaps I fear losing my friends. Perhaps I fear not being the Doctor …' I offered.

They liked that a little more.

'Perhaps I fear doing this alone.' That was a little closer to the truth. 'I'm just a gallimaufry from Gallifrey, doing my shambolic best against impossible odds … And there's you lot, watching from the Pavilion. You could … help.'

They reacted to this with fury.

'Surely you didn't just say that!' the Zero Nun purred. 'We called you here to account for your actions and you tell us to alter ours! Why … that would make us as bad as you!'

'Oh, I'm not suggesting you make a habit of saving the universe. The Time Lords of Gallifrey are no one's idea of an emergency service.'

The fury dimmed a little.

'But –' and they hung on my next words – 'perhaps, just occasionally, when a threat comes up, one that's so severe that the pendulum of existence hangs in the balance, you'll step in. You'll stop it.'

Slowly, the mood of the room froze over. The Zero Nun turned to me, wringing her hands with sincerity. 'Forgive me,' she said, 'but you've lost me.'

'I thought so,' I said sadly. 'You know, you don't have to do it at once. You could … take your time about it. You could set up committees. You could have meetings. You like all that, don't you? But, I urge you all, consider it. Consider being the last resort that the universe needs. I beg you.'

I waited for the shouting to stop, and when it didn't, I held up my hands.

'I thought so,' I said.

'Thought what?' demanded the Zero Nun.

'You've missed the point,' I told her. 'Scratchman wanted to know what I feared. But what I fear doesn't matter. Because what he really wanted to know was what the Time Lords feared. When you know what the most powerful race in the universe fears, then you can control them. And I know what you fear.'

You could have heard an angel quaking on a pinhead.

'When you dragged me here, I promised you a lecture and a warning. Well, here it is. I've told you what you fear. You're immortal and yet you fear death; you exist but you're afraid to live; you observe the universe but you're afraid of the beauty of it; and what you fear most of all is change. That's the reason this trial is a charade – you'll happily haul me over the coals, but you'll never do anything about me. Because, much as you hate it, you're content to leave saving the universe up to me.'

They went very quiet. The Zero Nun gave me a final simpering glare and turned her back on me, melting back into the crowd.

The beam of light around me flickered and went out. I looked up at the Sword of Never – as empty a threat now as it always had been.

'Listen,' I said. 'One day a challenge will come. One so great, you'll need to throw out the rules, roll up your sleeves and get involved. You need to conquer your fears. Before it's too late. Will you? Because, if you don't, then Scratchman's won.'

I turned and left them then. No one tried to stop me. Of course they didn't.

They shouted and jeered at me. They made more threats. They ordered me to come back and hear them tell me why I was wrong and that they were right. That they would carry on forever because they were the Time Lords of Gallifrey and I was just the Doctor.

But I didn't go back. I left them to it.

I had someplace, somewhen better to be. I always did.

EPILOGUE

Sarah and Harry were setting up rounders on the beach. I had promised to go and find them some really useful sticks.

The woman with the rainbow striped across her hearts was waiting for me, skimming stones out to sea. I went and stood beside her. I picked up a pebble, and tried to throw it. It sank with a plunk.

'Not bad! You get better at it, though,' she said kindly, and then sent another pebble bouncing across five sets of waves.

'I'll try not to look jealous,' I said, watching another stone sink.

'You just have to put the time in,' she told me. 'And you will.'

We skimmed some more pebbles, some more, some less.

'A lot of people died here. More than I'd like,' she told me critically.

I nodded. 'The argument that more would have died if I'd done nothing is my least favourite kind of tidying up. But it's done.'

'And now you're playing games?' She raised an eyebrow.

'Harry was so eager for a bit of fun. It's like having a puppy.' I sent another stone to a swift burial at sea. 'It was nice of you to turn up, when you did, back there. I don't mind confessing, after all Scratch had done, I was at my lowest ebb. And you bucked me up.'

'Did I?' She looked all innocence. A pebble skipped once, twice, three, four times and then slid easily beneath the surface. 'Surely that was just a figment of your imagination, conjured up by Scratchman?'

'Was it?'

'Well …' She considered. 'It'd be far easier than imagining that I'd drop everything and hurl myself into a parallel dimension just to be kind. That's be ridiculous.'

'Wouldn't it?' I nodded. 'But it is so very me.'

'There is that,' she acknowledged. She started to sift the sand beneath her feet, tracing out a pattern in it. 'It never stops,' she sighed.

'I very much hope it doesn't,' I said, crouching down next to her, piling a few stones into a fortress. 'People will always need defending, and I'll always be there. In some form or another.' I paused, balancing one tricky stone atop another. 'I told Scratch our little secret, you know,' I confided, tapping the side of my nose. 'Harry – bless him – thinks he fought off Scratchman somehow. And I'll let him think that. It's easier than the truth. Sarah suspects, of course.'

'Ah, Sarah Jane,' she grinned.

'Scratch wanted to know what frightened me. What really frightened me.'

She frowned. 'And you told him?'

'Of course.' I leaned back, concentrating on building a good, solid pebble wall. 'He thought I was frightened of what I was. Instead I showed him I was frightened of what I was not. What I can never be. Not even for a moment.'

'The Doctor's darkest secret,' she smiled.

'Oh, I like that,' I told her. 'I showed him everything I've ever faced. The secret to being me is that I've never run away. I've never been afraid. I can't afford to be. That's what being the Doctor is all about. Don't you think?'

'Isn't it just?' She accepted the point, smiling gently.

'If I once give in, then the universe is lost. All my bottled-up fear, I gave it to Scratchman.'

'And it cost him everything.' She stood up, dusting the sand from her boots.

I joined her, and we both regarded the fortress we'd built.

'Do you think it'll stand the test of time?' I asked

'Oooh, long enough,' she said. 'The waves will keep coming, knocking it down, but we'll rebuild it, keep it going.'

'Does it even serve any purpose?' I smiled.

'Who knows,' she told me. 'But it's nice that it's there.'

We both laughed at that.

The wind turned a little, and I offered her my scarf.

'I've been dying to try it on,' she said, taking it.

'It suits you.'

'No, it suits you.' She unlooped it from her neck and handed it back. 'There's a lot of me in you,' she told me.

'And there's always some of me in you,' I told her.

Then, with a cheery wave at the future, I turned and went to play on the beach with my friends forever.

PS FROM THE DOCTOR

Well, hello, I must be going!

I hope we've managed this more or less in the right order. I always worry about that when entering a room (though I'm a master of not letting it show).

I do so enjoy being me. Sometimes I find it hard to imagine being anyone else. But then again, I look around at all those people, all those magnificent people who fill up a universe with their days lived somehow from one to the next and always in the right order – and never cheating, not even a little – and I wonder.

Am I doing it right?

To smile so much that children catch it like measles; to laugh at boring people till they laugh too; to leave every room better than you found it (if not tidier, happier); and of course – to remember that, no matter what you're doing ... is there anything better than having a little nap by a sunny stream on a long afternoon?

Those aren't the rules I live by – my other rule is to have no rules – but they feel about right to me.

I hope I've been a good Doctor. I hope you've enjoyed having me around. And I'll be terribly sad if I ever have to stop being the Doctor. So, I won't. But if it happens, then I hope you'll always remember me fondly.

Mind you, if someone like me could get away with being the Doctor ...
Well, who's to say you can't too ...?

Happy times and places,
   The Doctor

Acknowledgements

I would like to mention Ian Marter as a friend and a good egg.

A NOTE FROM
SARAH JANE SMITH

Hey!

What? You didn't think I'd let the Doctor have this to himself, did you? I write for a living! If you didn't think I'd sneak something in then you don't know me at all.

Besides, there's a question you're dying to have answered, isn't there?

Well, don't worry, of course I asked him about the Jigsaw Room in the TARDIS. Eventually.

We were walking around the ship and he was giving me the grand tour with the practised ease of a man who's making it all up on the spot. Throwing open doors, trying not to blink in surprise and then confidently declaiming about whatever was inside. Like a drunk duke showing a charabanc of tourists around his stately home. 'This – well, this is Dick Turpin's bedroom. His 'orse slept next door. Inseparable, they were.'

It wasn't the first time the Doctor had done this. I liked to call it 'The Naming of Parts'. I guess, when you own a nearly infinite time machine, you must sometimes fancy a wander and a daydream. The rest of us do a bit of spring cleaning. The Doctor potters off to see what the East Wing's been up to.

'What about the Jigsaw Room?' I asked him. It had been nibbling at me for a while.

'The what now?' He was all dangerous innocence.

'You have a room,' I prompted, 'with a big jigsaw in it.'

'What's it of? Chelsea Flower Show? The Haywain? Dogs playing poker?' He was being facetious.

'You know the room I mean. The floor is a jigsaw. I stepped on it.'

'That room?' He was sharp as November wind. 'That room's locked.'

'Well, I unlocked it.'

'You shouldn't have gone in there, Sarah.' His eyes were screwdriver sharp. 'What did you see?'

'Well, I saw my whole life.'

A hand rested on my shoulder. At first I thought it was to grip it, but it was a gentle pat. 'The whole of it?'

I shook my head. 'Not to the very end. It got … fuzzy.'

'I should think so too!' The Doctor's hand relaxed. 'You escaped by a cat's whisker. I wish you hadn't gone in there.'

'I was being chased by a scarecrow. Why, what's so dangerous about it?'

'Seeing the whole of your life? Knowing when you're going to die? Waking up every day knowing every mistake that's coming? How can you ask?' He snorted. 'The human mind would explode.'

'Well, why's it there? What's it for?'

'It's a Time Lord invention,' the Doctor rumbled. Of course it was. The Doctor's species couldn't invent a trouser press without it being ominous. 'It's supposed to be calibrated to where you land and generate a probabilistic pattern of forthcoming events.'

'Eh?'

'It's like a weather forecast for time travellers.'

'A time forecast!'

'Exactly.' The Doctor smiled, and I did like that smile. 'A useful little device. Only, well, mine … it's not properly set up.'

'It doesn't work.' I wasn't surprised.

'Not so much, no. It's peculiarly introverted. Focusing lens is broken. Doesn't look outside the ship.' The Doctor threw open a door and strode into another room. It was a vast space. On the floor was an old copy of Mallory Towers and a lot of empty shelves. He placed the book reverentially on the shelf and then backed out. 'Library,' he offered without much conviction.

'And that's why you've got a lock on the Jigsaw Room door?'

'Exactly.' The Doctor was patting the dust off his hands. 'Out of harm's way.'

'You're worried that we'll go wandering in and …' A lightbulb lit up in my head. 'Oh! Wait – this isn't about us. It's about you! You're worried about you.' I nudged him in the ribs. 'Come on – have you gone in there and had a look? Crossed your palms with silver and seen your future? You have, haven't you!'

'Never! The very idea! Well, once or twice.' The Doctor grimaced. 'Didn't look that far ahead.'

'Really?' I wasn't buying it. And he could tell.

'Sarah!' The Doctor looked pained. 'It's not like me to skip ahead to the last page.'

'Of course not,' I vowed. It was absolutely like him.

'Exactly,' the Doctor said.

We walked on for a bit, in silence.

'Besides,' said the Doctor. 'The last page? That's a myth. The killer's normally revealed about six pages before, and the last page is reserved for a hasty wedding and a joke. If we're going to be precise, the real last page of a whodunit is given over to a list of other titles recently published and an advert for liver salts. It absolutely never tells you who slew old Major McGrew.'

And that was the end of that. But at least I did ask him.

That's the thing about the Doctor. He's an amazing, impossible, beguiling, wonderful man, but there's always something hidden about him. His pockets are full of bits of string and apple core and once, I found the keys to my car in them. But, maybe, somewhere on his person is the secret of the universe. And, until he finds where he's put it, I'll never stop asking him questions.

As we left the room the Doctor said one more thing. 'If you found my jigsaw remarkable, you should see my train set …'